ALTRUISM IN GOPHERS

ALTRUISM IN GOPHERS

Morgan Wolf

Acknowledgements

While writing is a solitary undertaking it would be a tremendous conceit to pretend that there were not many who bore me aloft with their encouragement and prayers throughout the sometimes joyous, sometimes arduous process of wrangling this story (and all the others) into submission. To my parents, David and Sylvia Wolf, I am too inadequate a writer to accurately express my gratitude to you for the love, steadfast support and the generosity that characterizes you both. I have not only been the beneficiary, but also had the supreme joy of belonging to you. Your example of faith, your wisdom and this gift of a family leaves me in breathless awe at the goodness of God. To my siblings Gabe Wolf and Camille Debrey and their incredible spouses, Miriam Wolf and Nick Debrey for the shared sensibilities, the laughs, the love of conversation and big ideas and the always delightful time we spend together. Only the good stuff came from you guys. For this outstanding cover design I owe heavy thanks to Cody Andreasen. Cousin, friend and original collaborator who first challenged me to write a story. Your creativity and humour have been a continual source of blessing and joy. Finding my superb editor Erin Parker among the sea of names was like finding a needle in a haystack. Her skill, professionalism and encouragement helped reenergize my love for the project during the fatiguing doldrums of rewrites. My cousin and dear friend Rachel Orregaard—who continued to read new chapters at the expense of her health and whose enthusiasm for Winston's story and desire to know what would happen next provided the motivation I needed to finish. And to my wonderful friends for the invaluable intangibles: Sarah Hamilton, who always tells me to swing for the fence despite our mutual uncertainty over the meaning of baseball analogies. Monica Janzen, indefatigable friend, who was always willing to read pages no matter their state. Sara Fretheim, who high-fived my successes and commiserated during the lows of writing. Jonathan Nikkel, who reminded me that there was nothing that God hadn't already provided for me—including all the wonderful friends at First Evangelical Free Church who prayed and kept asking how it was going as time ticked by.

And, to Tim Fretheim for scattering the seed of this story in the first place.

About the Author

Morgan Wolf is a writer from Calgary, Alberta. Her writing appears online and in print thanks to *live* magazine, Cloudscape Comics and more. *Altruism in Gophers* is her debut novel. She also blogs occasionally at www.anothergratuitousmdash.blogspot.com.

For Late Bloomers

ALTRUISM IN GOPHERS

CHAPTER ONE

How the Damn Foolishness Began

The big-time bad decisions made in life aren't made in a vacuum. If you are willing to look at the whole picture—dare to examine far enough backward—you'll find there were a lot of little compromises that preceded them. There was an edifice of choices; a gallows upon which the final choice—the damn foolishness—was only the moment when you put your head through the noose. Few people get married with the assumption that they will commit adultery, but one thing does lead to another if you let it. Few drug addicts start out with heroin because who wants to be a heroin junkie? No one. You step on those paths believing you're going somewhere else. But there are really only two actions in life. You are either building something or tearing it down. Creating or destroying. That's it. The only question is how fast you are doing it. Maybe it's Mach 5, or maybe it's glacial, but it is happening one way or another. You think you're treading water—going nowhere—but you aren't.

Maybe that woman at the office has a really suggestive sense of humour and after a while she's texting you, and calling to chat when your wife isn't home. One thing predictably leads to another and the next thing you know, your life shatters to hell because you left your phone unlocked and your wife happened to glance at it when it dinged on the counter while she was washing the lettuce for dinner. It wasn't leaving your phone unlocked that caused your life to tumble to the ground like a gigantic, wobbly Jenga tower. It was everything selfish and reckless that you did up to that point. The tricky part is that it never really looks like it at the time because—like in that Jenga game—you get away with precariousness for such an impossibly long time.

I didn't commit adultery. I don't have a heroin habit. Some people think what I did was a lot worse than either of those things, even though it was essentially a victimless crime. I'm not saying that to justify my behaviour. I'm just pointing out how screwed up the cultural moral sensibility has become.

The first block removed in my personal Jenga game was the news that my parents were moving out in order to separate from me—their son. I am aware that sons usually leave their parents somewhere around the time they get their first real job. (Or, for the folks living biblically, when they get married.) But I never got my first real job. I mean, I've had lots of jobs but I never arrived. I've never even felt like I was on the cusp of arriving. Instead, there I was, thirty-three and still living at home and, if I am going to be perfectly honest, I wasn't even that unhappy about it. And, no, not because my mom makes my lunches; she hasn't done that since I was ten. Rather, it is actually nice to live with people you don't hate. My friend Robbie once roomed with a schizophrenic drug user who kept going off his meds and starting fires in his closet and trashing the place. Robbie didn't know about those issues when they first became roommates. There is a crazy that you only find out about up close. While my parents are utterly helpless when it comes to operating their entertainment system, neither of them makes a habit of psychosis, threats, drug use or arson. It's pleasant to share a meal around a table instead of eating alone, your dinner for one illuminated by the faint glow of the television set left on for the illusion of company. There is something snug and homey about making coffee and knowing my dad will finish off the pot while he talks about the Arian Heresy or the collapse of the Roman Empire or whatever ideas might be percolating in his thoughts.

It isn't all upside, though. There is a measure of societal judgment that accompanies living at home so long, but as any old person will tell you, the more you age, the less you care. There was a nine-month period when I was twenty-seven that it really bothered me, but after I got over that, I wore my residence like a badge of distinction. I was the punchline of so many jokes. I was the acceptable prejudice. I was an object of contempt to the sneering classes. Within a century, bachelors like myself had gone from being known as the respectable and unobtrusive sons who seamlessly and competently took over the running of the family homestead, to cultural pariahs. It isn't the same for girls. They can stay at home with their parents and nobody thinks anything of it. Nobody makes jokes about them living in their mom's basement. It's pretty sexist, if you think about it. We at-home boys really need some loser male suffragettes (suffragers?) to take up the cause. We won't, though. Girls are much better at getting up in arms over bullshit nothings than we are. That is why you only see the really angry omega males in the dark corners of the internet railing against women while gorging on their masochistic pornography habit.

Those aren't my people.

If guys are going to actually fight something, there's probably going to be blood spilt, or else what's the point? The right to live with our parents sans scorn hardly seems worth all that hullabaloo—blood crying out from the ground and whatnot. We want something worth fighting for—worth dying for, really—but even I can see that the right to live with Ma and Pop without mockery shouldn't make that cut. What *is* worth blood and guts and death is the real question. Unfortunately, I've spent a good deal of time amassing a list of what doesn't apply, rather than what does. I mean, I've got some inklings—certain intangibles like principles and so forth—but the call to die for your principles doesn't come up as often as one might think, at least, not in Calgary. The worthy tangibles are people. A wife, if I had one. Kids. I occasionally craft daydreams about exacting a terrible revenge on those who threaten my imaginary family. But I don't have a family. I just have dreams.

"Doesn't it—you know—put a cramp on your love life?"

Everyone wants to know this, like it is any of their business. I see this question mark appear over a person's head within sixty seconds of his finding out that I have lived at home into my thirties. As though living by myself would be some kind of guarantor of a happening lifestyle; like I'm Christian Slater in the '90s or Will Smith in *Bad Boys*, and random scantily clad women are always showing up at my door in their lingerie at comedically inconvenient moments. Nobody really lives that life. None of my friends have, and not for lack of trying, either. Real life involves a lot less potential and a lot more humiliation and self-loathing. All the single people I know binge-watch Netflix in their underwear while glumly eating endless bowls of Cheerios for dinner. At least with my mom around I bother to wear clothes.

So—no, it barely affected my love life at all.

I've had relationships. In a fit of unqualified optimism a couple of years back (three years, two months and sixteen days, but who's counting?), I even asked Cassandra if she wanted to marry me. She said yes with a blushing look about her and I felt—unoriginally—that I was the luckiest guy in the world. But while other newly engaged couples planned their nuptials, Cassandra and I inadvertently (yet painstakingly) undertook the destruction of Us. By the time we limped to our respective corners, our breakup was a textbook example of what David Foster Wallace was talking about when he wrote that acceptance was more a matter of fatigue than anything else.

So, neither my career nor my relationships have ever managed to generate any real traction. And since the Cassandra Incident, which escalated into a personal end of days, I've been content to weather the post-apocalyptic landscape alone. Alone is survivable. I reimagined myself as a confirmed bachelor of the black-and-white era of fedoras and nightcaps (the drink, not the kerchief from *'Twas the Night Before Christmas*). I was Cary Grant or Clark Gable. Suave, witty and untethered by the romantic machinations of women who think not knowing what they want is an attractive quality. And inevitably, time just kept passing, as it does, without marker or notice and the next thing I knew I was being pushed out of the familial nest by my parents.

My dad refers to these confirmed bachelors as "beta males." He subscribes to that anthropological theory about human interaction and relational hierarchy in which men and women have to strive to attain alpha status. Age does not confer it. It is only achieved through the selfless raising of children; the sacrificing of one's own desires on the altar of parenthood for the success of the offspring. The beta members of the group are the unmarried juveniles. They may have great potential for alpha-hood, but they haven't had to strive and self-sacrifice yet, so in beta-dom they shall remain. The only other category is the already mentioned anti-social omegas. They are at the bottom of the social ranking and are unlikely to do or accomplish much except occasionally take a shotgun into a mall and start firing in a hate-fuelled rampage. In such a scheme, it seemed to me that being a beta was A-okay. Especially in light of the fact that my attempt to join the alphas had been a colossal failure. Beta was my -*dom*. My mother didn't see it that way, though. As I began to care less about my advancing age, she began to care more. She regarded it as a failing (possibly in her parenting), or a sign that I was intentionally avoiding maturity. I wasn't. It's just that things didn't work out. They really didn't work out.

The news of my parents' removal from me came with no warning. It was my day off and I was leisurely reading the newspaper and sipping coffee unaware when she dropped her own personal A-bomb like the Enola Gay.

"Winston—"

There was something in her tone, something about the way she said my name that disconnected my attention from the article about protests over a proposed pipeline. Something precise and pregnant with doom. Like she really was a bombardier and her fingers were hovering over the proverbial red button, a millisecond away from releasing her payload. It was that tone that caused me to glance up slowly from the newsprint and watch as my mother poured hot water from the kettle into the china mug with the Siamese cat on it. No tea bag. No coffee. Just hot water.

"Your father and I bought a condo. Our unit will be ready in three months. I only have to pick out the light fixtures. I'm planning on going with the brushed nickel, I think."

"Your unit?"

"At the complex." My mom held her mug close to her mouth, as if she was going to drink it. She wasn't, though. She would carry it with her around the house and then forget it someplace. Dad would probably find it in a few days on top of the washing machine or tucked behind the printer.

"Sounds cozy," I said, my thoughts extrapolating outward like some cosmic meteor shower. "Why would you want to do that?"

"We're doing it to help you."

"How does it help me?" Were they surrendering the house to me? That was totally unnecessary.

"You are thirty-two years old!" The mug was on the buffet now. She needed both her hands for gesticulating. "It's time for you to grow up and be a man."

"Thirty-three," I corrected her.

"What?"

"I'm thirty-three."

"Well. You're still not old enough to live at the Lancashire. You're going to have to find something else."

Too old and not old enough, apparently.

"What about Boomer?" I asked, glancing down at my parents overweight Doberman, who lounged at attention on the kitchen rug. "He isn't even fifty-five in dog years."

"Owners are allowed up to seventy pounds of pet. He needs to go on a diet, but he will be coming." Mom picked up her mug again and blew tentatively on the hot water. "I've cut him back to three-quarters of a cup at meals. He'll make weight."

Boom's expressive eyebrows demonstrated his apprehension. I leaned over and scratched under his chin, instantly regretting it as he smeared me with the thickest of dog saliva.

"What about me?"

"I'll cut you back to three-quarters of a cup at mealtimes, too, if you like. But you won't be coming with us."

"You guys don't have to move. You could have just asked me to leave."

8

"We have given you a thousand and one chances to make this move on your own. You have never once chosen to do it."

"That's not true," I said. "You've never said, 'Move out or we're going to sell the house,' or do you mean that I could have moved out at any time in the last thousand and one days?"

"Don't be ridiculous. You know this is overdue."

"There have been reasons. I've had setbacks."

My mother snorted. "You can't keep trotting out Cassandra like some war wound. That was forever ago."

"I wasn't thinking about Cassandra." I had been thinking of Cassandra.

"I'm sorry that it didn't work out, Winston. I really am. I liked Cassandra, too. But she isn't a good enough reason to throw in the towel on your life."

"I haven't thrown in the towel on life. And I certainly haven't thrown the towel in on my life based on Cassandra." Incredibly, this conversation, which had started with the revelation of sudden homelessness, was getting worse.

"Really? You've got this ridiculous romantic notion that you can never find anyone else, so you've just turned yourself into some hermit so that you will never be in danger of meeting anyone else."

"Whatever," I said. It wasn't my strongest argument.

"You won't let me introduce you to Eleanor's niece. She's lovely. But you act like it would be some terrible betrayal."

"Mom—" I closed my eyes and jammed my palms into my eye sockets. Living alone was looking brighter by the second. "—I'm not dating the blood relative of anyone I've called 'auntie' since I was born."

Mom waved her hand as though this perfectly cogent argument was nothing more than a pesky fly. "You have three degrees. Three! You dropped out of a master's program. You don't work in any of those fields. You have a casual position at the rec centre. As your father says, you are the most overeducated, underutilized bank of knowledge. Does that sound like someone making the most of his opportunities?"

"I like learning. Besides, it isn't like I asked you guys to pay for it. I work more than full-time hours most of the time."

"That isn't the point. This isn't about money. The point is that you are all untapped potential and now is your opportunity to capitalize on it. To stand on your own two feet. To jump into the unknown and find that you are strong and able to handle it."

"I get it, Mom. I'm moving out. Cue the ticker tape parade."

"This will be the making of you, I promise." Her face was bright with a mixture of relief and enthusiasm. It was the same kind of enthusiasm she showed when she'd bought my sister that tambourine and signed her up for a workshop—a tambourine workshop.

"You say that like it isn't offensive."

"A person can choose to be offended by anything. That doesn't make it reasonable." My mother had evidently been working herself up to this conversation for some time. Vaguely, I wondered why my dad wasn't participating. "Besides, I think you're going to get out on your own and love it. I think you're going to wonder why on earth you didn't do it years ago."

"You know, if we were Italian, this wouldn't even be an issue. You'd want me to be here."

"Well, we're not. We're Canadian. This is us. White Canadians don't live in multi-generational dwellings. Our allowing you to stay here long past the reasonable age hasn't done you any favours. You are hiding out here."

"I'm not hiding. How am I hiding?"

"Fine." She threw up her hands in exasperation. "You're stalling. I know you. I know that you think if you wait long enough, you won't have to make a hard decision. You won't ever have to make a choice, and then you won't have to be responsible for the outcomes."

"A decision about what?"

"Anything! Life. Career. Marriage. You're in some bizarre run-out-the-clock mindset. And I don't know why. You have everything going for you and yet you've spent the last few years hiding—sorry—*stalled* here."

"You've just spent the last few minutes telling me how I've got nothing going for me." I could feel the heat rising in my face. "Besides, if Eleanor's niece is such a catch, why would she be interested in me anyway? I should be ashamed of myself."

"It's not about shame; it's about maturity. It's about independence. Get some of that and any girl in the world would be lucky to find you."

"Lucky to find the guy who works casual at the rec centre? Man, we're all shooting for the stars here."

"Well, you'll need to get another job, obviously. One with a future attached to it."

"So, I'm getting a new job as well as a new place to live." I sighed heavily. "Every family has one failure. Why can't I just be ours? I mean, why can't we all just be okay with that? Tell your friends about Nat's and Jeremy's accomplishments. They've both produced children. Both have careers—sure, Jeremy is a sociopath, but no one's perfect all the time."

"That isn't fair and you know it."

"You know, 'you can be offended by anything but that doesn't mean it isn't true.'"

"I can't believe that my thirty-three-year-old son is arguing with me about whether or not it is time for him to move out. That my husband and I can't move into a new house without having to consider whether our adult son will be moving with us. It isn't like you have some handicap that would require our continual support."

"I'm just taking issue with the idea that somehow I should feel ashamed of myself. As if living alone proves maturity; that is just a cultural norm. It isn't a moral issue. I pay room and board. I pull my weight. I'm not just some loser who's been sponging off his parents."

"No one has said that."

"Then what are we even talking about? The fact that I'm not like Jeremy? As if anyone could bear to have two of him around."

My mom sat down at the table across from me as though gravity was particularly burdensome to her. She absentmindedly began scraping something off the table with her fingernail. I watched her progress for a few moments as the sound of her nail scratching the wood filled up the awkward détente in the conversation.

"You are very different from your brother," she said finally. "He just doesn't understand you."

"This was his idea, wasn't it?" I said as she picked up the newspaper that I had been reading and scanned it with a sudden intensity of interest that strained all credulity. "Mom?"

"What?"

Now who's stalling?

Certain conversations—like that one with my mom—inevitably prompt you to take inventory of your life. You want to assess whether or not the charges against you are true, whether you really do cut as unflattering a figure as others seem to suggest. The only question is how far back to go. I decided I would cut myself a break up until high school. A kid doesn't really make too many of his own choices before that. He goes to swimming and hockey practice because his parents started dropping him off there years and years before. It was a habit long before I knew that I had habits. I went to school because that is what you do—what all my friends were doing—and it was illegal not to. On my own I'd have stayed home and played Super Mario until that day in junior high when my mom smashed the Nintendo on the driveway. She believed that score displacement was inadequate justification for waiting for three hours in the emergency room at Rockyview Hospital to see if my arm was broken. Jeremy never was a good loser (whereas I have managed to perfect it) and after seeing his high score bumped to second place in the rankings of Street Fighter II, he tackled me over the back of the couch. My arm wasn't broken but Jeremy has always been too intense for anyone's good—particularly mine.

That isn't to say that he doesn't have any good qualities. One time he protected me from a couple of bullies at the wave pool. No one was going to beat up his little brother but him. It seemed nice at the time, and I was feeling all brotherly in a blood-is-thicker-than-chlorinated-water kind of way until he straight-armed me into the lockers in the change room for following him too closely. Jeremy has been an achiever since he was born. He emerged from the womb into the incubator at Foothills Hospital and would have patted himself on the back for achieving life had he not been all weak and blue-looking. He didn't stay there long; he was achieving optimal infant health as soon as possible. He went home to join my parents and older sister, Natalie, who has the uncanny knack of eventually mastering everything she attempts. I arrived some twenty months later to his perpetual irritation and the dynamic hasn't changed much in the intervening three decades. I am sure that the idea of a 55-plus living arrangement originated with him. He probably scouted the location and then pitched Mom and Dad the plan. He probably thought he was a genius.

Scratch that. Jeremy definitely thought he was a genius.

My brother has never been able to comprehend my complacency. He is always striving to attain the next stage. The next badge at swimming. The next grade in school. His degree. A master's. Now he's working on his PhD. Not because he needs it. He wants it because it exists. The white-hot intensity of his focus has always been on becoming the best future version of himself, so much so that he's never noticed how insufferable he actually is presently. At the end of his undergrad he arbitrarily decided that it was the appropriate time to marry. As though the successful completion of this goal was merely a matter of setting one's mind to it. (I don't even know a single eligible woman—Eleanor's niece notwithstanding—so how he pulled it off, I'm sure I don't know. If we were closer, I might've asked him for advice, but we're not; and I imagine that within eight seconds of asking the question, I'd be willing to make a Faustian bargain of being alone until the end of time rather than listen to the rest of his answer.) Jeremy met Beth in February of his senior year at—actually, I don't know where they met—but it was probably the modern-day Canadian equivalent of a USO mixer. My imagination comes up short trying to picture Jeremy saying anything winning or charming, but when Beth saw him, she must have known he was someone with whom she'd never have to suffer the spectre of the unknown. They married the following January in a tastefully coordinated wedding that was probably perfectly on trend. I have a pair of $38 teal socks from Harry Rosen in my drawer that have only been worn once. Now they (Jer and Beth, not the socks) together strive for their perfect marriage replete with date nights, matching figure skater smiles and parallel careers in which they wow at the Christmas party rounds. They accessorized their marriage with two excessively scheduled sons—because two is "the optimal number of children." I took his very vocal opposition to a potential third child as the personal slight that my brother meant it to be.

Jeremy—inexplicably—has always taken it personally when I drop out of something, as though it reflects poorly on him. It embarrassed him when I quit hockey. He rolled his eyes when he heard that I'd dropped out of my high school production of *Guys and Dolls* because I didn't want to rehearse three hours a day, five times a week, if I wasn't going to get to play Nathan Detroit. It irritated him when I didn't keep my job as a geologist after I got my first degree. I like geology well enough, but not above everything else. After nine months the economy tanked and I got laid off. Jeremy kept trying to set up interviews for me at his company but nothing came of it because nepotism is a real thing that most serious businesses want to avoid. I tried school again. I didn't really intend to get two other degrees in history and English—but I liked university, so I stayed. I got a job at the rec centre on campus, cleaning the machines, signing people in, that sort of thing. I liked it. I liked chatting with the people who came in to work out. I like hearing their stories and overhearing their conversations. I got to read a lot and studied while I was working. I didn't make much but it covered my expenses. I met Cassandra there, which was its greatest claim for a long time. Even after it all ended, my penchant for nostalgia tethered me in place. Jeremy hated that I worked there. He hated that I went back to school for another undergrad (two!) when I could have been doing a master's and then a PhD. He kept using the term "lateral move" like he'd invented it.

My brother makes almost everyone he encounters anxious. You can watch it happening in real time. First, those parallel lines appear between the eyebrows. Then an index finger starts tapping or a leg starts bouncing and you can almost see their blood pressure skyrocketing like some old cartoon. Jeremy does it on purpose, I think. He doesn't like to think that there are people who aren't "giving their best to everything they do." People like me. He'll be the best engineer. He'll be the best husband. He'll be the best father. I guess that is why the Nintendo score made him so mad. He wanted to be the best and wasn't, and I just wanted to play and still I beat him. Doesn't it seem obvious that someone in the family needed to relax? Natalie had her piano lessons, then exams, then competitions. Jeremy was hyperactive in an annoyingly productive kind of way. Someone needed to bring the mellow. It was practically my job from the womb. Laughing at Jeremy was an assignment. When Natalie was still dating Joel, Jeremy thought she could do better than a tradesman, because, in his words, "What does a plumber know about classical music?"

"Which of Beethoven's symphonies is your favourite, Jeremy?" I retorted. "Or, will you be pleading the Fifth?"

He looked at me blankly but Natalie appreciated it. Granted, classical music American jurisprudence puns are a niche market so it wasn't that big a deal that he didn't get it. But, still, he is just so damn pretentious. Natalie and Joel got engaged a few days later, much to Jeremy's chagrin. But I liked Joel and I'd rather my sister marry a good guy like him than some disdainful a-hole Jeremy would pick out.

Natalie is a prodigy of sorts; everything she touches turns to gold. From her looks to swimming, to piano, Natalie seems to float above the rest of us mere mortals on a cloud of graceful mastery. I was in high school before I discovered that not everyone had an older sister who was kind and beautiful and talented. Many of my friends had sisters who they disliked, but they all liked Natalie. It's impossible not to. (I was also in high school before I realized that my friends' unbridled admiration for my sister was not based on her sweet nature, her talent or her good heart.)

But you'd never know just how good she was at something, which could never be said of Jeremy. She would work with a single-minded determination that sealed her away from the rest of the world. She played because she wanted to play, because there was beauty and power in the playing. Mom still goes on and on about how Nat had never touched a keyboard before she heard Rondo alla Turca play on CBC Radio 2 on the way to a swim meet. From that moment on she wanted to quit swimming and master the piano. And master it she did. It was this attitude, I think, more than anything that made her exceptional, but at six feet tall, Jeremy and I—jerk little brothers that we were—used to joke that it was because of her big man hands.

So, you see, this has been my role since I began. And everyone thought it was great until my thirtieth birthday. Then the wind changed and suddenly I'm just this layabout loser who won't achieve anything. All the qualities they thought were great while Jeremy's ambition was nipping at their heels had somehow grown stale. What they had loved about me was now my handicap; they'd praised me to the skies for essentially being the anti-Jeremy for years and years, but now my personality was a problem. No one ever warned me that there was an expiration date on being me.

I want some vindication for that.

CHAPTER TWO

First, Some Deep Knee Bends

The entrance to Edworthy Park is a meandering single lane road that carves a see-sawing path through prairie bluffs down to the Bow River. A pedestrian path runs parallel to the river all the way to the downtown core and beyond, circling the city in looping ribbons of asphalt like water in a drain. It was late afternoon as I guided my car down the familiar road with the wheel spinning back and forth like the wipers on the windshield. The sky was already darkening to the kind of twilight that always comes early at this time of year and carries on its wings the frost that hangs in the air when you speak. That same air—that same cold—that would soon be stabbing at my lungs with each ravenous gulp.

My running lights illuminated a lone figure in the parking lot. Her familiar outline was hopping in place and swinging her arms in exaggerated bear hugs erratically punctuated by deep knee bends. I pulled up next to the only car in the lot, an ancient Toyota Tercel that used to belong to my aunt and uncle before it was inherited by my cousin Samantha, who kept it running through the power of prayer and frequent oil changes. I killed the engine and shoved my wallet under the front seat. It was stupid to leave it in the car but I did anyway. I got out and locked the door wishing I could leave the keys under the seat as well. They would soon be bouncing in the pocket of my sweats, bumping annoyingly against my thigh as I ran.

"It's freezing," I said. "This is a horrible idea."

"Start moving." Sam gestured for me to follow her warm-up motions, which I did, half-heartedly. I hate jogging. Of all forms of exercise, jogging is the worst.

"If you would do this earlier in the day, I wouldn't have to come."

"I had to work late. I was trying to find housing for this client and her daughter. Besides, look around. You want me out here alone?"

I glanced at my watch. It was only five thirty in the afternoon, but already the last light of the day was silhouetting the tops of the trees against the western sky. "You could get a treadmill. Run on a track at a gym. There are countless solutions to this problem that don't involve destroying the cartilage in my knees."

Sam pulled on an elasticized headband with a flashlight attached that graced her forehead with Cycloptic utility. "You're supposed to be taking glucosamine. You know that after thirty your body basically goes into an accelerated disintegration."

"All the more reason not to do this." I tucked my hands into my armpits for warmth wishing I'd remembered to bring gloves.

Sam turned on the headlamp, temporarily blinding me. "Sure you don't want yours? I've still got it in the car."

"I'm good."

"Suit yourself, cool guy." Sam began to jog lightly, the soles of her running shoes crunching against the gravel of the parking lot.

"If I did, I would be doing almost anything else."

"True. You are pretty easygoing."

"It might be the source of my downfall."

We crossed the railway tracks and I resisted the urge to stop and feel for vibrations in the rails like the kid in *Stand by Me*.

"What is it about train tracks that always bring to mind every book or movie with a traumatic train scene?" I said as we started down the darkening path.

Sam regulated her breathing as she said, "I always think of Snidely Whiplash tying Nell to the tracks and Dudley Do-Right rescuing her just in the nick."

"Wasn't it Dudley's horse that always managed to rescue her in time? Dudley was just a grinning dope."

"The details have grown a little dim," Sam admitted.

"It seems to me that Nell might have benefited from having a weapon. Nothing like a gun for female empowerment. Deal with Snidely once and for all."

"Maybe Nell should've just got Dudley to go running with her." Sam glanced back at me as she delivered her joke and blinded me with her LED headlamp.

"It's a good thing for you that I have a lot of free time," I said, sparks and fireworks temporarily erupting in my vision. "That might not always be the case."

"When do you need to move out by?"

"A week Tuesday."

Her nod was noncommittal. Even though Sam was on my side—she'd seen the whole history play out— she was reluctant to get too involved. I think she was afraid that I would sleep on her couch for the rest of my life.

"That's quick," she said. "Have you been looking?"

"I can't really afford anything."

Sam kept her eyes trained on the bouncing beam of light cast on the path by her headlamp. She had been footing all of her own bills for years. The cost of living didn't startle her the way that it did me. I made okay money at the rec centre but it would hardly cover rent in some dive in the Beltline, let alone a decent place.

"What about a different job? Maybe try applying for some geologist positions again?" The words came out in staccato-like bursts as she regulated her breathing. Our footfalls pounded on the pavement of the path and my keys jangled musically in my pocket as though I was the one who had taken the tambourine lesson.

"I have," I said, ducking a poplar branch that hung low over the path.

"Any luck?"

"I think I am too out of date."

I glanced over at her but she kept her eyes on the path in front of her feet. The shallow puddles that dotted the pathway had a skin of ice that the light from her headlamp would dance upon for a moment as the only warning of the danger of falling. "I would have thought that only computer-y people had to worry about that. How much has the geologic strata changed in eight years?"

"Maybe none of my references are still around."

"Maybe. It's a bad time to be looking for work, though. I was listening to the news on the way here and they were saying that the number of people accessing the food bank is way up."

Seamlessly, we moved single file—Sam taking the lead—to pass by an elderly man walking a schnauzer. In spite of myself, I was appreciating the run. It made me feel like I was doing something—moving forward, away from all of the thoughts that I didn't want to think. What kind of job was I going to find? The buyers of my parents' house would take possession in two weeks. My stuff wasn't even in boxes and I had no plan. No one had offered to let me stay with them until I got a place, not Nat, or Jeremy and Beth, not even Sam. It was like they were all playing some uncomfortable game of chicken and wondering who would crack first. I think that everyone's money was on Sam; my money was on Sam.

You can tell Sam is a soft touch just by looking at her. She attracts hopeless cases. Homeless people downtown zero in on her to ask for money, which she always gives despite my reminders that they are probably using it for alcohol or drugs and not food like their signs proclaim. They don't really mean the words *God Bless* when you say no to them. That's just supposed to make you feel guilty. Sam rolls her eyes at me for saying that, but she works at Friendly Horizons, which is a group home for pregnant and at-risk teenage girls, so what can you expect? She mentors them to make better choices and teaches them life skills. Mostly, it seems like she manages chaos.

"What about just getting a general labour job until you find something else? I'm sure it would pay better than the rec centre."

"Yeah, maybe."

"You can't be choosy right now, Winston."

"I promise you I'm not."

She shook her head like she didn't believe me. "These girls I work with—it's like they think that they have the right to be picky about everything. Sometimes the choices that you make preclude other options down the road. These are what we call 'consequences.' I don't understand how people make it this far in life without having run into that phenomenon before now."

"I know that, Sam," I said. "I waited too long to move out and now I have to do it in a rush."

She continued as though I hadn't agreed with her. "Sometimes you get dealt a bad hand from the get-go. I don't know why. No one knows why. But now you have to choose based on the remaining options. I'm not saying that you shouldn't be able to respect yourself. I'm just saying that not every option is available all the time."

"Totally."

Sam always picks up the pace when she gets going on some topic. I knew from experience that it was best just to let her work it out of her system. She'd tire faster that way. I sped up to match her speed. We weren't jogging anymore. This was running.

She began gesturing while running, despite the fact that her movements were jerky and didn't accentuate her points at all. "It's, like, if I want to get back home from here, I actually have to cover the physical distance to get there. I can't just automatically—magically—transport there. I'm in the park now. I have to make all the decisions that lead me back to my home. It's corrections and altering course until you find yourself where you want to be."

I didn't say anything. Sam is a better endurance runner than me. She can rant and run. I can only sprint for a while.

"There is this client I am working with right now. She just doesn't get it at all. She gave birth about six weeks ago—she's constantly leaving me messages about how she wants to go out and have fun because she's young, and will I look after her baby? She tries calling the guys, one of whom she thinks might be the father, to look after him—but turns out, they don't care. They aren't committed. She is only marginally more committed to that child than they are. It makes me crazy. You don't get to go out partying every night. You made the choices of a married woman—or the choices that women used to make after they had provided themselves with the appropriate situation for kids to thrive in. But you took something before its time and find out that it is actually really hard."

"You mean marriage."

"Women used to protect themselves by finding a guy worth marrying who was going to be a lasting part of the whole rearing of children. Now we just give it up without a thought about what we're getting out of it except for a few minutes of pleasure. I see first-hand how difficult it is for single moms. Marriage is a good deal for women who want kids—if they pick the right husband."

"Right," I said. "Except she—the girl with the baby—kind of still can do whatever she wants because other people step in to take up the slack. The stuff that husbands used to do, now we get the government to do. The government gets to be the husband. People like you—social agencies—make sure that nothing too terrible happens. She's got a safety net strung taut over any consequences."

Sam looked at me with what I assume was an expression of incredulity. I couldn't actually see her face since she'd blinded me with her headlamp. "You think I'm enabling bad choices?"

"Not intentionally. But if you think about it, the whole point of Friendly Horizons is to insulate people from the natural outcomes of their choices."

"It's *New* Horizons. And, there are kids involved! We're just supposed to let them face the consequences?"

"Take the kids away."

"That's cruel."

"Not to the kids who get adopted by stable people who want children. Honestly, how many of these girls make the most of the opportunities you guys provide for them? Is it even 50 percent?"

"So—the government comes in and forcibly removes a woman's baby? What a lovely world that would be."

"Not forcibly remove—but we let people face the music. Maybe more kids would be adopted if we weren't incentivizing single motherhood through freebies."

"You're one to talk," Sam said. "You've had loads of options but you've never been great maximizing your opportunities. Seriously. Isn't that a little rich—a little judgmental—coming from you?"

"Why?"

"Because not everyone has the same opportunities that you have. You started life with good cards."

"Sure, and some have done a lot more with a lot less," I answered. "Most of them, actually. I applaud them."

I could see that Sam was getting exasperated but also exhausted.

"I'm glad to hear that is your opinion, actually. I was going to offer to let you crash on my couch, but now that I know how you feel about freebies—I'll forego it."

I had walked into that one. "I'm just saying people manipulate situations in their favour."

"Not everyone. I don't believe that."

"Most people, Sam. Human nature. You don't want to believe it because it would mean that your job is counterproductive. Pretty discouraging to be working so hard just to compound a social problem."

"I don't know why we're having a hypothetical discussion when you need to sort yourself out in reality. Find a roommate situation. Get a higher-paying labourer job. Use one of your three degrees to get your foot in the door somewhere. People would be much more eager to offer to help you if there was some sign that they weren't adopting you forever."

Adopting me, like that stray dog that you see running around but you don't want to get involved in case you end up its owner. The dog might be nice, but you weren't really looking for that kind of responsibility. Plus, you'd probably have to make a lot of phone calls or put an ad in the paper or online or something like that. You hope someone else will step up, though.

I could see her point.

"Those people out there with a lot less going for them? They are able to do more because they just do more. You've got lots of talent, Winston, but none of that is worth much if you don't use it for anything. That is what is so exasperating about you."

My lungs were starting to burn. I glanced down at my shoes, hoping that one of the laces was coming untied so that I could stop. And then, maybe she would stop. But I had laced myself in too tight.

"What about the people who are either born with disabilities or end up in accidents and they don't have any safety net? They aren't trying to manipulate anyone. They have to find places to live. They have to find means of support, too. They have it a lot harder than you. Is there no marginalized group that deserves help?"

"I'm not saying that no one should be helped. The problem is with the way that help is given. Especially when it is through the government. It creates this cushioned pseudo-reality. People don't do for themselves as a result. They end up relying on someone else to carry them because somebody always does." Breathing the cold air was like taking shards of glass into my lungs. "Even in my own situation. I acknowledge that I wasn't motivated to move until I absolutely had to."

"Do you ever ask why you are incapable of taking anything to the next level?"

Of course I'd thought about it, but the only reason I could come up with was the fallout with Cassandra, which seemed like a stupid reason to be a screw-up for life, so instead I just said, "Not really—laziness, maybe."

I didn't want her to make this about me. It's one thing to talk about these sorts of things as hypotheticals, but it was much harder to hold the line when a disabled person was suffering in front of you, or the bastard child of some single mom was looking up at you with an expression that a World Vision ad campaign would have approved.

"Look—I'm not saying we shouldn't help anyone, but we need to recognize and mitigate the negative effects of these social programs. Maybe the ones for disabled people are less ripe for fraud. I do think we should help the disabled." Cassandra's brother, Gus, had Down's and he was—is—the sweetest human being. I certainly wasn't opposed to carrying people like him. He was vulnerable.

"Congratulations. You aren't a total monster."

We ran in silence for a few minutes as we both tried to recover our breath.

"Actually," Sam said after a while, "I just heard yesterday at work about a new government housing program for people with some manner of disability who can't work. Up until now most have had to live in group homes—which can be great or horrible depending on the situation—but now there is funding available for people to live on their own. Providing, of course, that they are able to manage on their own."

"What, like the government will pay their rent?"

"I guess—although I got the impression that the government would actually purchase the house."

"That's great," I said, my thoughts straying from disabled people and their housing needs to the last time I had seen Gus. Cassandra and I had taken him to see one of the latest Marvel movies on opening night. Gus was part of the weird collateral damage that happens in a breakup. You never know that the last time you see someone is going to be the last time. Cassandra, on the other hand, always hung over my thoughts like a spectre. She was like laundry still on the line in the background of my psyche until a thought or a word blew by and the next thing you knew, she was dancing in a frenzy that was impossible to ignore.

"I know. Amazing, huh? I mean, these poor people who have been forced into poverty-level housing, unable by virtue of their physical or mental state to work, who have been living on assistance—which is never very much, by the way—are finally getting a break. I was so happy when I heard about it."

"Yeah, that's awesome. Now—if only they had some sort of housing-assistance programs for losers." It's funny how you don't notice the moment when an idea is planted, because that was it. That was the moment when the seed of my damn foolish idea fell into the fertile soil of my ripening desperation. Like every seed, it had a germination period. But that right there was the moment it was planted.

"They do. It's called hard work."

We rounded a bend in the path and the lit sentinels of Calgary's economy beckoned to us, towers against an inky canvas dotted with light.

"Can we stop for a sec?" Sam dropped out of my peripheral vision. "Shin splints," she grimaced.

The city's low-wattage street lamps cast faint watery reflections on the surface of the river and the frost that was creeping slowly from the banks like Old Age. Soon the whole surface would be frozen, but no one ever noticed the exact moment when it happened.

I fought to regain my breath as Sam rotated her ankles and tried to relieve the pressure in the legs.

"Any better?"

"No." She turned around. "Let's head back."

We ran back more slowly than we'd headed out and maintained an uncharacteristic silence. I was thinking about what Sam had said—so, really, it is sort of her fault, if you want to trace it back to root causes. Why wasn't I able to get anywhere? Why didn't I even want to get anywhere? It was true what I had said. If my parents hadn't been moving, I wouldn't have had any desire to change anything. I was fine. I was content with being the overgrown juvenile living with his parents and their dog. It wasn't like I was unhelpful to them. I pulled my weight. I did all the maintenance and yardwork and cleaned up after dinner and stuff. I wasn't a slob. I was useful. I just wasn't motivated to have to do it all on my own. Maybe I was worried about moving away and being lonely. It's not like there wasn't any friction. They kept the house too warm. It was a little confined, but I was used to it. I'd never really even thought seriously about leaving.

Except for that one time with Cassandra.

Except for that one time that cost me way too much. Clearly, those kinds of stakes were only for the high rollers, or maybe the small-timers who just didn't know when to stop betting. I wasn't one of those. I knew when to say uncle. I was better off at home. It was a little restrictive, maybe—but it wasn't that. Anything was better than that.

I spent the next day scouring the internet for apartment rentals. I made phone calls to strangers—which I hate doing—and eventually found an illegal suite that I could rent for an exorbitant amount. Well, exorbitant for my paycheque. I took it, sight unseen, and then called Sam to go for another run.

Suddenly, thirty-three was sounding really old. Way too old, like I-don't-even-know-how-I-got-here old.

CHAPTER THREE

My Beltline Basement Lair

My sister's face, adorned with that particular expression of exasperation only moms of small children wear, was framed in the dingy, narrow window of my new front door when I answered the bell.

"Joel will come by with the truck next Saturday morning and bring the couch from our basement. You know, the extra long one with the flowers?" Nat said as her daughters, Mandy and Frances—age four and nearly six and decked out in ballet class pink—darted in front of their mother as I held open the door. The crook of Natalie's right arm bore the weight of my new nephew Jonas in his enormous baby carrier while her left arm braced an overflowing laundry basket against her hip.

"Girls!" Natalie's voice was taut. "Get back here and pick up your jackets! You don't just dump them when you come in the door! Someone's gonna trip and break their neck on these stairs. And it's rude! Who's raising you, some incompetent?" My sister shoved a laundry basket full of donations at me.

"Helpful, aren't they?" I said. The cord of a handheld vacuum hung stubbornly over the side, resisting all efforts to gather it into the basket.

"Industrial England could have taught them a thing or two," she answered. "I brought you hangers and a laundry basket. I had too many but you can always use more. There is also a towel at the bottom. I thought I had a set of them for you, but I haven't found the rest yet; they might be in the camper. I'll keep looking. I really hope Joel wasn't using them out hunting. Oh—and the Dustbuster. It works; you just have to hold the cord up while you're vacuuming. You'll get the hang of it. It just requires a firm hand." She looked down the stairs into the basement. "This is narrow, isn't it?"

Undeterred, she plunged down the stairs with the baby carrier hooked over her left arm. Jonas—whose eyes I have yet to see open—slept unperturbed as his carrier bumped unceremoniously against the handrail. Once she reached the bottom and rounded the corner out of sight, I heaved a garbage bag full of my clothes down the stairs, and watched it roll end over end until it slumped piteously at the bottom. Balancing the laundry basket on a box of my books I had brought in from my car, I followed.

My place was too small both for the stuff and for the people who had brought it. Boxes of books and grocery-store bags stuffed with my various possessions littered the cramped floor space. The carpet was a muddy shade of brown with a well-worn pathway that led from the stairs to the wet-bar sink to the bedroom. Looking around the room, I recognized very little. News of my moving out had attracted a mismatched detritus of other people's cast-offs—collected like a planet sweeping up stellar dust by the force of its gravitational pull. I had my clothes, bed, a lopsided Ikea dresser and the contents of my overstuffed bookcase. My parents' coinciding move had created a swell of hand-me-downs. There were pots and pans with a collection of lids that didn't seem to fit any of them. The assortment of dishes that my mother had decided to part with were hastily packed with a holocaust of paper towels. Two end tables, a TV cabinet that was too small for Joel's old tube TV, an outdoor café table and two rickety, rattan dining room chairs that my dad had acquired before he was married. These were splattered with a medley of paint colours that had adorned the walls of our family home over the years. There was also a bedraggled spider plant that had been purposefully placed atop the fridge by my mother "to green things up a bit."

Even so, it was too much stuff for my 500-square-foot dive. After its delivery, the extra-long, floral couch left only a foot-wide pathway between itself and the wall in order to access my "living room area." A donated coffee table from my auntie Joan had to be abandoned due to the tightness of the space, as did the TV cabinet, which Joel and I took to Goodwill on Saturday after manhandling the couch down the pinched stairway.

Jeremy and Beth showed up in what I can only assume was meant to be a gesture of support, though my brother spent a good portion of the time examining the walls as though he could see the cracks in the foundation and musing philosophically how it was a shame that I "was so far behind."

"I get it. You're the hare. I'm the tortoise. Your insight is your greatest gift."

"But better late than never, I suppose," he answered himself gravely as though I hadn't spoken.

"'Better never than late,'" Natalie answered him buoyantly. "What is that from?" She looked expectantly around the room. "Is it a movie or a book?—Also, the tortoise won in the end, remember? Slow and steady wins the race."

Jeremy snorted. "So it isn't the best analogy."

"But, really, what is that from? 'Better never than late'?"

"Isn't that a James Bond movie?" Dad asked as he set down some grocery bags on the counter.

"That's *Live and Let Die*," Jeremy answered. "Or *Never Say Never Again*."

"I was never a fan of Roger Moore," Dad said.

"Roger Moore wasn't in *Never say Never Again*," Jeremy said. "That was Sean Connery. He was the only good Bond."

"What's the one in China where the plot hinges on some cheap source of MSG?" I asked.

"That was terrible," Dad said as he went back up the stairs. "But I still like Connery the best."

"Everyone likes Connery the best." Jeremy was rooting through the grocery bags on the counter and pulled out an apple and ran it under the tap before taking a bite.

"It's only nostalgia that makes you think Connery is the best. None of those movies, old or new, are very good," Nat said. "And, yet, still no answer to where 'better never than late' comes from."

I shrugged and Jeremy ignored Nat's question completely. A notorious conversational plagiarist, he never gave credit where it was due, nor did he bother to know where anything came from. As far as he was concerned every word that issued forth from his tongue was a new creation.

"My brothers are uncultured buffoons."

"Because I don't know your stupid movie line?" Jeremy answered peevishly, tossing the half-eaten apple into the sink. "Besides, culture is a phony concept. People talk about it but no one really knows what it is. It's just like the emperor's new clothes."

"Culture is a real thing."

"Really, Nat? What is it? Mommy groups and pottery?"

"Where do you want me to put this?" My father held up the disconnected pieces of a lamp that had languished in my parents' basement since Calgary had hosted the Winter Olympics.

"Is Mom just off-loading broken junk on me?"

"Among other things, yes. Although those are really more cultural artifacts than culture itself," Natalie answered Jeremy breezily. "Only our culture could have produced someone like you, Jeremy. That's a condemnation, I suppose, if you're looking for a criticism. But claiming it doesn't exist is silly."

"I wasn't saying it doesn't exist. I was quibbling with your use of the word." Jeremy waved his hand dismissively like he was Socrates or someone.

"You just said it was a phony concept." Natalie shoved the garbage bag of clothes that lay abandoned at the bottom of the stairs into the small bedroom with her foot. "But, undoubtedly, you have many opinions on the subject."

"What kind of an idiot doesn't have an opinion?" Jeremy said, throwing a pointed look in my direction.

"What kind of an idiot has an opinion before he knows what he's talking about?" I said.

"Winston?" My dad gestured at me with the lamp.

"Set it down anywhere, Dad, I don't have reserved spaces for broken sh—" I glanced at my nieces. "—junk."

"If you're going to throw out insults, Natalie, you should back them up."

"Jeremy would prefer evidence-based insults, if you please, Nat. I wonder if it will take him another thirty-six years before he can recognize a joke—" I said, but Natalie interrupted me.

"I take it back. You're as cultured as Yoplait. I stand by the 'buffoon' part, though," Natalie said lightly. "From the Latin 'buffo,' for clown."

"This is a stupid conversation. I've got to get going, anyway. Where's Beth got to?" My brother looked around as though his wife was hiding in the foundation or something.

"She's waiting in the car," Dad said. "She said the mould was bothering her allergies."

The mould? Great.

Jeremy took the first of the steps heading outside before turning back suddenly. "What's your problem, Nat?"

"Nothing. But I'm not the one going over Winston's life with a magnifying glass all the time. Cut him a break."

"He's been cut way too many breaks already. Maybe if he hadn't been he'd be further ahead."

"Further ahead of what, exactly? My point about culture was that your opinion is only your opinion based on your cultural assumptions. They're just cultural artifacts, too; not statements of objective truth."

Jeremy shoved his hands in his pockets. "Just because an opinion is a cultural artifact, it doesn't mean it doesn't coincide with objective truth."

"Isn't it funny that you feel the need to qualify 'truth' with 'objective'?" Dad said absently as he tried to assemble the lamp. "As if there was actually another kind of truth? If there was, truth would cease to be truth."

"Winston is far behind," Jeremy said. "That's the truth." He threw a glance at my father, who was once again absorbed with the lamp. "Look at anyone else his age and you'll see that they have careers or families or whatever. They aren't moving into a dump because they work minimum wage and their parents finally got the nerve to kick them out."

"That's not true," I said. "Periodically a movie will depict some sad-sack guy who lives in his mom's basement. Then he gets accused of being a serial killer or something. I know my people."

My dad cast me a sly smile, but Natalie ignored me completely.

"Nice, Jeremy." My sister took out her car keys. "Come on, girls. Let's get going." Mandy and Frances emerged from the cupboard under the sink, their winter boots catching on the shelf.

"What are you doing under there with your boots on? Apologize to your uncle for getting his cupboard all dirty!" My sister pulled her daughters out from under the cupboard and searched hopelessly for a rag or a paper towel.

"Don't worry about it," I said. "I don't think some muddy water is going to make or break this place."

"I'll get Joel to get you a big thing of paper towels from Costco the next time he goes. You always need paper towels."

Beth appeared at the top of the stairs and called down to Jeremy that it was time to go. "We've got to pick up the boys from martial arts."

"In a minute," Jeremy answered. "My opinion is that Winston is far behind. And popular wisdom—objective truth—is on my side. Good things come to those who hustle. Winston has never hustled for anything in his life. He just sits around and waits for—whatever it is he's waiting for."

"Did you read that on a bumper sticker or a T-shirt?" Natalie asked, clearly annoyed. "Popular 'wisdom' is not the same thing as objective truth."

"Good things come to those who prostitute themselves," I said, imitating his lofty tone as I wiped out the cupboard with the sleeve of my shirt, which was a mistake since there was a lot more grime on that shelf than two little girls could have brought in on their boots. "It's always nice when you come by to pump me up."

"That's not the only definition," my brother said peevishly. "And even if it was, at least you could have explained what you had done with all your time. You could have hit rock bottom and that would have led to a transformation that could have been tidily summed up in a book proposal. You'd have something to show for yourself, then."

"Like a venereal disease," Nat said indignantly.

"Don't sweat it, Nat," I said. "I know that we're almost at the end of the visit when Jeremy starts wishing I were a male prostitute."

"I'm not saying it would be preferable. I'm just saying that no one is going to accept the book proposal of someone who did nothing for their whole life. A hustler is something."

"I didn't know I was going to have to write a book proposal. Will you be grading it for style and grammar?"

Jeremy ignored me and put on his jacket to leave. I could tell I was getting to him when he began flexing his jaw like that. It was a weird tick. It had looked even weirder when he was a kid.

"Is it too late, do you suppose? Have I lost my innocent look already? Maybe I could sell a book proposal about turning to a life of prostitution as part of a mid-life crisis—after much soul-searching, of course. I found that it was a choice I had to make for me. To put me first. Another cultural artifact worth preserving."

"You're such an idiot—"

Beth laid a manicured hand on Jeremy's arm before he could finish. "Your new place is going to shine up nicely. It's real bijou, Winston." She smiled brightly as she buttoned up her red wool coat. "I'm sure everything is going to work out great."

I nodded to Beth. "Uplifting, as always, Jeremy." I watched as they disappeared up the stairs. Natalie looked as though she was going to follow them out, but she stopped and turned back to me.

"You can't let him get to you, Winston. That's all about him. He doesn't understand that you do your own thing."

"No sweat, Nat. I'm sleek. Anything Jeremy says just slides right off."

"Deep down he means well; at least, I hope he does." Natalie smiled and squeezed my shoulder.

"Don't kid yourself. He's an egomaniac. I'm used to it."

"Are you okay, though?" My sister peered into my face in a way that made me feel uncomfortable.

"Relax. Jeremy's opinions—whether coinciding with objective truth, or popular wisdom—have no effect on me. I haven't let him connect since *Johnny Tremain*."

"I'm pretty sure there has been blood spilt since then." My sister turned to locate her daughters, who were now trying to climb into the dryer I shared with the people upstairs. "What are you doing?! Get out of there right now! We never climb into dryers! Do you want to suffocate to death?" Mandy and Frances once again rushed past me and up the stairs in a flurry as my sister retrieved Jonas's carrier. "Just remember what I said, okay?"

"Okay."

"And," she said, turning back to face me one more time, "if Beth is right about there being mould here, you can't live here. You could get really sick."

"What are the chances Beth is right and not a hypochondriac?"

Natalie was thoughtful for a moment. "I'd say, 50 to 60 percent." My sister gave me a hug. "See you on Sunday."

After everyone else had left, I surveyed my new place and tried to organize it into some semblance of a home—my home. There was just no room. The massive TV perched (uselessly, I might add, as I had no cable or internet) on the narrow end table gave the appearance of a bobble-headed media idol presiding over my dank little basement lair. There wasn't really a kitchen. It was an old rumpus-room wet bar equipped with a straw-coloured fridge that partially blocked the entrance so that I had to turn sideways to get to the sink. A single hot plate set up on the counter was the stand-in for a stove. When taken in its entirety, my new living arrangement was a homely mishmash of other people's cast-offs, fluorescent tube lights and a vague sense of being the loser at a lifelong game of musical chairs.

It wasn't entirely true about me having always bested Jeremy since the *Johnny Tremain* incident. It was mostly true; it was psychologically true. If it wasn't true, it should have been. But Jeremy had stubbornly remained bigger than me until my senior year in high school. He was thick and lumbering while I had been gangly and overgrown like some leggy plant. I topped out at six-foot-two to his 5'10, two-hundred-pound frame. And, despite a continuous eating regimen, I could barely keep the scale above a 149 pounds for most of that time. But his size made him slow and mine made me awkward. In such cases there will be blood. But, gradually, as I grew accustomed to the size of my feet and limbs, I began to avoid him, and that agility afforded me more glee than most things in life. My brother stopped wanting to wrestle me when he began to lose, but for the first seventeen years of my life, I lost. I lost big.

To this day I have never read *Johnny Tremain*. I don't even know what it's about. I remember the golden-yellow paperback cover. I remember the youthful titular character standing boldly in his leather vest and breeches, holding a long rifle as though he knew how to use it, tall ships sailing in the background with their banners caught in the breeze and the ominous redcoat approaching from behind. The seal that marked it as a winner of the Newbery Medal was suspended boldly over Johnny's shoulder. I remember all of that—but I never read it. I wanted to. I was the one who picked it out at the library along with *Number the Stars*. (Another Newbery winner—I was nothing if not fastidious about quality children's literature in those days.) I had looked forward to reading it. Boys with their own guns possessed considerable power over my imagination. As a Canadian, I was somewhat less interested in fighting the redcoats, not having much of an idea who they were or what the stakes were. I was more interested in fighting the Germans since both my grandfathers had; hence, the dubious selection of *Number the Stars*, which was about a girl who, as far as I could tell from the book jacket, never touched a gun despite being in the middle of the Second World War, and it possibly had something to do with a necklace. But the book jacket seemed to indicate that she might outwit some Nazis, and that was almost as good as shooting them. I only planned to read the girl story if I finished *Johnny Tremain* early, but I never got the chance. Jeremy had to read *Johnny Tremain* and give my mother a book report as punishment for the incident. His resistance to punishment precluded my ever getting a chance—well, that and the fact that Jeremy broke my nose with the stiff spine of that paperback. If anything, *Johnny Tremain* owed me.

In those days my parents drove a 1975 Chrysler Town & Country station wagon—beige with wood panelling, round headlights, a chrome grill and a hood as big as a double bed. It wasn't new when my dad bought it, but it was the first time in my life I encountered that intoxicating and illusive New Car Smell. The wagon's other attraction was that it contained the jewel of all childhood seating arrangements. A third-row, rear-facing bench that allowed its occupants a privileged view—watching the road fall away—while everyone else sat facing forward. The very back was the privileged position and my mother had to devise a strict seating rotation in order to keep the peace. On the day of the incident, it was my turn. It was legitimately my turn. I was reiterating that when my brother—the sociopath—picked up *Johnny Tremain* and wielded it like a battle club. The whole family can recall the vivid brightness of my oxygenated blood spraying across the rear window of my parents' Town & Country like some discarded scene from *Aliens*. I got to watch movies during my recovery. Jeremy had to write a book report with far stricter standards than his sixth-grade teacher would have exacted. After three drafts totalling two months' work, Mom finally allowed that he had completed the assignment. There is no adult equivalent to sitting in the very back. I wept when Dad sold the Town & Country and bought a black-and-grey Dodge Ram van like we were a rock band on tour. My mom denies it, but I think they got rid of it because they feared for my permanent disfigurement.

My Beltline Basement Lair was damp in a city known for being dry. After delivery of the couch, the worn pathway in the wall-to-wall carpet dead-ended at the sofa's floral upholstery, whose corners had been shredded into candy floss by Joel and Nat's indomitable Maine Coon cat, Chekov. Besides being nearly the width the basement, the couch crowded the door to the tiny bathroom, where the peel-and-stick linoleum squares on the bathroom floor had slid out of their places like ice cubes melting on a counter. Between the obstructionist fridge and couch, I began to lend credence to the whole loony notion of feng shui because constantly having to turn sideways to access the kitchen or bathroom was incrementally driving me insane, causing my will to live to drain away or become constipated or whatever it was that feng shui claimed. The size of the bathroom itself was comparable to one of those Ikea showroom bathrooms where everything from shower to toilet to sink fits in ten square feet, but in my case it was not—as Beth claimed— bijou. With the corners dingy and the tiny fluorescent light above the sink flickering, the bathroom was a refuge for thick, black basement spiders and the curled, brown exoskeletons of dead centipedes, both of which creeped me out. Fortunately, I was armed with Nat's temperamental Dustbuster to hold back their onslaught.

While the ugliness of my new home was a drag, it was the comparative isolation that got to me. For the first time in my life I was aware of my loneliness—my aloneness. Life at the family home had bustled with comings and goings as my siblings and their children blew in and out again like dramatic summer storm fronts. I missed the fact that I could chat with my parents. I even missed Boomer and the way that his head always seemed to find its way under my hand for a pat. I found myself listening to the people who lived above me for company. People I never saw, but whose footfalls and idiosyncrasies were the only indication that I wasn't living in a crummy dream or a discount version of the Matrix. At first I picked up on my neighbours' habits out of irritation. The sound of the bathtub always filling and the way that they used all the hot water available in the house so that my hard-water-encrusted shower head only dribbled forth tepid water between the hours of 7 a.m. and 11:45 p.m. The one guy upstairs who clomped around like he was going to come through the false ceiling at any moment and coughed like he was dying of lung cancer. After a while, though, I appreciated the predictability of it. There were rules and structure to this new life I was living. One week, a month or so after I moved in, I didn't hear the water running for several days in a row and felt a pang of panic that my neighbours had all died in a violent home invasion while I was at work. Or maybe one of them had drowned in an overflowing bathtub and the others had gone in to help and slipped, cracking their skulls on the sink yielding a pathetic scene of accidental carnage.

Maybe there had been a carbon monoxide leak and they couldn't get out in time. Or, damn it, perhaps they had finally succumbed to the mould Beth had sniffed out and it was only a matter of time until I, too, would develop a persistent cough and expire; my body lying undiscovered for weeks until some poor cop was charged with breaking down my deadbolted door and finding my bloated form face down amid a gallimaufry of dead insects.

Actually, it was just Reading Week.

CHAPTER FOUR

A Slow Snap

Ever since my freshman year of university, my thoughts periodically stray back to the gophers of Psychology 205. Those damn gophers haunt my psyche, popping up out of the hard-packed landscape of my mind like—well, like gophers. The class was populated by two hundred uninterested students who sat, soporific and warm, trying to follow the tiny ferret-like professor with the thick Eastern European accent as she repeated the material in the textbook line by line. And, while little of the course material stuck with me beyond the exam, I have always remembered the gophers. Gophers—of all God's creatures—regularly display altruistic tendencies in defiance of evolutionary biological theory. When a predator appears, the gophers without jobs or families will pop up out of the ground and draw off the predator by loudly cheeping to attract the menace to themselves. They do this. The maiden aunts and bachelor uncles—the betas—distract the predator so that the gophers with families can escape to safety and survive. Altruism in gophers is an observable phenomenon and a conundrum because it is the loser gophers who never get married and never pass on their genes to the next generation who martyr themselves for the greater gopher good.

Presumably, if all of that was circumscribed by the genetic code, such behaviour would be deleted out of the gene pool in relatively short order. And yet, in each subsequent generation, the altruistic pattern repeats itself. Did the little nieces and nephews observe their aunts and uncles throwing themselves unto the breach and develop selfless aspirations? If altruism isn't in the genes, then where does the impulse come from? Gopher colonies aren't the Borg. It isn't like a lemming colony following the crowd off a cliff to their individual and collective doom. It is a distinct act of self-sacrifice on the part of a solitary rodent. A rodent who isn't going to pass on his genes. It isn't the parent gophers. It is the lonely maiden aunt who never got asked to dance who raises her head out of the hole to draw off the predator. It is the gamer uncle who lives in his parents' basement who gets his head torn off for the sake of others. It's so damn heroic, it almost makes me weepy to think about it.

Even when I first heard it, I identified a little too heavily with the tiny martyrs. It was enough to make you a little resentful: having to save the very group that looks askance and judges all your ventures as failures. The betas who haven't been able to make a relationship work. The ones who haven't moved out from their parents' gopher hole. They can barely keep a job or aspire to a better one. But, boy oh boy, when that predator shows up, the family gophers sure are happy that their overgrown, immature gophers are around to be eaten in place of the young. And

maybe that is the point, really: maybe we aren't failures—
us solitary gophers. Maybe we just haven't gotten our
chance yet, but when the threat is revealed, that will be
our moment to shine. It is possible, I suppose, that the
moment might never come. Just because you have a fire
extinguisher in your house doesn't mean you will ever
need to use it. The lack of fire doesn't say anything about
the worth of the fire extinguisher, only the relative needs
of the situation. But in the days when fires are rare and
everything is made of flame-retardant materials, that
once-necessary extinguisher just becomes a piece of junk
collecting dust around the house.

It really bums you out, you know? Thinking about
everyone else's expectations of what your life should be. I
always assumed I'd marry and have kids and generate all
the associated trimmings of a house and a lawn to mow
and so on. I thought those things would eventually come
along at the right time. They hadn't, though, and I didn't
have the faintest idea of how to generate them out of thin
air. I thought about Nat's cultural artifacts and Jeremy's
popular opinions and Sam's assessment that I just needed
to meet the challenges in front of me and everything
would turn out fine. But "fine" is pretty relative and kind
of a low-water mark to shoot for anyhow.

I started having recurring dreams that I was
wandering down endless windowless corridors looking for
an exit and never finding one. One hallway turned into
another, turning right, turning left, but always the same
dull outlook. Each day that passed, I felt like I was filling
in time. I used the university's computers to apply on jobs,
but the weeks ticked by like Nat's metronome without me
hearing anything. Every night I went to bed conscious of

the fact that nothing had changed, and likely, nothing would change the next day, either. I had nothing that anyone wanted. No connections, no current references for anything other than cleaning gym equipment.

As my bank balance began to plummet under the pressure of my new expenses, I started going down to the cash corner on 13th and Centre in the hope of picking up some day labour. It only worked out a couple of times. I was either too late or too early or there were too many of us, or sometimes nobody came with a job. When I did get some work, it was digging fence-post holes in the rapidly freezing November ground. I kept my head down and didn't talk much to the other guys working. I didn't want to look at the sadness of their lives that covered them more completely than the jacket that hadn't been washed since 1999. Seeing it—letting it invade my notice—might make me feel like I had to do something to help them and I was barely able to help myself. What did pass in front of my eyes only filled me with a nervous foot-tapping energy. I didn't even have a drug habit. How had I even ended up here?

Through one of those hole-digging gigs, I managed to pick up a job as a helper to a bricklayer working on the construction of an office building downtown. The work was hard—shifting around fifty-pound cement blocks to build the parkade at the roots of a new office tower—but my fellow labourers were harder. The experienced bricklayers were mostly immigrants from Denmark and Ireland. The helpers were mostly ex-cons and crack addicts, less likeable than the cash-corner crowd. As much as I hated it, it was better money than I had ever made. But the steadiness of that awful job put me out of favour at the U of C Rec Centre. Iqbal, my unpredictable and frenetic twenty-two-year-old manager, who had always depended on me to make up the difference in the schedule when someone didn't show, was nonplussed when I arrived late for the third time in a week after refusing a couple of shifts because of the concrete-block gig. I just wasn't used to having so many balls in the air all the time.

"Wincey, what's up, old man? You are just crumbling, crashing and burning like the World Trade Centre. It's that epic, dude. What is that? Dust?" Iqbal asked, gesturing to the fine coating of cement dust that rested on my hair. "I hope so. Otherwise you are Old Man River not caring about plantin' taters. You're supposed to be white, not grey. That is not a normal skin colour. You are scaring the self-identifying females. Showing up late looking like some homeless Grim Reaper isn't doing anything for you. Bill and Ted have left the phone booth, man."

I tried to brush the cement dust from my hair. "'Strange things are afoot at the Circle K,' these days."

"I don't even know what that means."

"It's from *Bill and Ted's Excellent Adventure*—never mind. It won't happen again."

Iqbal was in one of his moods. Nature and his parents' genetic coding had begat him a slight Pakistani build with delicate features and narrow bone structure. Dismayed by his lack of burly genetics, over the last year he had become an avid user of internet-purchased steroids. His use of the juice coincided with his development of profound linguistic changes and overdeveloped traps. I towered over him in everything except attitude.

"I don't have the first flipped-out clue, nigga. You've got to stop speaking in code like some crazy CIA mofo. Speak English, man, the King's English—so that Prince William and his progeny would understand. I am Prince William to you, John Wincey Adams."

"Prince William."

"You better not be giving me attitude. Not Wincey-Baby, not my best guy. He's not giving me attitude when he comes in late and then says he can't cover my Saturday-morning shift when he knows full damn that I will be hungover or possibly still drunk from my Friday-night frolicking, because that would be seriously stupid. That would be some seriously impaired thinking. That would be like saying 'bomb' in line at airport security when you're headed to Pakistan on a one-way ticket paid with cash and travelling with no luggage. Dumb dumb. But you wouldn't do that. Not the guy who has been written up three times in the last couple of weeks. Three letters going in his permanent file because he's not up to the task of wiping ass sweat off the bench press. I know it isn't attitude because the Wincey I know wouldn't risk it. He knows that another letter would mean he was out on the street selling his body or at least his dispensable organs."

Oh, the old letter-attached-to-my-permanent-file chestnut. As though it was the police or the government who kept track of my work habits, and not the U of C Human Resources Department. As if it would matter. As if it would ever see the light of day. Still, I saw no reason to antagonize my infantile boss whose personality may or may not have been affected by his use of controlled substances. Especially one who talked about bombs in the airport on the way to terrorist training camps in Pakistan.

"It won't happen again, Iqbal. But I can't cover this Saturday morning because I am working at my other job."

Iqbal scowled. "It seems to me, Wince-o-matic, that you aren't giving this job your all. Like you are giving your career a no-show. I wanted to send you places, white man! I wanted you to be the guy with the mop bucket cleaning up the puke of future Olympians. I wanted to make you that guy. The Olympian guy. But you won't. You won't play the corporate game. You show up late looking like ten kinds of recycled shit; you refuse to cover shifts, which is in your job description, bee tee dub, and you still haven't filled out your personal evaluation that was due a month ago. Don't make me into the bad guy, here, Winston-banana-fana-fo-Finston. I am Prince William. That is how you know I am the good guy. My face is on tea towels and china and shit."

"I'm going to fill it out today. I have all kinds of ideas for areas of improvement."

"You bet your ass that section should be chockablock full. That section should be heavy-laden with low-hanging fruit, my pale friend. You better have some attached pages detailing all the ways that you are going to improve in your Areas of Improvement. I want to shed tears of joy like slavery just ended and I am going to get forty acres and a mule when I read your personal evaluation."

"Only brown people can get away with saying that kind of thing."

"You bet your bottom dollar that's so, whitey. We've earned it Bollywood dancing for your pleasure and laying down our Chinese lives to build the railroads."

"Lay off the juice, Iqbal."

"No way, Josie Pye. You should see my junk. It's colossal. It's a thing of beauty and a joy forever."

"It looks like you're growing breasts, carny."

"Bull kaka, Jazz Hands." Iqbal threw up his hands in an exaggerated shrug as he began backing up while maintaining intense eye contact. "Haters gonna hate."

"Fakers gonna fake…"

"Hey—by the way, town meeting after work tonight. Bring your self-eval. No excuses, no exceptions. Failure to comply will not be tolerated."

"A staff meeting? That'll be a first."

"Downtown at the club. Cuz I am the World's Best Boss. Be there or be square, Winchester." Iqbal mimed shooting at me with a rifle. "I'll text you the deets. Wear your boots, cowboy."

"I work until ten."

"You don't show and this whole damn town will know you're a yellow-bellied city bastard from the East." Iqbal whistled the familiar strains of the theme to *The Good, the Bad and the Ugly* before meaningfully adding, "You feelin' lucky, punk?"

"That was *Dirty Harry*."

"'Draw, ya stinkin' coward! Draw! Or Imma bash your head in!'"

"Fine."

"That's my boy. I'm going to check on the women bodybuilders. Make sure they's still female. No Adam's apples allowed."

"It's creepy when you watch them."

He walked away with exaggerated swagger; I spent the next hour searching for my self-evaluation forms. I was mid-paragraph coming up with my professional goals for the next five years when my phone buzzed three times in quick succession.

C U 2nite, yo. 10pm. 8 st between 1 & 2 ave.

Use the alley door. Bring ur dolla dolla billz and yo comin of age story

Don't forget your eval, Jason Bourne. Treadstone wants your testicles.

I shoved my phone back in my pocket and went back to filling out my self-evaluation form. I lingered over it for the rest of my shift, making sure to staple extra pages and filling it with Aragorn's speech at the end of *The Return of the King*. Iqbal wouldn't read of a word of it, anyhow. I rushed through my closing tasks, leaving the sanitizing spray unmade for the morning shift, and locked the doors at 9:50.

As I parked my car downtown, it occurred to me that there was a halfway-decent chance that I was going to a drug deal, that being my boss's idea of a wicked prank. But when I turned into the alley that Iqbal had indicated, it was well lit and a small lineup of people were waiting outside a steel door. I scanned the queue for Iqbal, but he saw me first.

"Hombre! You made it."

"I didn't realize attendance was optional. This is a staff meeting?"

"Don't rush the big reveal, Winter Sport."

"What is this place?"

"This? This is destiny calling, my man."

"White slavery ring?"

"You're not that good-looking, yo."

"Where are the others?" I looked down the alleyway to see some of my fellow employees.

"You'll see," he said as the steel door opened and the line began to disappear inside the building. "Got your eval?"

I nodded and followed him inside down a dimly lit, claustrophobic corridor that led to a steep, narrow staircase. We waited as the people in front of us navigated the staircase, eyes straining in the gloom to see the steps.

"If there's a fire, nobody is making it out of here." I braced my palms against the black walls as we plunged underground.

"Up with your chinny-chin-chin, Winky-dink. The only thing that better be on fire is your self-evaluation," Iqbal said over the growing noise of a live band playing down below. The bottom of the stairway opened into a low-ceilinged lounge with a small stage at the far end. Iqbal navigated the matchstick furniture and claimed a table opposite the stage.

"You want something? It's on the U of C," he said, gesturing toward the bar.

"Bourbon. Neat."

Iqbal whistled. "I always knew you were one of those sad alcoholics. You'll fit right in. Hold the table."

He disappeared into the crowd heading toward the bar. I took my seat and looked around. It had been a long time since I had been to this kind of place. Probably since Cassandra at least. Back then, I'd felt the need to try to come up with cool places for us to go. By the looks of it, most of the people my age had stopped going to these trendy bars. Most of the other patrons were pretty young—younger than me; they were all hipsters, emaciated and tattooed and wearing a carefully "curated" look of homelessness. Most of the guys were working on scraggly beards. There were also a couple of middle-aged women dressed in billowy, black garments wearing variations of the same butch haircut.

"The bartender has the hots for me, so he always gives me free drinks." Iqbal set the drinks on the table and threw himself down into the seat opposite me.

"He?"

"You got a problem with the gays, dude?"

"Depends," I said, tilting my chair on its back legs. "Am I on a date against my knowledge?"

"You wish, Lost Boys."

"What am I doing here?"

"You are here to perform, my narrow-minded friend."

"Are you being extra creepy today or is that just me?"

"Your performance review, Stephen Hawking. Why else do you think I'd tell you to bring your self-evaluation?"

The band stopped playing and there was a shuffling as they moved their instruments and equipment from the stage until there was only a solitary microphone stand remaining. An emaciated, slump-shouldered waitress in a tight black dress announced that they'd be starting any minute and advised us to get our drink orders in.

"Well—" I said, taking a swig from my drink and then pulling the wad of papers from my coat pocket and sliding it across the table to Iqbal, "—go ahead. Probably want to get through it before the music starts again."

"Drink your drink. Don't be a hasty Ent. You'll get your chance, Treebeard."

I leaned back in my chair and looked around the room. I guess it didn't matter much to me whether he read it with a soundtrack or not. The whole thing was a joke. The questions had no bearing on my actual job. Where did I see myself in five years? What were my professional development goals? How did I meet or exceed expectations this past year? Ridiculous. I made sure students swiped their IDs properly and called the Lifecycle repair people to service the machines when something was busted. The unwritten portion of my job was doing damage control with female students to make sure no one took my boss too seriously.

Iqbal dropped his shot of Jägermeister into the glass of Red Bull and downed the lot in what appeared to be a single gulp. "You ready?" he asked with uncharacteristic earnestness. "You want another drink first? I'm all about success."

"Is this going to take a while?"

Iqbal assumed a quizzical expression. "As long as it takes." He signalled to the bartender for another round.

"Okay—Slammers, sorry for the late start." The slump-shouldered woman was back at the mic. "We've got a full ticket tonight so we are all in for a transcendent ride. I'm not going to waste time. We're just going to dive in. First up, we have local favourite and regular here at Spoken Word Slam. Give it up for M.K.!"

"Are we really doing this during a Poetry Slam? Is that what this is?"

Iqbal laughed gleefully—his white teeth gleaming in the low light. He said something but I couldn't make it out. One of the women in billowy black made her way up on stage. The sleeves of her top were long and gave her the appearance of having a cape when she flung her arms out wide, which she did as soon as she took the mic.

"So this is a poem about life and death and the rafts we make to float over the abyss. This is a poem about swallowing the tide of lies that conventional society pours down our throats and regurgitating our own truth with the shrill ring of a whistle. This is a poem about power," she declared and held up her fist. "Fight the power!"

I rolled my eyes and thanked God for Kentucky and the invention of bourbon as M.K. began a poem that—as far as I could tell—seemed to be about Jack fitting or not fitting on the floating door in *Titanic*, which was inextricably related to leaving her marriage and sending her children out in lifeboats or something. Around the fifteen-minute mark, it also had something to do with Marxism and "bare-breasted Wiccan priestesses." At the half-hour mark, I downed my third drink. I had to figure that Jack—whoever that poor bastard was—was probably just as happy to have metaphorically drowned and/or frozen to death. She got wild applause at the end, particularly from one table of women who could have been believably cast as the Weird Sisters in *MacBeth*. They kept holding hands and raising them into the air like they were cursing some poor sailor's wife.

M.K. bowed low and flapped her wings when she was finally finished, and the emcee reappeared and praised her as a visionary artist.

"Up next: a spoken-word virgin is about to be deflowered. Join me in welcoming newcomer Winston Bedlow reciting his personal work 'Self/Eval.' Give it up, poets, for Winston Bedlow."

What did she just say? I felt both hot and cold. My thoughts felt sluggish with alcohol. Applause filled the room and I looked at my boss with horror. Iqbal was clapping politely and gesturing to the stage with his head. This was worse than being sent unaware into a drug deal. Much, much worse.

"Self-evaluation time."

"What the hell, man?" There was no way this was actually happening.

Perplexingly, Iqbal started snapping at me like he was trying out for a role as one of the Sharks in an amateur production of *West Side Story*—and then—and then the whole room was snapping at me.

"Everyone is shy their first time," someone in the crowd shouted.

"We'll be gentle—" The room burst into laughter at that gut-buster, and I felt all bristly in my neck.

"Wins-ton! Wins-ton!" they chanted and snapped at me.

Ah, what the hell. Bat woman had blathered on about her middle-aged crush on a young Leonardo DiCaprio for thirty-three minutes. I couldn't do much worse.

I climbed the two steps up to the stage and raised the mic six inches to a better height.

"Good evening—" I said, because this suddenly seemed way more difficult than thinking *What the hell*. The mic slipped down to its original position. The crowd started snapping again. I adjusted it again and pulled out the self-evaluation. "This is my self-evaluation. I work at the U of C Rec Centre." I fumbled with the pages because whatever I had scribbled down this afternoon seemed inadequate for where I was right now. I began to read it, trying to lend it some sort of rhythmic quality because as far as I could tell that was really the only rule.

"Name: Winston Bedlow. Employment Position: Recreation Centre Technician. 'Technician.' You heard that right. Describe your duties: Make sanitizing solution. Inspect equipment. Damage control."

I could only see the silhouettes of the heads of the people in the crowd. My knees felt like they could either lock or buckle at any second. What the hell was I doing up here?

"What is your greatest strength? Being satisfied with the humdrum."

I wrote that this afternoon, but I was struck right now by the fact that it wasn't true. I wasn't satisfied at all. It was like I had been asleep and I was just waking up.

"What's your greatest weakness? My left rotator cuff."

There was a titter of laughter from someone in the crowd. Their laughter helped me to relax.

"That's the official answer on the form," I ad libbed. "If I were honest, I'd say my greatest weakness is lying to myself. Self-deception. The most dangerous of the deceptions."

"Tell us about a time when you demonstrated success? August 1999, when I won a regional swim meet even though I stress-fractured one of my ribs. I was the *Chicken Soup for the Soul* story of the meet. If I'd been Michael Phelps, they'd have made a movie about the winner with the broken ribs who overcame adversity to have a sportsmanlike win at Regionals. I was Daniel Larusso at the All-Valley Karate Tournament coming back in to fight after the dirty tactics of the Cobra Kai. But I'm not Michael Phelps. My greatest strength is being satisfied with the mediocre. But since then? Since August 1999—?"

I paused dramatically. This was supposed to be spoken word poetry, for crying out loud. "—I peaked too soon."

Another ripple of laughter and I lost my place on the form. My gaze slid back and forth over my handwriting, searching for the next question. How had it disappeared? The silence elongated and I half expected to hear crickets. Instead, someone started snapping. Slowly. It was a slow snap instead of a slow clap.

"Tell us about a time when you needed support in order to be successful. Tell us about a time when you felt valued. Tell us about a time when you did not feel valued. What are your development goals? Where do you see yourself in five years?" I blew past my answers because the answers were stupid.

"As if I owe my boss a story about when I felt valued. Would it get me a raise? I'm pretty sure I've topped out the hourly wage for Casual Rec Centre

Technician at the U of C. I don't owe Human Resources my humiliation, either. I'm not a conspiracy theorist; I just don't think having the gall to ask me personal things on an official form means I owe you the answers. People think that they owe an answer to anyone impertinent enough to ask a question. No, thanks." The spotlight on me made it impossible to see Iqbal's face in the crowd.

"Let's talk about duty while we're at it." The bourbon was definitely talking now. "Sanitizing solution? Are you kidding me? Men owe duty— their lives—to country, to wife, to God. List my duties? Those are them. Not putting a sign on a broken elliptical. But I shirked them. I shirked the real duty for the mundane. Five years. What if five years from now I'm still right here? Not right here but—" My thoughts were swimming wildly like a bait ball and my head felt heavy and off-centre on my neck.

"Forms don't ask the right questions. Human Resources aren't human. If they were, they'd know to ask me what I fear—ask me about my dread, if you want to know something about me. I dread that tomorrow and next Tuesday and the week after month after year will all be exactly the same. That five years from now, I'll be the same. Because I was the same five years ago and filling out these same forms. And—" I squinted out into the audience because it occurred to me that five years ago, my boss was still in high school.

"And—nothing has changed."

Maybe this is what Hemingway meant when he said you should write drunk and edit sober. It all sounded a lot better when you were drunk. I stepped back from the mic and out of the spotlight. There was some polite applause and I heard the emcee thank me and introduce someone else as I made my way back to the table.

It was empty.

I looked around the room for Iqbal but he was gone. Of course he was. This was his prank. Send me up there like a lamb to the slaughter. I grabbed my coat from the back of my chair and headed for the stairs as my phone buzzed in my pocket. He was probably outside killing himself laughing at my expense. I climbed the narrow staircase and pulled out my phone to see a text from him.

Wincey Jonze, U got 2 go. Keep it real. Keep on Rockin' in the Free World. Keep on keeping on. Keep Calm and Carry On. Keep on truckin'. Keep on the sunny side of the street. Keep on taking the hobbits to Isengard. —Iqabald Crane

It is the ultimate asshole move to make someone read their self-evaluation as a spoken word poem and then fire them in a text message after the fact. But that's what he did because that's the kind of guy he is.

I hit the panic bar of the emergency exit door to the alley extra hard, sending it flinging open as I reeled in my newly unemployed state.

"Watch it, man," said an angry voice hidden behind the door. He sent it flying back toward me.

"Sorry. I didn't realize you were there."

Two guys and the slump-shouldered waitress from below were smoking cigarettes and looking disaffected.

"Didn't you see the sign? There's a sign." The waitress said with that pissy voice that women sometimes develop. "'Open door slowly.' So open the door slowly and don't be a dick about it."

"I would have. If I had seen it."

"Well. It's there," she said, dragging on her cigarette. "Learn to read."

"Thanks, Tips." They had the whole alley but they had to huddle behind the one door that was bound to open?

"Watch your mouth, loser, or else—"

"Or else what? You'll watch it for me?" I knew it was probably just the perfect storm of alcohol, humiliation and anger, but I realized I was totally happy to fight this guy. Besides, he was smaller than me and too well dressed to be looking for a street fight. He was probably just trying to impress the girl—but from the looks of her, that was a losing battle.

The second dude decided that he wanted to be in on whatever fisticuffs might ensue and so he interjected, his voice dripping with sarcasm, "Hey! Nice poem. I really enjoyed it."

"Patriarchal bullshit promoting misogyny," the round-shouldered waitress said as she tossed her cigarette butt onto the ground and extended her praying-mantis-like arm to open the door to head back inside.

"Yeah. Your poem sucked, asshole."

I'm not sure why this stung. I hadn't written my self-evaluation with the intention of reading it as a spoken word poem.

"Thanks, Harold Bloom." Seriously, I was going to pound this guy and not feel the least bit bad about it.

"Your poem sucked," he said again.

"And I don't like the cut of your jib. Want to do something about it?"

I'm not sure how many fights in the history of the world have included insults to unintentional poetry and telling someone that you don't like the cut of their jib, but I feel like it must be a fairly exclusive number. I would have emerged unscathed, too, if it hadn't been two on one.

CHAPTER FIVE
Bagels and Slimfast

My mother's face registered shock at the sight of me when she opened the door to their new condo to welcome me for the first time. "What on earth happened to you? Were you mugged?"

I caught sight of my reflection in the mirror that hung adjacent to their front door. I hadn't been too sure when I had examined my injuries in the bathroom last night, but in this light there was no doubt about it—I looked misshapen, but the bruising hadn't showed up yet. Nothing major, though I could feel my pulse in my face.

"No, I was—working." Technically, I had been leaving a work-related event.

"At work! Are you alright? What happened?"

"You look like you were in a brawl," my dad said from his chair, the newspaper in his lap and his finger holding his place in the article he was reading.

I didn't feel like explaining it. "Just some guys looking to spar. MMA type of thing. No big deal." It was only sort of a lie. I mean, I don't think those idiots had any training. They just mixed everything they'd seen on pay-per-view.

"I don't think you should do that. It's so violent. You don't have any experience with that sort of thing."

"I had enough. Jeremy is a more ferocious opponent."

"Does it hurt?" My mom reached out with her fingers and lightly pressed against my swollen cheekbone.

I winced involuntarily. "No."

"This isn't very promising. You move out and look at what happens to you. Are you losing weight? You look like you've lost weight." She gestured for me to follow her into the kitchen. The plush, new white carpet felt springy under my socked feet as I trailed after her. The smell of a beef roast permeated the condo and set my mouth watering.

"Maybe." I had lost eight pounds. The truth was I was barely making my new arrangement work financially and the only expense I could cut to try to stay in the black was food. I was scouring flyers for bargains and listening for radio promotions promising free hotdogs on the weekends. I'd found a giant can of strawberry-flavoured SlimFast shake powder on sale at Liquidation World. It was revolting, but breakfast only cost me eleven cents a day.

"Not maybe. Definitely. You don't need to lose weight." She threw open the oven door with the same excess of force she always used for everything that she did. She pulled out the roasting pan and jabbed the electronic thermometer into the lump of meat.

"What's beef supposed to be at?" Her head weaved in and out, as she tried to find the right distance so that she could read the thermometer. "Peter," she called out to my dad. "What's beef supposed to be?"

"One sixty." Dad's disembodied voice came from around the corner where, no doubt, he had taken up residence behind the newspaper.

"What is it?" Mom peered at the digital display of the thermometer again. "It's at 190.8 and still climbing." She chucked a spoon she was holding into the sink, where it landed in a dirty dish of water. "I hope everyone likes beef jerky."

"I'm sure it'll be great," I said, unable to tear my eyes from the glistening roast.

"Well—you look like you should eat the whole thing yourself so—" she said as she began scooping roasted potatoes and carrots from the pan into a bowl.

"Did you get all new dishes?" I asked as my stomach rumbled loudly—loud enough for her to hear.

"What are you eating these days?"

"Food. I eat food. It's fine." In addition to the SlimFast, I ate day-old bagels I found on the discount rack at the Wholesale Club for lunch because they were cheap and filling. Sometimes, depending on the day, I had them for dinner, too. Already I hated the sharp, yeasty smell of the doughy bread that I could taste even when I wasn't eating them.

"Maybe this wasn't the best idea."

"Oh sure, now you say that."

"I'm serious. Your clothes are baggy. Your skin looks—" She paused and I waited for her to say "saggy" because that had been my thought yesterday before the swelling started, but instead she asked, "Do you need money?"

There was no way I was going to take a cent off of my parents. "No."

"Because we could lend you some."

"Thanks. I'm fine."

"I'm worried about you."

"Mom. Please. Enough."

"You look awful."

"And you look lovely." I said as I wandered out of the kitchen and threw myself down on the couch opposite my father. My mother followed closely and stood towering over me, arms akimbo and frowning.

"I'm serious. You have an unhealthy pallor. You look sort of— Peter, tell him we'll lend him money."

"Babs. Leave him alone." My dad did not re-emerge from behind the paper. "Come eat dinner here if you need to."

My mother waved the tea towel that she kept slung over her shoulder dismissively at my father and returned to finish the tasks in the kitchen.

"Can you carve this, please?"

I jumped up to comply. Absolutely. I would happily carve and sample as I did.

"You need to let the meat rest," my father called out. "Otherwise all the juices will run out and the meat will be tough."

"It's at 190 degrees, pet. That ship has sailed." She turned to me again. "Can you get the serving platter from the cupboard above the fridge for me, please?"

I walked over to her fridge and opened the high cupboard door. "It isn't up here."

"Yes, it is."

"No, it isn't."

"I put it there when we moved in. It's there. Get a chair and you'll see it."

"Mom. I don't need a chair. I'm staring at half a dozen liquor bottles, two vases and a popcorn maker. It's not here."

"I wouldn't have gotten rid of it." She looked thoughtfully around her foreign kitchen. She started throwing open drawers and cupboards in pursuit of the illusive serving platter.

"I really can't stand the look of your face," she said from the depths of the pantry. "Oh, here we go!" she exclaimed as she emerged victorious with the familiar platter held aloft. "Maybe you should move back in with us."

I snorted. "After all this fuss? After you moved out of your house to get away from me? You want us all trapped together in this little space? That'll be the day."

"You've always needed a little more help than the others."

"What? No, I haven't. I'm not an imbecile. I got hit in the face. It happens."

"Honey, I'm not saying that I think you are stupid. It's just that—" She looked at me earnestly, like I was in kindergarten and I needed validation. I started to cut the meat into slabs, feeling stung, even more than when she first dropped her bombshell about them moving out.

"How reassuring," I said. "It's just what?"

"I'm just saying that there are certain things that you've found more difficult than your peers."

"Like what?"

Mom started pulling plates from the cupboard to set the table. "The others will be here soon. Can you pull out the TV trays for the kids, please?"

I moved to do as she asked but stopped when I realized I had no idea where they were. "Are they above the fridge as well? You didn't answer my question."

"Spare-room closet." She sighed. "You just don't seem to be as elastic. You never bounced back after Cassandra broke up with you. You never wanted your independence the way that your brother did."

"First of all, I broke up with Cassandra," I said loudly as I walked to the spare room and wrestled four wood TV trays out of the closet. "Second, just because I am not like Jeremy doesn't mean that I am special needs. Jeremy makes Steve Jobs look unmotivated." Dad rattled his paper noisily in the living room.

"It's not just those things. Those are just some examples. There are lots of other things." She said as she dumped frozen peas into a steaming pot.

Lots? Great.

"I blame myself, honey. You probably got it from me."

"Got 'what,' exactly?"

She was getting flustered. "This—this—behaviour. It is like pulling teeth to get you to finish anything. Think of all the sports, the classes, all the jobs you quit because—why? No one knows. Do you even know?"

I'd thought I did at the time. I could feel heat coming into my face. I had moved out. I was living on my own. I was supporting myself—just. Why was I still having this conversation?

"And why would you break up with Cassandra? She was the best thing that ever happened to you. She was wonderful. But you ended it for some mysterious reason."

I rubbed my eyes. "Well, if I am inflexible and delayed in some mysterious way, then I did her a big favour. Did you ever consider that as a potential reason?" This conversation was giving me a headache. If it veered into Cassandra Land, I would likely end up marooned there.

My mom was still talking. "You are the most creative of our children, Winston."

I snorted. This was the most offensive part: the compliment to gild the insult.

My mother persisted despite my obvious contempt for her efforts. "It's true. You're the most curious. The most interested in the world around you. But somehow that never translated into anything. Nothing ever came from any of it. You are like the rosebud that only partially opened before it started to wilt."

"Babs." Dad was still holding up his newspaper, but my conversation with Mom had broken through that normally impenetrable sound barrier. He was watching. He was listening. He said my mother's name as though it were some code word. Some code that she knew but wasn't interested in following.

"It sounds harsh, but it is true."

"Babs."

She turned to Dad. "You know what I mean. You've fielded those questions, too."

"I told people to mind their own business. Nobody's life is going to look exactly the same as someone else's."

"I'm just wondering whether we made the right decision. There's nothing wrong with questioning yourself to make sure you made the right decision."

"Sure. Except you're also questioning whether or not your son is an idiot who needs constant tending," I said. I finished carving the meat, forgetting to sample it because I was distracted by the fact that my mom not only thought I was a loser, but a stupid one. I wandered out of the kitchen, returned to my seat opposite my dad and reached for one of the discarded sections of the newspaper.

"So what really happened to your face?" he asked quietly, bringing the paper down to his lap.

"Just got into a fight. It wasn't a big deal. It was a lot less painful than that one." I gestured toward the kitchen with my chin.

"Did you win?"

I shrugged noncommittally. "I didn't lose."

My dad stared at me a moment longer before returning to his paper.

"What?"

He was saved from answering me by the phone ringing. My mom called out to him from the kitchen. "That'll be the kids. Peter, will you answer, please?"

"Anything for you, light of my life," Dad said cheerfully as he set his paper aside and stood up. "She hasn't figured out how to buzz anyone in yet. All you do is press nine. I don't mind. It's good to know she needs me and won't run off with the super."

"I did press nine," she answered indignantly. "It doesn't work for me."

Soon, the rest of my family had squeezed into the small entryway like clowns piling into a clown car. I waited for Natalie or Jeremy to comment on my face—prepared as I was to present my mixed-martial-arts sparring story—but neither of them looked at me closely enough to notice. They were preoccupied, as they always seemed to be: keeping track of shoes, jackets, sweaters and backpacks; cutting up food; and worrying about whether or not one of their kids had pink eye. My nephew, Michael, seven years old, stared at me wide-eyed and forgot to remove one of his shoes.

"Why does your face look like that?"

"I'm lucky," I said. "I was born this way."

"But why is it all weird like that?"

"Were you in a fight?" His older brother, Bret, asked as he came in close to my face to inspect the damage. (I know. Neither Jeremy nor Beth had any idea that it looked like they had named their sons in tribute to an aging glam rocker who regularly wore eyeliner.)

"I got jumped by some bad guys."

"Was it the Foot Clan?" Michael asked.

I raised my eyebrows at him. "You know, I think it was."

"Don't be dumb," Bret said. "The Foot Clan are in New York."

"They could be here," Michael protested. "You don't know."

"I thought they were in Japan," Jeremy said. "Micheal. Take off your shoes in Grandma's new house."

"This isn't a house. It's an apartment."

77

"Whatever. Just do it." Jeremy sidled past his son to escape the crowded entryway. I waited for my brother to comment on my fight with the Foot Clan but he didn't.

"Did you win?" Michael asked.

"How could he win against the Foot Clan? There are like a million of them."

"If he had the right weapons, he could."

"Which are those?" I asked.

"Nunchucks, or a bo staff."

"If he was a Ninja Turtle?" Bret said. "Uncle Winston isn't a Ninja Turtle."

"Little do you know," I said. "Maybe I transmogrify at night into a turtle."

"That would explain a lot," Jeremy said.

"What's 'transmogrify' mean?" Bret asked.

"Shape-shift."

"Will you take us to the rec centre?" Michael asked, evidently uninterested in learning a new word.

"Sure—" I said slowly. "What did you want to do there?"

Michael shrugged. "Dad said that you could take us on Saturdays after you pick us up from martial arts."

I peered around the corner to look at my brother, who was inspecting the gas fireplace. "You want me to take Bret Michaels to the rec centre after picking them up at martial arts?"

Jeremy didn't turn around but examined the woodwork closely. "It's just an idea. Beth's doing her recertification classes for the next couple of weekends and I've got hockey on Saturdays. You could do it, right?"

I glanced toward Beth, who was exclaiming over the built-in organizers in Mom's new cupboards and drawers. Her back stiffened and I could tell that she was listening for my answer.

"Yeah, sure—I guess—no problem." It wasn't like I had a job anymore to worry about.

Beth turned, cutting herself off mid-comment about the necessity of magnetized knife boards. "Are you sure, Winston? Because if it is a problem, I can cancel my classes or figure out a workaround."

"No sweat, Beth. Seriously."

"Are you sure? I don't want to trouble you."

"It's fine. No trouble at all."

She was smiling at me nervously when suddenly her face fell. "My goodness!" she exclaimed. "What happened to your face?"

Jeremy looked up briefly from the edge of the baseboards, where he was now examining the quality of the inlaid carpeting. "Forget your helmet in hockey again?"

"Pretty much."

"Winston, I was thinking—" my mom said as she was putting the finishing touches on the table. "Maybe you could start your own gym. You know all about running the university rec centre. You could have your own business. I think it would be a really good fit for you. You know so many people at the rec centre. Once they graduate they will be looking for somewhere else to go. You have a built-in market."

Jeremy snorted at Mom's suggestion. "With what money? How come in all of your schooling you never managed to take anything useful?"

"Why don't you loan him some, money bags?" Natalie said. "You could go in on the business together."

"He's got geology," Mom said.

"Big help that'll be running a gym. You should have taken a business degree. That would have been something, at least. Good grief. Your whole life is a how-not-to lesson."

It has been my natural response to always provoke Jeremy—whatever he accused me of, I would take a step further. But as we all attempted to cram around this new dinner table— my shoulders hunched to avoid touching Beth or my dad—I felt tired and brittle. Maybe I should have taken a business degree instead of geology. Maybe he was more right than wrong, even if it pained me to think it. I doubt anyone sets out to make a mess of their life. It just sort of happens and you wind up looking at all the broken pieces and wondering how so many things fell down.

"Last time you said you thought he should be a hustler," Natalie said lightly. "I'm not sure your advice is solid gold."

My mother set her fork down and looked at my brother. "What? Why on earth would you say such a thing?"

"I didn't say he should be a prostitute. I said it would explain some things about his life if he was."

"You said that he would have a solid book proposal."

"Who wants to read about male prostitutes?" Jeremy attacked a roasted potato with his fork.

"I took it as a compliment," I said, trying to regain my footing. "Jeremy has always been a fan of my Adonis-like physique. He knows I'd be a high-priced call boy."

"The term is 'gigolo,'" Natalie said blankly, picking up a section of Dad's discarded paper and settling herself on the couch.

"How do you know the term?" Mom asked, taking the newspaper from Natalie and folding it away.

"Probably because I'm thirty-eight years old."

"Well, no need to shout that from the rooftops."

"Is this really appropriate for little ears?" Beth asked. "Besides, human trafficking is not funny." She was preparing her sons' plates by cutting their meat into impossibly small, un-chokeable pieces. "There are somewhere between twenty-seven and thirty million people enslaved on the planet right now."

Mom wasn't prepared to let go of her gym idea without a fight, no matter how many people were currently enslaved, proving Stalin's line about one death being a tragedy while a million is just a statistic.

She sat down next to Natalie on the couch. "Wouldn't you like to run your own gym, Winston? You know everything about it. You would have a bunch of people who like you at the rec centre who would probably move over to your gym if you had one."

"I doubt it. I got fired. Besides, I know what it would take to run a gym, but Jeremy is right. That would be a lot of capital upfront to start one."

"You lost your job?" Dad finally joined the conversation. "When? How?"

"Friday. In a text about hobbits."

"You were fired in a text message? Is that what the fight was about?"

"What fight?" Natalie asked.

"Only obliquely. My boss is twenty-two, prone to impulsive pranks and currently jacked up on steroids, so I can't say that it was a total surprise that the bottom fell out eventually."

It's possible I was getting too old to work at the rec centre, anyway. Or maybe I was just starting to look too old to work there. Maybe it was ageist profiling and prejudice. I'd heard some women in line at Walmart complaining that weight loss did bring out the wrinkles. Maybe my SlimFast-and-discounted-bagel regime was responsible for losing my job.

"It was a dead end, anyway," Jeremy shrugged.

"But he needs money to pay rent and for food," Mom said, worry pulling the skin on her forehead together. "Have you got anything else lined up yet?"

"It's Sunday. It happened on Friday."

"How much could that hole possibly set him back each month? They should pay Winston to stay there."

"I always thought you would make a good fireman," Joel said. "You'd get to work out, make food and rescue people. It'd be right up your alley."

Natalie perked with enthusiasm at that idea. "You have to do that, Winston. You'd be the best. Seriously. I can totally see you doing that."

"Winston is the last person I would want to rescue me—or any of us."

My mother shot Jeremy a warning look.

"What? He'd be late. He'd forget his gear. He wouldn't be properly trained—need I go on?"

"I think the fire department trains their people pretty thoroughly," Joel said, unruffled by Jeremy's criticism. "I have a friend who is a firefighter. Want me to ask him about their application process? It's pretty competitive, but I think you'd have a good shot at it."

I nodded. "Yeah, sure. Thanks, Joel."

"Three degrees and you're going to be a fireman," Jeremy said with disgust. "What a waste."

"I'll dedicate my photo in the calendar to you, Jeremy, because you've always been so supportive."

"I've wasted so many job postings and interviews on you; I'm not helping you this time."

"Who's asking you to?"

"Whatever. Waste Joel's efforts this time around while you languish in that hovel."

"I'm touched, brother."

My mother placed her hand on my arm. "You just need to paint that place of yours. A fresh colour will make all the difference in the world."

"I'm not allowed to paint. It's in the rental agreement."

"I love the colour you chose for this place," Beth said to my mother, clearly trying to change the direction of the conversation. "What's it called? I'm thinking of having our place repainted. This is such a nice shade. Very bright, but also soft, you know?"

"I've got the swatch. Colonial cream, I think. I was afraid it was going to be too grey but it turned out more yellow-y."

"Very classy. It's like Jackie O in a colour." Beth began fiddling with her left earring—taking it out of her ear, looking at it in such a way that implied it had offended her and then putting it back in. Boomer, my parents' previously overweight Doberman, only roused himself from his wicker-basket bed when my nieces and nephews sat on the couches with their dinners on TV trays. He stared at their plates with that forlorn intensity known only to dieters. Silvery strands of dog saliva stretched to impossibly long lengths before succumbing to gravity's pull and forming perfect, round circles on the shiny laminate floor. His canine surveillance was uncanny and any food that did find its way to the floor disappeared immediately, as though Boom were a firm believer of the five-second rule.

I sat silently during the meal while the conversation criss-crossed over the table like an ever changing web of cat's cradle. Natalie needed to decide if she was going back to work after her maternity leave. Joel's promotion. Jeremy heading up to Fort Mac. Mandy and Frances were going to join soccer this year. Bret got 100 percent on his math test. Michael's art teacher thought that he showed real promise as a painter. I didn't have anything to say. I didn't have anything to add. I didn't even have anyone to sit across from and share a special code with. When Cassandra had been around, we'd had our own language of *Seinfeld* quotations and inside jokes. She was a terrible storyteller. She dragged out the parts that should have been summed up. She rushed over the punchlines. But she would laugh, and it didn't matter that she sucked at telling stories because she was laughing so hard that you just had to laugh, too. I missed that. There wasn't room for her at this table anymore. It was cramped as it was, but I found myself wishing that she were here, because if she were here, none of this would have happened.

After the dishes were cleared away and coffee mugs drained, I offered to take Boomer to the off-leash park. I wanted to get away from everyone but I didn't want to go back to the basement suite. Boomer was an acceptable companion, though even he was ahead of me in terms of achievements, what with his successful weight loss. I used to think that it was impossible to be unhappy at a dog park while watching their canine exuberance. That afternoon, watching the late-winter sun ooze toward the western horizon, with Boomer trotting disconsolately beside me, I knew that wasn't true.

CHAPTER SIX

Inception

"You need to go to the doctor." Sam opened the door to the fridge as though it were personally responsible for my misshapen face. The open box of Arm & Hammer baking soda that my mom had placed in there slid down the otherwise empty shelf until it struck the end of the row and released a self-pitying puff of white. "I shouldn't even have to tell you that."

"This place is a dump. If depression has a cause, I'm pretty sure this place is the source." But for the sticky jar of grape jelly, the almost-empty container of cream cheese and a few unidentifiable crumbs on the bottom, the fridge was bare. She closed the door again with a thud and threw open the cupboard door, exposing the mammoth jar of strawberry shake mix. "SlimFast? Are you kidding me?"

"It's cheap."

"You look horrible; your body is cannibalizing itself. With that swollen eye, you look like Chunk from *The Goonies*."

86

"You mean Sloth."

"Huh?"

"Sloth from *The Goonies*. Chunk was the chubby kid they made do the truffle shuffle to get them to open the gate."

"Sloth. Chunk. Whatever." Sam waved my correction away with indifference. "When was the last time you ate anything green?"

"Sloth was actually pretty strong." I hopped over my long couch from the "kitchen area" to the "living room area" instead of sliding between it and the wall.

"Seriously, are you in danger of heart failure or something?"

"You're a downer. Let's hang out more often."

"You need to go to the doctor."

"I don't need to go to the doctor. It's a black eye and a couple of bruises."

"Did you even call the cops? Every time I see you, I think, 'This is as bad as it is going to get.' But it isn't. I'm honestly afraid that the next time I drive up, you'll be dead."

"This is a false ceiling—" I said, rapping the panel that hung a few inches above my head with my knuckle. "—and, besides, I think it is too low to hang myself from it."

"Not funny." Sam flopped down on my floral couch. "So what really happened? I don't buy the story my mom told me about you sparring at work."

"Bar fight."

"Since when do you go to bars?"

"Okay, fine. It happened in the alley outside the bar."

"What bar?"

"I—I actually don't even know. I was there for a poetry reading."

Sam dismissed me with another wave of her hand. "If you are embarrassed that you walked into a pillar or something—"

"Pillars don't gang up on you."

"Seriously?"

"He didn't like my poem."

"What poem? Since when are you writing poetry?"

"It wasn't really a poem. Iqbal thought it would be hysterical to have me read my employee self-evaluation in front of a crowd of people expecting spoken word poetry."

"Did you know ahead of time?"

"Nope."

"That's horrible. That's like the nightmare where you're naked."

"My naked soul exposed for all the hipsters to see through their horn-rimmed glasses."

"I'm almost afraid to ask—" Sam looked all sympathy. "Did it—did it go okay?"

"Of course it didn't. It was my U of C Rec Centre employee self-evaluation, for crying out loud. If it weren't for the fight afterward driving the humiliation from my mind, I would be mortified."

Sam shook her head in disbelief. "I can't in a million years imagine something like that happening to me."

"If only you had the soul of a poet, then you, too, could encounter these low-lifes."

"If only—" Sam said with mock wistfulness. "Instead I get to pick up the pieces of their girlfriends and 'baby mamas.' I still think you should go to the doctor. You were bleeding. What if he had hep C or HIV or something."

"Awesome. I was feeling cool about fighting that asshole and now I have AIDS. No good deed goes unpunished."

"I just think you should get checked out." Sam said, studying my face. "The funny thing is, you don't even really look like you were in a fight. You just look like you have a really odd-shaped face. Sloth-like, if you will."

"Thanks a lot."

Sam laughed. "Don't take it personally. AIDS doesn't have nearly the stigma associated with it that it used to. We'll all start wearing ribbons for you."

"That's a real comfort."

"Speaking of stuff for you, I got you a housewarming gift." Sam retrieved her purse from the counter and dug around in its cavernous depths. "It's a can opener. No one ever donates one of those, unless it sucks and they want a new one. I bought you the Rolls-Royce of can openers. Tupperware. Lifetime guarantee."

She'd tied a ribbon around it.

Truth be told, I kind of wanted everyone to see how bad I had it, but nothing ever really goes how you want it to. People don't play the characters you want them to, say the lines that you script for them when you are feeling sorry for yourself. The errant lover doesn't return contrite and beg to be taken back. The child boss who fired you doesn't come to you hat in hand in order to speechify about how he should have promoted you and not fired you. In my whirlpool of self-pity, I never paused to realize that I actually wanted to be promoted. I suppose that was as much a sign of growth as anything. I'd gone from loser-slacker who didn't want any extra responsibility to a poor loser who did. Your parents don't regret their decision to push you out of the nest. Your blowhard brother never sheds tears of repentance because he was an asshole. No one ever does those sort of things—except in the movies, where it happens all the time, thereby creating unrealistic expectations about life and people. People just don't come back. Adults rarely say that they are sorry, almost as though they can't. Sure, they say doctor-y things like "I'm sorry that you felt that way," as though the problem is your feelings, not their actions. Or they say really annoying things like "We both had a part in creating this situation... I am sure that we are both sorry..." As though we must be socialists in our dealings with one another, with everyone allotted their fair share of blame.

"I'll drive you to the walk-in clinic right now."

"I'm not going to go wait for hours at the walk-in because I haven't eaten a vegetable in recent memory. Being diagnosed with nutritional stupidity would be a waste of health care dollars."

"Stupid, maybe—but that isn't what I think you should go to the doctor for. You are obviously depressed or something."

"Is it really 'depression' if you have stuff to be depressed about? I need medication because my life has actual difficulties? Besides, I get out of bed. I cope. I just don't have a job."

Sam surveyed my surroundings, which, granted, were looking a little mangier than usual. There was a backlog of mismatched plates and butter knives sticky with jam and cream cheese. I had to fill a large bowl with soap and water to do my dishes because the sink was too small to fit anything in it. I had grown accustomed to my insect squatters and hadn't bothered to vacuum them up for a week or two, resulting in a larger contingent of arthropods than she had perhaps seen before.

"I think you should go to the doctor and ask about depression—maybe AIDS. In fact, I will buy you lunch if you agree to go to the doctor."

"Why didn't you say so?" I grabbed my coat. "Let's go."

"I'm making you order a salad, though."

"I'll get one with my steak. I'm probably iron-deficient."

Sam pulled her keys out of her pocket as she headed up the narrow stairway to the grey light of winter above. "Fine. I need to stop at my work to pick up a package for one of my girls on the way there, though."

"Whatever you need to do, money bags."

Sam left her car running in a loading zone outside of her office building with me sitting in the passenger seat. She always pulled over wherever she chose and left me waiting in the running car with the injunction to move it if it looked like a truck was pulling up. Inevitably, there was always a truck about to pull up that would lean on its horn until I moved. I waved to the other driver as I walked around to the driver's side door. The Tercel was small. I slid the seat all the way back but still felt jammed behind the steering wheel in a disorganized assortment of knees and elbows. I circled the block three times before I returned to see Sam standing on the sidewalk leafing through a packet of papers. I pulled the car over and she jumped in the passenger side.

"To the Keg, maestro. I got my bonus finally."

"Big spender. I was kidding about the steak," I said as I pulled the car out into traffic once more.

"I know. But you've had it rough and I meant it about going to the doctor." Sam didn't look up but continued to flip through the materials on her lap. "This is amazing! I can't believe how fast this worked out for Alesia."

"Who?" I was now cruising down Crowchild Trail.

"Alesia. She's one of the girls in our group home. She got into that program I was telling you about, where the government buys you a house and assigns a support worker." Sam shook her head in disbelief. "I just can't believe how quickly that happened. She only applied two weeks ago. Nothing ever works that fast. Ever."

"I thought you said that program was for mentally disabled people."

"It is. Alesia's story is super sad. But she's getting a break here. That makes me so happy." Sam stuffed the papers in her oversized purse and grinned as she looked out the window.

"What happened to her?"

"She got pregnant from some low-life. She wanted to keep the baby. Her boyfriend wanted her to have an abortion and beat her up until she miscarried. He also caused brain damage."

"That's horrible."

Sam nodded.

"If she miscarried, how come she ended up at Friendly Horizons? I thought you had to be pregnant to stay there?"

"She got pregnant again shortly thereafter. Same guy. A lot of these girls go back to the guys."

"Are they all brain-damaged?"

"Don't be a jerk."

"What good is all this charitable effort if these girls are no better off after the help than they were before it?"

"A kindness is a kindness regardless of whether or not it solves the root of the problem. Alesia needed a place to live and some help. Hopefully she'll take the help and make more productive choices as a result." Sam shuffled through the pages on her lap. "Hey, want to see the place that the government bought for her? It isn't too far from here."

"They already bought her a place?"

"They must have had a bunch of houses ready for when they rolled out the program. Maybe it was just a matter of approving and assigning." Sam read off the address and within a few minutes we were turning down a tree-lined street in Lynnwood. Sam was peering through the frost-scraped windshield looking for the correct house number.

"There—at the end!" Sam was so enthusiastic you'd think we were pulling up to her new government-funded house. I parked the car behind a construction waste bin lying at an angle to the sidewalk.

"It's a new build?"

"This is unbelievable!" Sam's whole face was lit up with delight. "You have no idea how little money people get when they live on assistance. It usually means living in horrible cramped places where they can barely scrape by."

"Yeah, I have no idea what that's like."

Sam rolled her eyes. "The regulations up until now have been so punitive that even people who could work a little bit haven't been allowed to earn more than a couple hundred extra dollars. It condemns them to a below-poverty-level existence through absolutely no fault of their own. They can never save anything."

Sam threw open the car door and ran up to the new house. It was a small bungalow. The finishes were basic, but it was new. Sam cupped her hands around her eyes and stood on her tiptoes to look in the window.

"I can't believe it!" She turned, her face animated with joy as she gestured emphatically for me to get out of the car. "Come here and look at this! It looks like it's furnished." She glanced again at the house number as though she was pinching herself in order to believe Alesia's good fortune. Her good, tax-payer-funded-government-provided fortune. "This is the right house and it is furnished!"

I trudged through the snow, feeling self-conscious as I peered through the windows into a furnished living room where dark grey couches faced one another over a coffee table and a framed print of mass-produced abstract art adorned the wall behind a kitchen table with matching chairs. It looked like a minimally decorated show home.

"Who pays for all of this?"

Sam didn't answer. She was too busy trying to hop high enough to see in the bedroom windows. "I think that's a kid's room!"

I craned my neck to see the dark laminate floor. There were no segmented-bodied insects littered across it as though a massive battle had occurred during the night and the dead were left where they fell. We walked back to the car, Sam hopping through the snow with absurd little leaps.

"This is incredible!" I saw Sam wiping what looked suspiciously like tears from the corners of her eyes. "Seriously. This is the best day of my career."

I put the key in the ignition and tried to be happy for Sam and for Alesia and her unnamed child. It was good that they had a place to live. I wanted to be happy about it. It wasn't that I resented her a stable house or anything like that. I just wondered how some people could make all the wrong decisions over and over again and yet, still, someone made it all work out for them.

At the restaurant, the inadequately clad hostess glanced at me warily as Sam asked for a table. Maybe I should have put a Band-Aid on my face somewhere so that it would be obvious it was an injury.

Note to self: save up for Band-Aids.

I ordered the Sirloin Oscar and a Keg-Sized Caesar. I told myself that one day I would be well off enough to buy Sam a lunch like this. While we waited for the food to arrive, Sam talked more about Alesia and how great it would be for her to get a second chance in life. How this girl had had such a hard life. How it was only getting harder. How this program would give so many people like her a pleasant place to live and the dignity of semi-independent living.

"Group homes are just not the ideal arrangement for everyone," Sam said.

"Didn't she already get her second chance?"

"What do you mean?"

"When she miscarried." My stomach growled noisily. The smell of steak permeating the restaurant was almost more than I could bear.

"Nice, Winston."

"I meant that the bad guy was out of the picture then. Or, at least, he could have been."

"Unfortunately, those bad guys are never really out of the picture." Sam leaned back against the oversized booth and sighed.

"So, the government just bought him a house."

"Well—he's in prison now."

"For what?"

"Sexual assault. Not Alesia—a different woman."

"This is a beautiful story. I'm glad my tax dollars get to be a part of it."

"With what you earn? Fractions of a cent."

"Yeah, me and the poor widow in the Bible who gave two copper coins."

"Are you really comparing your tax dollars to the widow's charity?"

"Not really. She had the freedom not to give at all—unlike taxpayers. But the point stands: I'm contributing to Alesia's boyfriend's house out of my poverty, not out of my wealth."

"But we're taxed based on a percentage. So, in terms of income, I bear a greater burden than you but it is equal and based on my ability to pay. Besides, there are things I can't do because of the taxes that I pay. But I think it is worth it in order to help those less fortunate than myself. People like Alesia."

Our waiter appeared, set down our plates and offered us freshly ground pepper. We waited in silence while he covered both our meals with a thick dusting.

"A large part of the reason she's 'less fortunate' is self-inflicted. Doesn't it ever bother you that the people who continually make all the wrong choices are rewarded? I mean, personally? You've done things right, but where's your newly furnished house? Where's your baby?"

Sam unwrapped her cutlery and gave her plate an inexplicable quarter turn. "I don't want to talk about this."

"Why not?"

"Because it doesn't lead anywhere good, that's why."

"I'm not criticizing you. Seems like if you try to do things the right way, the unselfish way, you get penalized, whereas the people who just don't give a shit get everything. I mean, moral choices matter or they don't. Seems like they don't."

"Winston—"

"Am I wrong?"

My cousin put down her utensils and leaned back against the booth again. "Maybe not. But I don't think it is a good avenue to explore."

"Why?"

"Because things are morally right whether they reward you or not."

"But shouldn't there be a reward for good and a consequence for bad?"

"In a perfect world——"

"But the world isn't perfect. So, why should any of us act morally if there is no natural consequence if we don't?"

"Where are you going with this?"

I wasn't even sure. It wasn't that I cared or didn't care about Alesia or even the tax burden of public assistance programs. "It just seems like we're enabling." My stomach growled again—louder this time. Insistent. I picked up my cutlery and looked at my plate for the first time. What I cared about was my empty stomach and how I was going to get a decent meal. I cared about steak. If I had been eating my last meal on earth, I would have died a happy man. The sirloin was smothered in Béarnaise sauce and shrimp and scallops, which spread out onto the plate and enveloped my baked potato in a rich, golden ocean.

"So—who decides what's morally good, then?" I asked.

"What do you mean?"

"Who decides what's right or wrong?"

"We all know what's right and wrong."

"Do we? You and I don't agree on a lot and we were basically raised the same way."

Sam took a bite of her steak salad and chewed thoughtfully. "It can't be public opinion—majority opinion—otherwise, Nazi Germany would have been morally right when everything cries out that it was morally evil to exterminate people."

"Right. So—what makes something right? Or, maybe more importantly, what makes something wrong?"

"If it hurts someone else?"

"Too subjective. You might hurt someone to prevent a greater injury. Besides, look at the abortion debate—or Nazi Germany, for that matter; all you have to do is declare that you aren't hurting someone else. A fetus is a clump of tissue. Jews are subhuman. No harm, no foul."

I looked up to see a couple of women at the table next to us glaring at me. "I wonder if they are mad about the babies or the Jews?" I said to Sam.

Sam glanced over at them momentarily before returning her attention to the conversation. "Fair point."

"Do you think democracy gives people this false idea that majority opinion is morally right? We seem to think if everyone has a say, that something is somehow good."

"I suppose it could lead to that. What's a better system, though?"

"I'm not saying that there is one. I'm just wondering if, culturally, we've elevated democracy to this inherent good when maybe it isn't. Maybe it is just as prone to corruption as everything else."

"Maybe—but more people involved makes it harder to hide the corruption."

"Still raises the question of what is actually good—or what makes things bad, though."

"It would have to be something outside the human system that sets the standard. That would be incorruptible, right?"

"You're talking about God."

Sam smiled with surprise. "I guess I am. But then—how would we know for sure that we got it right? The moral standard? Or is it just believing that Moses on Sinai got it right and we follow that?"

"Maybe it has to require a certain amount of faith. You know, deciding to trust something or someone greater than yourself. But not the government, because that's just people with power."

I dug into my food with gusto, momentarily forgetting what we were talking about as the taste of red meat took over every conscious thought. I focused on my plate with a previously unknown intensity of feeling. I forgot about doctor's appointments for depression. I forgot about hideous abodes and existing in mediocrity. I was eating and it made me feel as close to euphoric as I have ever felt. It was the kind of experience that you close your eyes for.

My plate was almost empty when I returned to the conversation. "So, how do you square away the deserving from the undeserving?"

Sam's plate was still nearly full of her steak salad. "What do you mean? I don't."

"You don't have a way of determining whether someone is in legitimate need?"

"Everyone has legitimate needs."

"Right, but I mean, like, if a homeless guy asks you for money, you can pretty much assume he's not using it for bus fare. He's going to buy booze or drugs."

"You don't know that for sure."

"Let's call it an educated guess with a slim margin of error."

"I don't judge my clients, if that is what you mean."

"Let me get this straight. Friendly Horizons helps—"

"It's called 'New Horizons,'" Sam interrupted irritably. "Quit being obtuse. You're mocking my job. I get it. Let's move on."

"My apologies," I said. "*New* Horizons helps everyone the same regardless of whether or not they are willing to make lifestyle changes that would ensure that the help you give them allows them to stand on their own feet. You don't turn anyone away—for anything?"

"No," Sam said and I could tell she was getting annoyed. "There are kids involved. Why should they suffer? Besides, it's not like people end up where they are randomly. Bad things happened to them to make them this way."

"So—they have no power, no agency over the situation? Bad things happened to them so they go about making bad things happen to their own kids?"

"I'm not saying that they don't have the choice of making better decisions, but I wouldn't be able to face myself in the mirror if I didn't try to prevent the innocent ones from suffering."

"Those kids won the loser's lottery in terms of parents. They are going to suffer, regardless."

"So, we'd be better off if all those kids were aborted?"

"I'm not saying that. I'm just wondering if there is a single situation that you've come across at New Horizons that doesn't qualify for financial aid."

"No. We help anyone who comes to us."

"With money."

"Among many other services."

"That's kind of amazing."

Our waiter approached the table to clear my plate. "Can I get you anything from the dessert menu?"

My shrunken stomach was protesting against the sudden onslaught of rich food, but despite the fact that my baggy pants were feeling way too tight, I ordered a Billy Miner Mud Pie and a coffee that appeared almost immediately.

Sam eyed me from across the table. "I'm going to put your cranky mood down to the fact that you've had it rough for the last couple of weeks and ignore this conversation. Your situation is also of your own making, Winston, and yet here I am, buying you steak and mud pie. Everyone deserves mercy."

"Nobody deserves mercy. That's the point," I said, digging my fork into the enormous slab of ice cream and fudge with reckless abandon. "Otherwise, it wouldn't be mercy. It would be a wage. Incidentally, I am very grateful for your charitable impulses and wouldn't want you to be any other way."

"*Incidentally*, you promised to go to the doctor in exchange for this meal, so I suppose you're right. This is a wage. Not mercy. And you'd better get the doctor to check your vision, too. You look—" She searched around for an appropriate adjective and settled on gesturing toward the mirrored wall across the aisle from where we were sitting. "You don't look like you at all."

The light in my bathroom being what it was, I hadn't really gotten that close a look at the damage done to my face. The swelling filled in my somewhat angular features and my left eyelid appeared to be decorated with a regal shade of purple. It wasn't super obvious with my eye open, though.

"At least I can open my eye again."

"Not fully," Sam said.

I tried to raise my eyelid but there was too much me in the way. "Not fully," I conceded.

Sam watched as I scraped the plate clean. "That was quite a performance. Ready to go? Your clinic awaits."

CHAPTER SEVEN

Yu, Me and Unnatural Disasters

SIGN IN REQUIRED!!!!
WE WILL GET TO YOU
WHEN WE GET TO YOU!!!!
VERBAL ABUSE
WILL <u>NOT</u> BE TOLERATED!!!!!

The sign taped on the wall over the reception desk at the walk-in clinic was emphatic despite being faded from the sun and dog-eared. Sam had dropped me in the parking lot with a sympathetic look that made me feel like one of the hobo down-and-outers (a.k.a addicts) that she hands out spare change to downtown.

Looking backward, I can honestly say that there was no planning. There was no malice of forethought that makes me more culpable than I already am for what ended up happening. I'm not saying that to justify it; I'm relating what happened. I ended up in Dr. Yu's office because I was doing what I was asked. Good grief, isn't going to the doctor supposed to be the responsible thing to do? Isn't the medical community supposed to shed more light on a situation, not add to the confusion? The answer: not always.

Even by the time we were leaving the restaurant, my stomach had been loudly protesting my gluttony. Turns out you can't go from a starvation diet to a rich-food overload without consequence. I signed in at the reception desk and then spent the next forty-eight minutes sprawled uncomfortably in a waiting room chair trying to ease the pressure on my distended gut, which grew outward by inches as the minutes ticked away on the giant analog clock above the reception desk.

Multiple exclamation marks on cranky signs make you sound like an irritable jackass, I don't care how busy you are. I flipped through ancient copies of *Macleans* that countless other sick people had touched. My knee bounced continuously as though that might somehow relieve the growing pressure in my stomach. The receptionist at the desk ignored me completely and seemed to have some eerie sixth sense about when I was about to ask her how much longer she thought it might be, because she always avoided my gaze and left the room whenever I tried to catch her eye. I scanned the miles of patient folders on shelves behind the reception desk. Does anyone even look at those anymore? After nearly an hour of shifting uncomfortably in the Alcatraz-inspired chair, the unfriendly receptionist with the brush cut led me to an examination room. My stomach churned uneasily as I shuffled carefully past her into the claustrophobic room and sat down tentatively on the examination table.

"Doctor Yu will be here shortly." Her eyes narrowed as she took in my pained expression. "What did you say was the matter with you?"

I couldn't remember what I had filled in on the form. That felt like eons ago. Depression? Who can focus on a medical form when their stomach is performing acrobatic feats?

"What's wrong with you?" She asked again, minus, it must be noted, any note of concern.

"Kinda a loaded question," I muttered. "Currently my stomach is upset."

"Have you been poisoned?"

"By whom?"

"Food. Do you have food poisoning?"

I shook my head vigorously. "Do you have any Pepto-Bismol?" I was starting to sweat.

"Drugstore is across the plaza," she said unsympathetically as she began to close the door behind her. "And the bathroom is down the hall."

In desperation to ease the pressure on my stomach, I lay down on the examination table, which was too small for me by half. My legs dangled limply off the end and the white tissue between me and all the other sick people that had sat there crinkled and tore as I shifted myself into place. My stomach was rolling and beads of sweat were forming on my face as a growing sense of panic began to take over my thoughts. I wasn't going to be sick, was I? That would be a terrible waste of all that good food.

There was a slight tap on the door before it swung open. "Comfortable—" the doctor said as he entered, pausing to look at his clipboard. "—Winston?"

Dr. Yu was younger than me. Suddenly, everyone who was a professional was younger than me. He wore thick-rimmed designer glasses and gay pointy European dress shoes that had slightly curled at the toe from walking.

"No." The word came out clipped. Why was I holding my breath? Having my legs hang unsupported from the thigh down was beginning to bother my lower back, but my stomach would not permit any other position without consequence.

"What seems to be the problem today?" he asked.

Maybe if I hadn't gotten such a stomach ache, I would have thought about what to say to the doctor in advance. I didn't really believe Sam's diagnosis of depression. Nothing that was going on with me had a medical origin, and yet here I was, hoping for a medical solution. I thought about just telling him about the bar fight and maybe concern about contracting hep C or something, but the food distending my stomach was loudly gurgling that I owed Sam more than that.

"My cousin says—" The words came out stilted, almost garbled. A sharp stab of pain shot through my stomach to somewhere else that I couldn't identify but feared. I couldn't breathe. If this pressure didn't let up, I was going to shit myself right here in the doctor's office.

Dr. Yu watched me for a moment before scanning his clipboard. "You wrote here that you're depressed?"

I couldn't answer. Nothing. No words. I may have grunted.

"Can you tell me about it?"

I shook my head emphatically. I wanted him to stop talking to me so I could think, so I could make a decision like a responsible adult. Could I get to the bathroom in time? Where did she say it was? Down the hall? What if I needed some doctor's office key attached to a giant wad of tongue depressors? The pain was rising to a crescendo, accompanied by a dreadful feeling of inevitability. I clenched my hands into tight fists so that even my short fingernails were digging into my sweaty palms. There was no way I was going to make it. I was going to have an accident. Like a dog. Perspiration was running into my hairline from my forehead and it dampened my armpits. I was going to be sick. I just couldn't tell exactly how. Oh please, God, don't let me be sick. Not like that. Don't let me dirty myself.

Dr. Yu looked down at his clipboard again. He was bored. I was having an honest-to-goodness health crisis in front of a doctor and he was bored.

"I need to go to the bathroom!" I said suddenly, struggling to sit up from the exam table. I had to get out of here before disaster struck.

"You can go to the bathroom in a minute. Let's just talk a bit. Are you having trouble getting out of bed in the morning."

"I need to go real bad!"

In my desperation to get out of the exam room and to a room with a toilet, I knocked a compendium of doctor-y implements off their place on the wall. The blood-pressure cuff went swinging as did that funny little reflex hammer, which hit Dr. Yu on the shin, spun sideways off his elf shoe and slid under the examination table.

"Sorry—" I started to chase it across the room but changed course mid-movement since I needed to conserve every extra moment and movement in order to make it to the toilet.

Dr. Yu cocked his head to the side like a contemplative Labrador. "Maybe you need to bring someone in to help explain your situation?" he asked slowly. Every word seemed to take a lifetime to get out of his mouth and I am too frickin' Canadian and polite to run out of the damn room when someone is asking me a question.

"What? I need a—" I was nearly bent in half in agony and this guy wanted me to fetch my mom?

Suddenly, the pain and pressure eased without warning and I laughed in sheer relief of a personal hygiene disaster averted. Dr. Yu cocked his head to the other side and looked at me with puzzled interest.

"Depressed," I said, chuckling. "I'm depressed." I had gone from grimace to laughter in a matter of seconds. I probably looked nuts.

Dr. Yu gazed at me blandly, seeming to take in my sweaty face and grubby, ill-fitting clothes. I hadn't been to Natalie's to do my laundry for a couple of weeks.

"Are you taking enjoyment in your usual activities?"

I looked at him blankly. I couldn't think of a single thing that I did. Did I do things *usually*?

He looked at his fingernails as he tried again. "The things that usually bring you joy—that make you feel happy—do you still enjoy them?"

"I guess."

"How are things going at work?"

I probably paused for too long, now that I think about it—I should have been able to answer that question quicker. I was trying to think about the least humiliating way to explain it. I failed.

"I got fired."

"And that makes you feel sad?"

"It didn't make me feel good—?" What was this, emotional kindergarten?

"What was your job?"

"I was a U of C Recreation Centre employee."

"Why were you fired?"

"I think it was because I forgot to make sanitizing solution."

"I see."

"I'm not totally sure. There was this poetry slam and then I got in a fight and then my boss sent me a text. I think it was the sanitizing solution."

Dr. Yu crossed his leg and laced his fingers together around his knee. "Do you have any other source of income?"

"I've been going to Cash Corner and getting day-labour jobs."

"That must be scary."

"Scary?"

"You don't find it scary?" He pushed his expensive-looking, rectangular frameless glasses up the bridge of his nose. There is something extra-humiliating about recounting your failures to a high-performance stranger.

"No. There are some rough types but I'm not afraid of them." This was the weirdest doctor appointment I'd ever had.

"Are you worried about having enough money? Where are you living? With your parents?"

"No," I answered slowly, wondering just how much of my history to tell him. I should just tell him the whole story. The ship of good first impressions had already sailed. Besides, Sam would give me the third degree if I didn't tell him everything. She'd claim I'd welched on the Keg deal or something. There was nothing else to do.

The good doctor listened to my story with the practised expression of one used to forming their features into an inscrutable arrangement, but said nothing in response. He merely took my blood pressure and listened to my heartbeat.

"I'm sending you for some blood tests."

"My cousin thinks I might also have AIDS," I said, laughing a little to lighten the mood.

Dr. Yu scanned the requisition form and ticked a couple other boxes as though he hadn't heard me. "Tell me about your sexual activity."

Oh geez.

"Why do you need to know about that?"

"Sexual promiscuity can be a symptom of certain mental health issues."

"Well. I don't engage in promiscuity."

Dr. Yu glanced up at me. "Do you use protection during sexual contact?"

This is why people hate going to the doctor. Where was the modesty? Where was the decorum? Where were the polite euphemisms? "Sure thing, doc. I pull out all the stops."

"There's nothing to be embarrassed about," he said indifferently.

"Who's embarrassed?" Dr. Yu's unreadable expression was beginning to get on my nerves.

"I'm sending you for some blood tests," he said finally and began ticking off boxes on the yellow lab requisition form with medical abandon. "That means that you will need to go down the hall to the lab and give them this form." He tore the page off the pad and handed it to me. He had scrawled something illegibly at the bottom of the page. I was peering at it, trying to decipher the words, when he grabbed my arm.

"I want you to go immediately so that you don't forget," he said, looking at me with a bizarrely intense expression. "As in, when you leave here."

"I won't forget," I said, pulling away and sliding off the examination table. I shoved the lab requisition form in my coat pocket.

"I want you to go immediately. No exception. No stops along the way. I am also writing a referral for you. My receptionist will call you with an appointment."

"A referral for what?" Suddenly the pressure in my gut was mounting again, sending paroxysms of pain throughout my abdomen.

The doctor lazily tore another note off of his prescription pad. "It's just for an evaluation. I don't want to prescribe antidepressants if that isn't the right thing for you."

"Right," I said, easing myself off the table. "Where's the bathroom?"

"Down the hall."

I slid uncomfortably off the table but was unable to straighten. Dr. Yu went to the sink and began meticulously washing his hands. I didn't go directly to the lab as instructed. I went to the bathroom and stayed there for a long time.

Where u @ Winnebago? Ur country needs u.

I squinted against the brightness of my cell phone screen. Iqbal was not a person I wanted to wake up to. The shafted predawn light that filtered through my basement windows did little to drive the grogginess of sleep from my brain. I dropped my arm over my eyes, turning the puzzle pieces around in my mind trying to make them fit into some semblance of a rational picture. He had fired me. Why was he texting me like I was late for work? Overhead, the sound of water rushing through the pipes. My neighbours were up.

After a few moments, I squinted back at my phone and began typing, sending several messages in succession.

Sleeping.

You fired me nine days ago, my abstracted Pakistani fiend.

*friend

whatever.

I blinked several times trying to clear my head. Something was weird. Why did my life never make sense anymore?

My phone lit up again with his response.

4 ur racism u gots 2 stay late

Iqbal had evidently changed his mind about firing me. It's possible I had misunderstood his text about taking the hobbits to Isengard but it was more likely he had firer's remorse when it meant he had to work more hours. Or, for all I knew, he was using me as some sort of lab rat for some psychology-class project. I rubbed my eyes hoping to clear my thoughts. If he had changed his mind, I suppose I could go work a shift. I ran my fingertips lightly over my still-swollen eye. I didn't have anything to do other than that specialist appointment Dr. Yu had set up for me at 4:30 p.m. today. It was better than waiting around at Cash Corner for some day-labour job. My phone dinged again.

> & bring me a mcmuffin, muffin
> & a coffee. 6 sweet and lows.

Sitting up, I swung my legs over the side of my bed and yelped. Almost as soon as the soles of my feet touched the carpet, I yanked them up from the ground in a panic. Holding my wet feet off the ground, my growing revulsion in abeyance, I squinted through the gloom at the floor. The carpet was dark, way darker than it should have been.

"Awesome, just amazing," I said with as much bitterness as a 5 a.m. flood can yield. I gingerly set my feet down on the ground again and stood up. Cold water pressed out of the carpet and in between my toes.

"Please, please, please don't let it be sewage," I muttered to God because it seemed like He might take pity on me. Bridling my disgust, I took an exaggerated stride to the light switch. The fluorescent bulbs flickered to life and cast their uncompromising glare over the ugliness of my latest disaster. Water everywhere—seeping into the old, disgusting carpet that had absorbed the skin cells of the countless other degenerate losers who had lived here like lees at the bottom of a barrel. Even the arthropods had scrambled for higher ground. The flood was spreading from the bathroom to my bedroom to the living room and siphoning its way up the too-long floral couch.

I took another stride and flicked on the bathroom light. I glared at the source of the problem as though my hatred would stop the water that was dripping steadily from the ceiling over the toilet. It was probably grey water, maybe from the tub upstairs. Whatever the cause, I was looking at the end of the flood, not the genesis of it. I took several cold, wet steps to my kitchen, where the floor was still dry, and pulled on my shoes. I grabbed one of the mismatched pots my mother had bequeathed to me and set it under the drip in the bathroom. I pulled on some clothes, doing an elaborate balancing act to avoid stepping with my bare feet on the wet carpet. I wondered why I didn't feel angrier. I glanced hopelessly around my small world to see if there was anything I could save but almost everything was contaminated. A couple of paperbacks that I had left on the floor by my bed were bloated and rippling like an accordion. I moved them to the counter in hope they might still be readable when they dried out. There was nothing else to be done. Utterly dejected, I didn't even lock the door on my way out.

At least I have my car, I thought as I unlocked the door and flung myself into the driver's seat. At least the Blazer had never let me down. I fought a superstitious urge to cross my fingers lest it suddenly burst into flames. I felt an almost juvenile kinship with it in that moment. As though it was the only friend I had who was partner with me in my downward spiral, like a cowboy's trusty steed who nudges him back to life when he's lying face down in the dirt with a tomahawk in his back. The streets were nearly empty as I pulled into the McDonald's drive-through to pick up Iqbal's Egg McMuffin.

As I paid, I wondered why it is that God seems more willing to answer crisis prayers—ones like "please don't let this be sewage,"—but seemingly ignores or refuses the bigger imprecations. I prayed the most fervently about saving my relationship with Cassandra but that was a no-go. Maybe I was too vague. Maybe God only answers crisis prayers because those are usually the ones that we bother to get specific about. "Please, please, please don't let it be sewage" is much clearer than "Save my relationship." What did that even mean? Change her? Change me? Make us fit together better? After it all ended I used to believe that maybe it would have been a bad thing if He had intervened, but on this morning that felt like sour grapes. Cassandra made the world run smoothly. If she were around, none of this stuff would have happened.

And it's weird that I was thinking about her that morning, because that afternoon I saw her again for the first time in three years.

"If we'd had an arranged marriage, we would have made it work. But no one in their right mind goes into it with so much against them. You did us both a favour. I didn't have the strength—the guts—to pull the plug," Cassandra said to me that afternoon because of course—of course—that would happen the day that my hovel flooded, when I still looked like Sloth from *The Goonies* and was possibly working for Iqbal for free. That would be the day. Why wouldn't it be that day? If I were superstitious, I would have believed that the day was out to get me, like some unlucky planet was passing over head or through my astrological house or whatever, and its gravitational pull was yanking out the stitches of my life one by one. That day—the day of the specialist appointment—it wasn't enough that I was subsisting on diet shakes and my cousin thought I was depressed and I had a fast-tracked referral to a specialist of No Name diseases. That wasn't enough. No, that was the day when I also saw Cassandra again. That was the day when I behaved like such a jackass that she left thanking God that it was over between us forever. Some people just bring out the worst in you. And Cassandra, in her near perfection, brought out the worst in me.

It wasn't until I saw her that I realized how much I had wanted to see her again. I wanted to know what she was doing. I wondered if she missed me, because I'm self-centred and want people who reject me to regret it— possibly for forever in a forlorn Brontë-like fashion. Besides, before we tanked, it had been good. Really good. We had trained our steps to fall in time. I hadn't been able to walk with anyone since. Whereas she was able to walk away grateful for her lucky escape from our entanglement, I had to shut myself in the janitorial cupboard only to be plagued by the comfort of a twenty-two-year-old, steroid-using idiot.

I saw her through the window first; I almost anticipated her. She was decked out in an assortment of violently coloured spandex workout clothes with random cut-outs and an oddly placed diagonal zipper. She had lost the weight that she had gained toward the end of our relationship. It wasn't much, maybe twenty pounds that came on probably as a result of stress. I didn't mind it, but she hated it. It had rounded out some of her sharper corners, making her features softer, though she generally seemed sadder. Her hair was longer now than it had been and her face was happier than I remembered. She was laughing with some girl I didn't know—some friend she had made since the time when we shared friends. She'd taken most of them with her. I got to keep Sam by default of family connection. She denies it, but I think she liked Cassandra better.

I am ancient history to Cassandra. She had probably gotten over me in the first six months. She probably never even thought about me anymore. People spend so much time worrying about what others think about them, but the reality is that other people aren't thinking about you at all. They are thinking about themselves. For all Cassandra knew, or thought about it, I was married to a great wife with precocious little tykes who looked like their mother and had the maturity of their dad. For all she knew I was doing amazing. Everyone is always looking on the bright side of their old breakups. The one that got away is just a myth for those of us who feel worse off. Cassandra was not the type to be worse off. She was probably happy. She was probably married. She probably had some cool husband who went on surfing holidays. He was probably a skydiving, manly man type from Finland or someplace cold and competent. Maybe he had guns and a motorcycle. He probably hunted his own game and skinned reindeer with a buck knife passed down to him from his grandfather—a buck knife he sharpened himself on an old whetting stone. Maybe his name was Axl or something cool like that. "Winston," unless attached to "Churchill," was such a loser name to have in the twenty-first century.

"Cass." I just walked right up to her and referred to her as "Cass." I had never called her "Cass" during the whole course of our relationship. Cassandra had always seemed to me something higher for whom a nickname would have been an abortion. I guarantee that Marc Antony never referred to Cleopatra as "Cleo" ever.

"Winston?" Cassandra turned off her treadmill and coasted off the back of the conveyor belt. "What are you doing here?" She gave me a hug as though that were her official duty. "It's great to see you."

"Is it?" I asked with a false cheerfulness that made me hate myself.

She ignored the barb. "What happened to your face? You look—you look different."

"This?" I said, touching my face. "A latent deformity. A birth defect that only emerged recently."

She raised an eyebrow. "A latent birth defect?"

"Yeah, I mean, can you believe that?"

"Not really." She smiled and I felt a flash of warning, of danger. No matter what writers or anyone might say about men being attracted to sad women—how sorrow makes them the most beautiful—that's a lie. Or, possibly, the sign of some sort of sociopathy. Sad women make me uncomfortable, like I am supposed to do something about it. A smile is a woman's great asset, her greatest weapon, and only really weird guys aren't disarmed by it. It's sad-sack losers who fancy themselves poets who say melodramatic bunkum like "sad women are beautiful." Even Jeremy—the most pretentious blowhard I know—wouldn't spout garbage like that. I had enough working against me as it was without adding a preoccupation with doleful women to the list. Crap. Seriously. Was I still in love with her?

"You're still working here? You must be running the place by now."

If I had been given a choice about where I might run into her for the first time since the last time, I wouldn't have chosen this, as though I was some loser whose life had been on pause since she left. I began to sweat. In times like these, a confident offence is the best defence against personal humiliation. Or so I believed at the time. Now I know you should just head to the janitorial closet immediately and bypass the personal jackassery all together.

"Nope, still casual. He runs the place." I pointed to Iqbal, who was throwing up gang signs to students passing by the windows to the hallway of the Kinesiology Complex. "What are you doing here? You're not a student."

"I am. I'm in the first year of my PhD."

"Of course. Great. Good for you."

"Seriously, what happened to your face?"

"Car accident. Deformed for life. You had a near escape. Imagine, our children could have looked like this."

She smiled again and rolled her eyes. "It was hardly an escape. You made the hard decision. I appreciated that."

"You don't think we could have made it work?"

"If we'd had an arranged marriage, we would have made it work. But no one in their right mind goes into it with so much against them. You did us both a favour. I didn't have the strength—the guts—to pull the plug."

I didn't like being reminded it had been me. I also didn't appreciate the realization that Cassandra would have been willing to make it work and I was the one who hadn't been.

"So, are you married? Kids?" I asked. She transferred her weight uneasily from one leg to the other, as though she was adjusting to the shift in conversation as well. Maybe we had both thought we could handle discussing it, but the ground was moving beneath us and the best thing to do would be to get out of there as quickly as possible. "Don't worry. I wasn't going to ask you out."

Cassandra laughed a fake little laugh. Her nervous laugh. "I wasn't worried," she said. She definitely was. She kept trying to brush a non-existent strand of hair out of her eyes. A Cassandra tell.

Instead of answering she asked, "What are you up to these days? How are your folks?"

"My folks are good. They just moved into a condo. Boomer went with them." I didn't know what to do with my arms; I was crossing and uncrossing them every minute or so. I was thirty-three years old and I didn't know what to do with my hands. I hated myself for letting Cassandra stay stuck in my mind—in my heart—like a record on repeat. Even the most loved song gets irritating after a while.

Cassandra brightened. "How is Boomer? I love that dog. He was such an adorable puppy."

"He's on a diet," I said. "Like you!" I was definitely an asshole. "Congratulations on losing, like, twenty pounds."

The brightness that had come to her eyes retreated and her features became masked. I recognized that. She looked once again like she had looked right before we broke up. She looked unhappy. She looked like someone bracing for her boyfriend to be jerk.

"Sorry." I said it. I wanted to mean it. "I meant that you looked great."

"Pardon?" Cassandra always said "pardon" when she was confused.

"Don't listen to me. I've had a weird day. It's weird running into you."

"Right," Cassandra said, sighing. "Well. Thanks, I guess. I had better get back to my workout. Christy is waiting. Take care of yourself, okay?" She said it as though it was a question. As though I would be letting her down if I didn't care of myself. I knew what she meant. Cassandra was kind always—even if I was jerk, she was kind. She could see I looked rough.

"Sure."

I walked back to the janitorial storeroom and shut myself inside. I didn't bother to turn on the light. Shame burned across my face in the dark. Even when you get a second chance or a third chance or a hundredth chance— you can't change. I had wanted to be different since our breakup. I wished I was a better guy. I wished Cassandra wasn't so kind. I wished she wasn't so unchangeable. I wished that I could have been different so that our relationship wouldn't have had to end. But even now, three years later, I watched myself be the exact same guy that I was then. I watched and saw the same battle play out over again and come to the same result. Cassandra was someone who moved forward and I wasn't. I watched the line of light at the bottom of the door. Someone passed by. I didn't want to kill myself, exactly; I just wished there was a way not to be alive anymore.

"Wincey?" Iqbal was outside the door. I flicked on the light and grabbed the handle of the mop like I was thinking about cleaning the floor as the door opened.

"Forget the broad, Wince. Forget them. She don't matter." Iqbal clapped his hand on my shoulder. "Bros before bee-yotch-ez notchez, my man. I was worried I was going to find you swinging from the rafters, Kurt Cobain. Get back to work."

I busied myself with the bucket. "Where is the cleanser for the floor?"

"Like I know. There are janitors for that. Seriously, el capitano. Lots of mermaids in the ocean and all that. Literally. Don't drink the bleach, man."

No. Not literally, you jackass. "I won't."

"I mean, she is pretty fine—for an older lady." Iqbal peered back out of doorway to the supply room. "If dames are your thing. You know I always say?" Iqbal was really warming up to the whole idea of cheering me up. "The best way to get over someone?"

I'd heard this before.

"Get over someone else." He laughed as though he were starring as Will Smith in a remake of *The Fresh Prince of Bel-Air*. "Get it? Get over someone else? LOL, my man." I started filling the filthy mop bucket with the hose from the sink. "Seriously, dude. I'm just glad to see that you aren't gay, my brother. No dudes for you. That is something to be happy about. Am I right? Am I right! No homos here! Not that there is anything wrong with that. I mean, seriously, be whatchu want, you know? Love is love and whatever. Lean into it, bro. It gets better... Literally."

I changed my mind. I did want to kill myself. Literally.

I mopped the floor in the guys' locker room. It wasn't even my job, but I didn't want to risk running into her again. I should have been mopping up the water that was spreading plague-like through my home. I slopped the mop back and forth. Three years of wondering. Three years of subconsciously hoping that there was some way to salvage the situation and that was what I'd come out with.

"Congratulations on losing, like, twenty pounds."

I was just a jerk. It had just spilled out like a toilet overflowing while I frantically, but helplessly, tried to stop it. If she had any rosy remembrance of things past, I had done my very best to eradicate it.

CHAPTER EIGHT

Dignity Begins at Home

You need to be careful about the things you say. Those statements of intent that you declare boldly to a friend over peanuts at the pub, words that he will forget but that will live on in your memory as the moment in which you decided to turn to the left instead of to the right. Those pivots of the soul that haunt your midnight turnings for years to come with the purgatory mutterings of "Why?" and "What if?" They are the decisions that come from the chaos of personal confusion, of half truths and misunderstanding.

I had decided at some idiotic moment between running into her and my appointment to once again pick up my long-discarded torch for Cassandra and blow life into the nearly dark embers of my feelings for her. In my malnourished and overwrought imaginings, I assumed that the awkwardness of our interaction was not the natural by-product of our dissolved mutual plans, but instead a fervent love of which the world was not worthy. I stated it like it was some objective truth rather than the fabrication of distraction that it was. I believed I was romantic and melancholy, like Heathcliff in *Wuthering Heights* but with fewer barbarian overtones.

The trouble is, the ideas that you get into your head matter. Sooner or later, no matter how slow moving you are, those ideas give birth to actions. I wasn't planning on pursuing her, though. Far from it. I would just be that incredibly fascinating bastard who was destroyed by that one woman who got away. I would be enthralling and horrible, like Charles Bukowski or Ernest Hemingway. It would be a melancholic life. Young women would moon over my scribbles (once I began penning poems) and cogitative young men would drink scotch out of Dixie cups and emulate my perfect despair.

It was idiotic, the kind of trouble you get yourself into when you spend too much time by yourself. We need other people to react to our bullshit and remind us that there is no such thing as a tortured poet; but there is such a thing as a melodramatic, self-indulgent wacko. Other people keep us from turning into weirdos. But I was especially alone at the time, and thinking of myself as a tragic figure, rather than a pathetic one, excused my lack of forward movement. Tragedies are inevitably downhill affairs, and as anyone could see, I had the prerequisites. I was downhill. I was Heathcliff with less moaning on the moors. I was Heathcliff on government assistance.

By the time I arrived at the specialist's office, I was in a Cassandra-induced fog. I had barely sat down in the waiting room to stare aimlessly into space before I was ushered into the doctor's office. This was a different kind of office than the small examination room in which I'd embarrassed myself on my last visit to an M.D. Dr. Mann had a sort of cozy little sitting room in which a tea service wouldn't have been amiss. It wasn't doilies and chintz upholstery but there was no examination table or tongue depressors in sight. The couch was abnormally low so that my knees stuck out at odd angles like I was some sort of lanky insect. The air conditioning was blowing out cold air even though it was winter. I shivered involuntarily. I felt cold but I was always cold these days.

Dr. Mann was a small woman with coarse red hair streaked grey and pulled back tightly into a ponytail. She didn't wear a lab coat. In fact, she didn't look much like a doctor at all. More like a high school gym teacher who loved hiking in Kananaskis on the weekends and knew all the best trails. If I were a doctor, I would always wear a lab coat and carry the stethoscope in my breast pocket. One should really look the part when asking people to defer to your expertise about their life and health. Cassandra had worn a lab coat when she worked at the veterinary office. Or maybe it was just scrubs. It was probably just scrubs but it looked like she knew what she was doing. Cassandra always knew what she was doing—or seemed like she did. She wasn't irritatingly Type A about it or anything; we weren't as badly matched as all that. She hated lists and making plans. She said that once she wrote something down, some part of her immediately rebelled against the task created. Instead she kept all her plans to her head—to hide them from herself—"so that everything always seems spontaneous and fun instead of foretold and lifeless." That was the sort of thing I found charming about her. Hiding her own plans from herself. Her irrational fear of birds and of developing a goiter. She used to ask me to feel her neck to make sure that she wasn't growing an iodine-related deformity.

"I'm serious," she'd say, looking at me with the utmost earnestness in the middle of watching a movie. "Feel this. I'm not kidding." She would grab my hand and bring it to her neck like I was either a doctor or a faith healer.

I'd probe around with my fingertips for a moment before declaring she was fine.

"You don't feel that?"

"You have a lymph node."

"That's not a lymph node," Cassandra declared, totally overshadowing Christopher Nolan's mumbly dialogue in whatever one of his movies we were watching. "It's the size of a walnut."

"Maybe you're fighting a cold," I'd say. "Or you've aggravated it by poking around so much.

"Nonsense. I am a picture of health."

"Except for the goiter."

Cassandra smacked my chest lightly with the back of her hand and snuggled in closer under my arm.

"Don't worry, I'll still love you even when your neck gets out-of-control big," I said.

Damn it. It was this kind of stuff that stays with you and hangs around your neck like the proverbial millstone (or the goiter), dragging you to the depths of remembrance of things passed by. Those innocuous, warm little memories that come back to you when you least want to remember. They went through my mind like a highlight reel as I waited for the doctor. Playing Dutch

Blitz with Sam and her old boyfriend, Charlie, and Cassandra cheating obviously and abominably. Cassandra car-dancing to the Backstreet Boys while I begged her to change the station. Cassandra with her head on my shoulder and turning her chin up to look at me.

I suddenly became aware of the fact that Dr. Mann was smiling at me and clearly waiting for something. She must have asked me something. "Sorry—did you ask me a question?"

"I asked you how things were going."

"Things?" I said. "Well, my neighbours are trying to drown me, or maybe make me kill myself. So, things are not great. Actually, not just my neighbours. My parents sold my home and my brother doesn't trust me to drive his kids to martial arts—so they're all colluding, probably. My ex-girlfriend is now wearing spandex to my workplace, so she's culpable as well—at this rate I'm going to end up fired again for the second time this month. Iqbal never makes it stick, which is both good and bad since I need the money for my SlimFast and bagels."

Dr. Mann raised her eyebrows. "SlimFast?"

"I got a tub. Cheap eats. Cool treats."

"I see. That's quite a lot of things to be going poorly."

I nodded. "Yes. Yes, it is."

"How often are you drinking diet shakes?"

"All day, every day. Except today. I haven't eaten anything today."

Dr. Mann stood up and walked over to a wicker basket on the table. "I can offer you a granola bar. Or six." She set the basket in front of me. "I hope you aren't allergic to nuts."

129

"I'm not," I said. "Thanks."

As I tore into the wrapper, Dr. Mann returned to her seat. "How have all these things made you feel?"

"My cousin says that I'm depressed."

"Why does your cousin think that?"

I shrugged and reached for a second granola bar. "I guess since things have gone downhill since I moved out from my parents'." I might as well tell the woman the truth. What difference did it make anyway? The most that was going to come of this was a prescription for something that I probably wouldn't fill because I'm casual and don't have any extra coverage.

"How long since that happened?"

"Couple of months." I had already finished the second bar. It was sickly sweet and I balled the two wrappers up in my hand so that they made a satisfying crinkly noise.

"Is this the first time you've been on your own?"

"Yeah." I contemplated reaching for a third granola bar. "I don't think it likes me."

Dr. Mann must have seen me eyeing the basket because she asked, "Would you like another?"

"You sure?"

"That's what they're there for. I'm thinking of replacing them with protein bars. More food value, lower sugar."

"I appreciate them, whatever they are."

"Why do you believe that your neighbours were trying to drown you?"

"That's the only explanation for the water."

"What water?"

"The water that is always running. Always. It's all I hear. When I wake up, when I go to sleep. Water rushing. Which is amazing, considering that there is never enough water for a decent shower. It's water, water everywhere but never a drop to bathe in. I mean, unless you count the water that's raining inside."

"It's raining inside?"

"It was this morning. Drip, drip, drip." I added the third wrapper to the others in my fist and crinkled it to punctuate my point. "Between the water and the footsteps, it's a wonder I've lasted this long."

"Whose footsteps?"

"The ones tromping around upstairs. My neighbours. But come to think of it, it is an old place and I've never actually seen them. Can I ask you a question?" I said, because I was feeling strangely comfortable with Dr. Mann.

"Go ahead."

"Can't you get a lab coat?"

Doctor Mann smiled. "A lab coat isn't really necessary for my practice."

"You'd look the part, though."

"You don't think I look like a doctor?"

"You look like you're a gym teacher," I said without thinking. "Sorry. Rude. That was rude. I meant I thought you looked like you were going wall climbing. There was a climbing wall in my high school." I could tell I was babbling. Total stream-of-consciousness talking and I couldn't seem to stop. Next thing I knew I'd be congratulating her on losing, like, twenty pounds. "Actually, it was my junior high. I took it in grade eight. I don't know if my high school had a climbing wall, but the gym teacher, she really loved it and looked like she bought stuff at Eddie Bauer or Mountain Equipment Co-op—" Good golly. Stop talking already. Someone please put me out of my misery. When it was clear that Dr. Mann was unlikely to do it, I had to do it myself. "I'm going to stop talking now," I explained abruptly.

Whereas Dr. Yu had been inscrutable, Dr. Mann's expression was warm and responsive in following everything that I was saying. Unfortunately.

"Very perceptive of you. I do like climbing," she said when I had finally shut my pie hole.

"I thought so. I meant that. That you looked like you liked the outdoors. Gym teachers always look like they like the outdoors. But I'm pretty sure the U of C bookstore sells lab coats. I could get you one," I offered. "Lab coats and stethoscopes. The bookstore isn't far from the rec centre."

"No, thank you."

That was it. That's what I remember about the whole stupid appointment. I know she must have asked me other questions because I was in there nearly an hour. But I know I spent a lot of it mooning over Cassandra and then left wondering if I was doomed to go about my life telling the various women I encountered that they looked like gym teachers and making inappropriate comments about their weight.

Oh, hell. I was going to be *that* old guy.

At the end of the appointment Dr. Mann had me wait around for a few minutes while she assembled some forms for me to fill out at home, which she gave me with the throwaway statement that I might need one of my parents to help me with some of the information.

That was it.

I heard the dull roar of the fans as I slid my house key into the lock of the door. The basement was dark but for a faint orange glow that cast ghoulish shadows in the dim light of the late afternoon. My landlord had left me a voicemail while I was in the appointment. He warned that I needed to turn off the fans before I could turn on the lights or I would blow a fuse.

"But, really, you want to keep the fans and heaters on until everything is bone-dry. Got to dry that sucker out before mould sets in. Remember the Flood."

I followed the cord of a heater to the socket, yanked it out of the wall and switched on a light. Dish heaters and three industrial-sized fans with twin settings of Loud and Louder were blowing heat in a scorching whirlwind reminiscent of Dante's second circle of hell. "Abandon hope all ye who enter here." If my Beltline Basement Lair had been uninspiring before, it now assaulted all five senses with an aggressive ugliness. The carpet was half pulled up and folded back on itself. The musty and stained underlay released decades of trapped odours so that the rank smell stung my nose and lingered inexplicably on my tongue. The heat was stifling and unbearable. The noise deafening. The whole aspect was drab and dirty and depressing as hell.

I tossed the stack of papers Dr. Mann had given me onto the counter. They fanned out like a deck of cards in the hands of a talented dealer until they rested precariously over the edge, the flap of paper waving briskly in the hot wind. I saw the logo bearing a house and a rising sun over the words "Dignity Begins at Home" and a faint bell of recognition sounded in my memory but I dismissed it as I evaluated my situation. I needed to live here. I needed to figure out a way to make this hole habitable. I picked my way through the labyrinthine spiderweb of extension cords, heaters and fans until I got to my bedroom. Though the flowing of water had ceased, the drywall behind the baseboards was exploding outward under its swelling load. The carpet still squeezed out water under the cracked soles of my Converse shoes. I could feel the bottom of my socks getting wet. Moving to the bathroom, I flicked on the light to observe the source of the catastrophe.

I didn't see it right away—that proverbial straw that broke the camel's back of my endurance, my ability to persevere and bear up under my present state of adversity. I was too busy looking at the ceiling, observing those droplets of water heavy under gravity's burden, yet still clinging to the sodden sponge of the ceiling. The flow of water had been stopped at the source. My gaze panned downward and that was when I saw it.

My towel. My one and only towel was inexplicably crammed behind the toilet. The water had been coming from the ceiling, not the toilet, and yet my landlord had taken my one solitary towel from the rack and stuffed it in behind the toilet next to the carapace of a crumpled and departed arachnid to soak up toilet water and dead dreams. It had been a light grey colour when it rested on the towel rack, but behind the toilet it was tie-dye, dappled, rusty brown.

And just like that, I was done. I was so effing done.

I filled out the Dignity Begins at Home form in ten minutes' time. I walked to the drugstore post office and mailed it. I didn't care if it was the truth or a lie. I didn't care at all. I was done with trying to make it on my own in my lone-towel-used-to-sop-up-other-people's-dirty-water existence. I was done. If the Canadian government was buying houses for unwed mothers too stupid to leave their abusive convict boyfriends, then they could buy perennial loser Winston Bedlow one as well. They could cut me a break. Besides, I rationalized, the Dignity People could still reject my application. I didn't lie on my forms. I told the truth. I just didn't correct their misunderstanding. I just filled it out like I was entitled to it.

I returned from the postbox with a hefty sense of self-satisfaction. I had done it. Up until now, everything that had happened, even the things that I had done, like going to those doctor's appointments, had all been someone else's idea. Move out. That was my parents'. Lost my job. That was Iqbal's. Regained my job: also Iqbal's. Sam literally drove me to the doctor. I had let myself drift along to the whims of outrageous misfortune, as it were, and it had landed me exactly nowhere. So, filling out the forms and mailing them in was my ironically perverse response to feeling led about by the nose from one crap heap to another. Weird, right? To feel like you have no control over your future, so you sign up for even less? But, hey, that's human nature. Esau sold his birthright for lentils. Lentils, of all things. Free stuff trumps freedom when you can't imagine that there is a bigger picture to your life.

The answer arrived seventy-six days later and without fanfare, as things often do when you have no one with whom to share the daily details of your life. It was sitting on the mat with a pile of fliers, all tumbled together from their fall from the mail slot in the door.

I picked up the envelope and kicked off my shoes and headed down the stairs to the overlong floral sofa and finally, when comfortable, I tore up the envelope to find a familiar-looking sheaf of papers.

Congratulations, it is my pleasure to inform you that your loved one, WINSTON BEDLOW, has been selected to participate in the Dignity Begins at Home housing program!

And the rest, as they say, is history.

CHAPTER NINE
The Aptly Named 'Potpan'

It is a peculiar kind of offence when you realize that everyone you know has ceased to expect anything of interest to happen in your life. As though you were just a bit part in some play, and narrative resolution is neither expected nor required for such inconsequential set dressing. No one comes to the end of *Romeo and Juliet* and wonders, "Yeah, they died tragically thanks to the impulsive stupidity of youth, but whatever happened to Potpan?"

Who, you ask?

Exactly.

Family, friends—they all stop asking because there is no anticipation that this plot of yours is going anywhere. It's not even a conscious decision on anyone's part. The change is glacially gradual until finally one day it occurs to you that it has been months, or maybe even years, since anyone has genuinely inquired as to what's going on with you. People forgot to ask and I forgot to tell them. I didn't tell anyone about sending the paperwork away. I didn't talk about the series of small, yet potent disasters and misunderstandings that had led me to leap from the narrow precipice of self-reliance onto the vast, sticky net of government dependence.

I only mentioned it to Jeremy because he was going to have to pick up Bret and Michael from a different address on Saturday afternoons after their martial arts class. I was a week away from moving into the house that Dignity provided. I'd already shoved most of my mismatched household junk into boxes that I'd picked up at a liquor store. Most of the donated furniture was damaged in the flood and Joel was going to help me take it to the dump. I only had a few belongings and many of them were already in my car when I picked up the boys at their martial arts class. I took them for lunch at A&W because I had a two-for-one coupon and then back to my soon-to-be-vacated basement suite, where we tossed around a football on the front lawn until Jeremy showed up. The boys were already loaded in his van and staring with slack expressions at the small TV screen that flipped down from the ceiling of the vehicle when I brought it up.

My brother had stopped to inspect the fogging of the headlight on the passenger side when I said, "I'm moving."

"Oh yeah?" Jeremy tapped on the plastic cover of the headlight with his knuckle but didn't look up.

"It's a place in Bowness," I said.

Bowness is a leafy, low-lying neighbourhood that hugs the river. It's hardscrabble and up-and-coming and I felt it suited me. We were both struggling to achieve. To attain. To finally get all of our roads paved like the rest of the city. I had only driven by the house, but even as I sat in my car and observed its plain, but tidy appearance I felt like I was Moses about to cross the Red Sea and leave Egypt behind for good. The house itself was a refurbished marijuana grow op. It was my new start. No floods. No more SlimFast or discounted bagel pucks. There was even a living allowance. It wasn't huge but it supplemented my abomination of an income enough that I would be able to afford better groceries. The modest little house came without a host of insect squatters. And it was mine. I wasn't just scraping by from dollar to dollar. I was building something. With each month that passed, I would be better off, not worse. I bought four towels in anticipation. I was ahead. I was happy.

"That's good. Beth was worried about the boys being here with the mould."

"Not worried enough not to have me babysit apparently," I said. "Look alive." My brother glanced up just in time to catch the football that I sent spinning through the air toward him.

"I said they'd be fine for a few minutes, once a week. What's the new place like? Another basement suite?" Jeremy placed his fingers over the laces and I took several steps back.

"It's a house. No mould."

"In Bowness? You'll be lucky if the basement isn't a dirt floor." He threw a powerful pass that came at me like a guided missile. Jeremy had always had a good arm.

"Fully renovated," I answered irritably, the palms of my hands tingling from the impact of the ball. I should have just texted him the address next Saturday morning.

"Oh yeah?" Jeremy backed up farther down the sidewalk. "How are you affording a new house? Did you get a new career as well, or has the rec centre upped you all the way to minimum wage?" he shouted.

"I don't make minimum wage." I threw the ball at him hard.

"Come on. Children in sweatshops have a better hourly wage than you. How are you affording this?" He bombed the ball high so that it sailed past my outstretched hands and bounced erratically on a neighbouring lawn several houses down. I jogged after it and was scooping it off the ground when I jumped to realize he had run up right behind me.

"Geez, Jeremy."

"Seriously, how are you affording a new house?"

I passed the football back and forth between my hands as I regarded his serious expression. "Maybe I've just been a really good saver all these years and I'm buying it cash. Or maybe I signed up for welfare and am about to reap the sweet, sweet rewards of subsidized housing," I said.

His expression was grave to the point of being comical and he paused theatrically before asking in a low voice, "Are you dealing?"

It took me a moment to understand what he was asking. "Why is it that whenever you and I start to have a nice time, you pull this kind of thing? There we were, getting along, tossing the ball back and forth, cracking wise and then—"

"—Are you?"

"Of course not. Besides, I've been living with Mom and Dad for forever. Think they would have let that slide?"

"Don't dick around, Winston. If you're doing drugs—or selling drugs—I don't want my kids around you. I mean it. They don't need a loser uncle leading them down the garden path. You may think it's no big deal, but look what it's done to you," he said emphatically and sprayed my face with a spatter of saliva.

A ripple of irritation went up my spine—like I was a cat and his opinions were the equivalent of being patted backward. "I don't do drugs, you jackass."

Jeremy looked at me with narrowed eyes. "You're not fooling anyone. Your pothead lifestyle is a dead giveaway."

"Sorry to disappoint you, brother. This is the loser I am without the help of narcotics. That's what you've thought all this time?"

Jeremy didn't say anything but I could see all the gears and machinery of his mind grinding away trying to come up with a retort. Finally, he said, "You've got to admit, it makes a certain kind of sense."

"Only to someone like you," I answered. "But I am amazed that you let Bret Micheals stay with me, given that was your opinion. That was a real lapse on your part."

That got under his skin. "Well, do you or don't you? How are you getting this new house? How do you explain yourself? Your whole life? I want an explanation for why you are the way that you are. Don't *you* want an explanation?"

"I don't want the explanation to be that I'm a pothead, no."

"Well, what is it, then?" He threw up his hands in exasperation.

"I told you. Government assistance. I applied for it and I got it."

Jeremy looked at me blankly. "How did you get on government assistance? On what basis?"

I sighed heavily because if it didn't come to blows between Jeremy and me, it came to heavy sighs. "I went to the doctor a while back and he sent me to a specialist who got me some forms to fill out and now I'm getting a new place to live."

"A doctor prescribed you a new house?"

"She said I should apply because I might qualify."

Jeremy looked like one of those cartoon characters who gets struck in the face with a mallet and stands there dumbly for half a second before all his teeth begin to tumble out of his mouth one by one. Jeremy's teeth didn't begin to fall out, but it was several moments before he said, "Because there is something wrong with you? What's your health issue, being lazy? Just get a freaking job already."

I shoved my hands in my pockets. "It must come as a great relief to you. All this time you had a simple brother. That explains everything."

I half expected him to laugh and mock me for this indignity, but he didn't. My brother's normally expressive face went suddenly—and startlingly— blank.

"I better go," he said as he took several steps backward toward his minivan. "I'll—um—Thanks for watching the boys." I watched him walk slowly across the neighbouring lawn and around the back of the van to the driver's side door. He still had that empty expression on his face as he pulled away from the curb.

So, really, that went better than I would have thought.

Sam, on the other hand, did not take the news with the same blank equanimity. Her response was likely the closest thing I will ever see to atomic detonation. She was apoplectic about the diagnosis in the first place; then she was irate about the fact that I planned to profit off (what she decided was) a faulty diagnosis.

"What do you mean you filled out forms for Dignity Housing? You need a doctor to recommend you for that!" she said when I showed her the acceptance letter. I watched as her eyes darted back and forth over the lines of print. Her green eyes grew wider as she read. "How did this happen?"

"She gave them to me."

"Who did?"

"The doctor. Doctor Mann. The specialist that Doctor Yu referred me to after you made me go to the doctor that day."

"But why did she give you the forms? There must have been some kind of mistake. She gave them to you by accident. That program is for the mentally challenged."

"So——" I said, letting the word linger in the air between us.

"——So you shouldn't have applied. You shouldn't have had access to those forms."

"I appreciate your vote of confidence but the medical community thinks differently."

"Shut up. You are not mentally retarded."

"You'll find that is a socially and politically incorrect term these days."

"Yeah, you're Mister Sensitivity. How did you let this happen?" She was sputtering. I almost wished I hadn't told her. I kept expecting people to laugh at the news, but no one really did.

"How did *I* let this happen? You told me to go to the doctor and I did. They're the ones who diagnosed me as being mentally incapacitated. What did you want me to do?"

Sam was gesturing wildly now, her hands waving in front of her face in a series of karate chops and wide, sweeping movements. "Tell the truth! Winston! You were supposed to tell them the truth! That you were depressed! You weren't supposed to go in there and pretend that you are somehow mentally challenged! I really shouldn't have to spell that out! This is despicable!"

"I did tell them the truth. I told them that I was there because my cousin thought I might be depressed. They were the ones asking the questions. They were the ones who made the diagnosis. I didn't even know what they were thinking until I got the stack of assistance forms to fill out. When didn't I tell the truth?"

"Then! That was when you should have corrected the faulty assumption! For crying out loud! I can't believe this!"

Sam would have been ranging all over my squalid Beltline Basement Lair had it not been for the fact that there was no room for it. She had to settle instead for pacing the three feet back and forth in front of my oversized, water-stained floral couch.

144

"This is absurd! This is unbelievable! This is wrong!"

"My parents didn't seem that shocked, actually. They were startlingly unstartled at the news."

"What do you mean? They accept it?"

Truthfully, I had expected this sort of response from my parents. Perhaps some indignation on my behalf would be coupled with disappointment in my lack of integrity that enabled me to consider going through with such a plan.

"I think it was a surprise," I said.

When I'd finally seen my parents at Sunday lunch and told them about it, their faces had been blank. Sort of like Jeremy's had been blank but with less surprise mixed in. It was as though they had deliberately emptied their expressions of all meaning. Perhaps they had been expecting such a diagnosis for a long time and it just confirmed what they had always feared.

"But it wasn't like they had a lot of questions," I continued. "I guess Jeremy gave them the heads-up, so I missed their initial response."

"I don't believe this! How can this have happened? How could you let this happen?"

"Hey—I'm an innocent bystander here. I went to the doctor because you told me to. Now I'm just doing what the doctor told me to do. Isn't that what you wanted me to do in the first place?"

"You can't accept this, Winston. Surely, you don't accept this—"

"If it gets me out of this place, I do."

"That's despicable."

"You said that already."

"So that's it, then?"

"What?" I wasn't sure exactly what *it* was.

"This is who you are now?"

"I guess," I said, shrugging. "I don't know what else to do about it."

Her face was flushed with anger and shock and who knows what else, and she kept grabbing handfuls of her own hair like she was Lady MacBeth desperately trying to maintain her grip on reality. "You fight it," she shouted. "You call or write back or whatever you have to do and say, 'I'm sorry, there has been a terrible mistake. I don't qualify. I don't deserve this.' You have to, Winston, before it's too late. Call whomever you have to call. I don't care if it is the prime minister himself. Just correct this mistake. If you don't, it—it says something about you. It reveals what kind of person you are."

"Right," I said tonelessly. "Calling people in the government to tell them that I am not mentally unfit is totally the behaviour of the sound of mind."

"You've got to."

"I don't, actually."

Sam stared at me for several tense moments before she said, "You know, Winston, when all of this falls apart—which it will, eventually—this is going to have been a terrible mistake. I want you to know that. I don't want you to pretend later on that there was no warning. You read the label, okay? When you get stuck in the system with this diagnosis, or when something is ruined by this lie, I want you to remember that I warned you. I told you to clean it up now while you still have the chance."

CHAPTER TEN

Don't Worry, I have Aid(es)

Nothing of true import is ever scheduled for a Tuesday. Every other day of the week has some feeling of expectation attached to it. The weekend needs no explanation; Fridays, likewise. Mondays—while generally dreaded—are occasionally holidays. Wednesday is hump day. The middle of the week. The marker. Thursdays are exciting because Friday approaches. American Thanksgiving is always on a Thursday. What is Tuesday? Nothing. So you can see how I wasn't expecting anything to happen. But glancing through the peephole on that inauspicious day revealed two unexpected women about my own age standing on my doorstep and looking for me. It was a Tuesday when Iris Naess and Gynnyfyr Brown showed up at my door.

"Good. You're home." A short woman with fire-engine-red hair and eyes thickly rimmed in black makeup said as I opened the door. "I'm Gynnyfyr with a G. And a Y. I'm your aide." She gestured to the woman following her as she pushed past me into the house. "This is Iris. Your other aide."

Iris extended her hand. She had wispy blond hair that seemed determined to settle in her eyes and a sun-bleached aspect to her person that made me think of a rancher's daughter in a Clint Eastwood Western.

"You're kind of a cute one. That's a nice switch," Gynnyfyr said as she turned to Iris. "Doesn't he remind you of someone? He reminds me of someone."

"Undoubtedly," Iris said as she smiled politely.

"Where does the 'y' go?" I asked, still spelling out "Jennifer" in my head.

"Everywhere," Iris answered.

Gynnyfyr glared at her companion—the first of many such looks during their brief visit—before turning to scan my house. "Not bad. Not bad. You've done alright. Did you get your family to help you move in?"

"Yes."

"Good." Gynnyfyr strode through the living room into the kitchen and began randomly opening cabinet doors. "Looks like you've got a good network. Would you say you have a good network, Sweet Cheeks?" She pulled out the unopened box of Wheat Thins I had bought the day before.

"I don't know what you mean. Like... the internet? I can't afford it. I just use it at my sister's."

"No. Not the internet, dum dum. A network of family and friends to help you."

"Nice, Gynn. Try to remember that you are the professional here," Iris said. "Put those away."

"I didn't get to eat lunch. I'm hungry. Besides, it's not insulting. I call all my babies 'dum dum.' No offence, okay?"

"Sure." I was still trying to figure out the "y" and "g" spelling. "Oh, I get it. 'Gwenhwyfar' like the Old English spelling of 'Guinevere'."

"Who the hell is that?" Gynnyfyr looked at me blankly. "No, like, JLaw... Jennifer Lawrence or Jennifer Lopez or Jennifer Love Hewitt, but uniquer. You're one of those savant types, hey?" Gynnyfyr threw herself down on the couch in such a way that there was no room for anyone else to sit down. "I haven't had one of those before. Cool. You probably can take yourself to the mall, huh?"

"Yes."

"So, anything else you want me to do here, Iris? Have we covered all the bases?"

"You haven't covered any of the bases."

Gynnyfyr made herself more comfortable on the couch and began adjusting her cleavage. "Trust me. I make sure all the bases get rounded."

Iris rolled her eyes. "Will you just do your job, please?"

"Such a prude. Winston, what happened to your last aide?"

"Uh—" Up until this point I hadn't told a single lie. I didn't think it was my fault if everything I said was misinterpreted. It didn't matter, though. Gynnyfyr didn't need my help with the conversation.

"I know who you remind me of—Ryan Gosling! Not as good-looking as him, obviously, but, still, you do remind me of him. Did you see *The Notebook*? I love that movie. You should bulk up a bit. Just my luck. I find a Ryan Gosling–look-alike and he's an idiot. Thanks a lot, God."

"I didn't realize that you were a stickler on that point," Iris muttered and I smiled even though they were talking about me being an idiot and I was right there in front of them.

"I'm not. But I need someone to get the collection agencies off my ass," Gynnyfyr said.

"I prefer the term 'idiot savant,' if it is all the same to you."

I kind of liked Gynnyfyr despite the fact that she was eating all the Wheat Thins and getting crumbs all over my new couch. I kind of liked Iris, too, but in a different way.

Gynnyfyr turned to me and smiled broadly, revealing some bedazzled teeth. "I like this one. I like you, Ryan."

Iris took the Wheat Thins box and returned it to the cabinet. "Everyone reminds Gynnyfyr of a celebrity. 'You look like Emma Watson, but not as pretty. Bigger. Older. But still…' She believes these are compliments."

"I don't know who that is," I said, glancing back and forth between the two markedly different women. Iris seemed like she could probably defend the ranch with a twelve-gauge shotgun from a Comanche war party in a Louis L'Amour novel. Gynnyfyr seemed like she belonged on some PG-13 version of SpongeBob SquarePants.

"You don't know who Emma Watson is? She's Hermione in *Harry Potter*. She's a UN ambassador."

"No, she isn't," Iris said, sighing.

"Whatevs, Fat Emma. Do you have a job, Ryan?"

"Yes," I answered, relieved that I didn't have to lie. Besides, it isn't often that women show up at your door and start a relationship with you, official though it may be. Yet here were Iris and Gynnyfyr asking me about my life like they were invested in it.

"Great." Gynnyfyr mimed ticking a box on a non-existent clipboard. "Where do you work? And do you need help getting to or from work?"

"The U of C Rec Centre, and no."

"Great!" Gynnyfyr ticked another box. "What about at work? Do you require any assistance?"

"No," I answered readily. This was easy.

"A home run and the crowd goes wild. I am not sure that you need that much support. What do you think? Once a week for a couple of hours should be enough, right?"

"If that," I said.

"Nice try. Do a standard assessment," Iris said.

"Fine. Boss Lady." Like a grade schooler, Gynnyfyr glared at her co-worker before assuming a fastidious tone. "When is your next shift? One of us will need to come with you to assess whether you can do your job without support."

I didn't like that idea at all. "I already told you that I could."

"Housing doesn't come for free, Breaker High. You got to tick all the government's boxes first. If we decide that you are able to do your job on your own, then great. If not? You get a lovely female to follow you around all day and help with your every task."

"Sounds kind of demeaning."

"It really does," Iris said blandly. "Can we cut the editorializing?"

"I meant for me," I said.

"Don't be lame. When is your next shift?" Gynnyfyr popped another cracker into her mouth but seemed to get momentarily distracted by her own cleavage.

"Tomorrow at 5 a.m. I'm only on there casual, though. The rest of the time I do day-labour jobs."

"No. I don't think you will."

"What? Why?"

"You can only earn $900 dollars a month. Otherwise, say goodbye to your assistance allowance."

"That isn't very much to live on."

"A mathematician, eh? You can always volunteer." Gynnyfyr smiled too sweetly. "I'm sure that it will be really rewarding—intangibly speaking. Besides, be glad you live in Calgary where the cost of living is so high; other places the 'tards get a lot less."

"Seriously," Iris said. "You should not be working in this industry. Isn't there a Hooters somewhere in desperate need of your skills?"

Gynnyfyr dismissed her co-worker with the wave of a bedazzled hand. "One of us—but let's be honest, it will probably be Iris since I am not really a morning person—will come to work with you tomorrow."

"That really isn't necessary. I've been doing this job for years. My boss doesn't think I need an aide."

Gynnyfyr waved my comment away indifferently. "The Canadian government will be the judge of that." She turned to Iris. "Tomorrow?"

Iris nodded.

Gynnyfyr clapped her hands together. "It's settled then. Iris will shadow your shift tomorrow and then we will reassess just how much help you need. Sponge baths are my speciality but that's a little above your pay grade, La La Land. Shame." She gave an exaggerated wink and Iris shuddered involuntarily behind her. "Know who I remind you of, Rain Man?"

I was fairly certain that there wasn't a person in the world who reminded me of Gynnyfyr. "I give up."

"Christina Hendricks. We're practically twins."

I don't know who that is, either.

At 5 a.m. Iris was waiting at the Olympic Torch Entrance of the Kinesiology Complex. The morning was still dark without a trace of the grey light of late winter. Hitching my shoulders up to my ears to keep the icy air from my neck, I crossed the dead campus streets to where my aide was waiting.

"Sorry, I hope you haven't been waiting long," I said.

"Couple of minutes. No worries."

"That's good." I didn't know what else to say as we turned to walk toward the entrance. Iris said nothing. She covered a yawn and then hugged her arms around herself as though she was chilled.

"You didn't have to wait for me outside," I said, wondering if that was the kind of thing that an idiot savant would say. Come to think of it, "idiot savant" probably wasn't an acceptable term—it was archaic, from a time before people worried about acceptable terms.

"I don't mind." Iris rubbed her arms. "It's just been a long time since I was anywhere this early. It's cold—or maybe I'm just tired."

"It's cold," I said. Good grief. We were talking about the weather. Our footsteps echoed on the concrete and between the buildings as though it were just Iris and me alive in the whole grey world. "I imagine this is what it would be like if the city were deserted."

"After the apocalypse?"

"Something like that."

"I work with a boy who is obsessed with survival stories." Iris covered her mouth as she yawned again. "Well—mostly zombie survival. He has contingency plans mapped out. Fallback shelters, supplies, the works." I held open the door for Iris to pass through in front of me. "He's not quite sure if he can trust me with the coordinates to the fallback location yet."

"But if you turn into a zombie, it won't matter to you where it is," I said. "I mean, hypothetically. Zombies aren't thinkers."

"Oh, it isn't Zombie Iris that he fears. That isn't his paranoia. It's Government Employee Iris who might raid the shelter."

"Well. That's not paranoia; that's a legitimate fear. 'The nine most terrifying words in the English language are: I'm from the government and I'm here to help.'"

Iris laughed unexpectedly. "Jamie would agree with you."

"With Ronald Reagan. He said that."

"I didn't know that."

"He was a card," I said, though I had never used the term "card" before in my life. Next thing you know, I would be saying things were swell and that all the fellas were loading their zip guns for the big rumble. Shucks. "I'm not really into survival stories, though. If there is an apocalypse, I am pretty sure I want to be wiped out in the first wave. No eating people to survive. If the civilized world is going down, I want to go down with it."

"That would make for a pretty short story. Survival is the point."

"Not every version of survival is preferable."

"You mean in terms of quality of life?"

"No," I said, pausing momentarily, ignoring a conscience that was protesting my own hypocrisy. "There are compromises to integrity that aren't worth your life." I asked, "Did you ever see *Sophie's Choice*?"

"Is that the one where she has to choose which of her kids goes to the gas chamber?"

"Yeah. Everyone talks about that movie like it was some impossible choice. It wasn't impossible. You take both kids by the hand and say, 'We're going to see Jesus.'"

"Let them kill everyone?"

"Killing everyone was always the endgame. You don't let them make you choose."

"Wasn't Sophie Jewish? What if you don't believe in Jesus?" Iris asked.

"Jesus was Jewish."

By now we were walking down the hallway to the rec centre. I unlocked the door and flicked on the light. It would only be a few minutes before the early risers would be standing at the door.

"So, what are your duties?" Iris asked, changing the subject.

"Maintain the equipment, mostly. I watch to make sure that people swipe in and stuff. It isn't hard."

"How come you are only working casual? Is it a long-term-disability hours thing?" Iris got up on a treadmill. "Do you mind?" She gestured to the machine.

"Go ahead." I picked up the remote to turn on the TVs and left them on mute. If I were by myself, I might have listened to the news but Iris's presence threw me off my routine. I began to analyze how she would interpret my every action. If I did things too easily, would she assume I was a liar? If she asked me straight out if I thought I was mentally handicapped or an idiot savant or whatever the appropriate term was, I wouldn't lie about it. She could ask if she was suspicious. Besides, I had real doctors and specialists recommend me for this program. I had told the absolute truth. There was either truth in their diagnosis or there wasn't—but a faulty diagnosis wasn't the fault of the patient. There was a doctor and a second opinion. According to the medical community, I deserved to be here. According to the government, I needed and was owed this help. I had been assessed by the large and the small. The many and the few. Neither had been able to determine the truth about me, but I went about my day and trusted in the collective wisdom of everyone but myself.

I told myself all of that, but that didn't dispel the faintly uncomfortable feeling I had let the well-meaning do-gooders *Sophie's-Choice* me into giving up my integrity.

Students, faculty and staff dribbled in and out of the gym over the next few hours. Iris shadowed me from machine to machine as I carried out my duties. The rhythmic whir of the stairclimbers and the ellipticals counted the moments until the end of my shift. Iris didn't say much and clearly tried to be as unobtrusive as possible, but I was constantly aware of her. I couldn't help it.

"This must be boring for you," I said as we sat behind the desk while students swiped in and out with their IDs. "Feel free to go do something else. Use a machine or whatever."

Iris looked at me strangely, as though her mind had been called back to this world from a place she liked better. "It's okay. I don't mind."

"So, will you be coming to every shift, or do you figure I can manage on my own now?" I asked.

"We'll see."

When my shift was over, we left together. She turned at the end of the sidewalk to head to the bus stop. She stopped and looked back for a moment. "See you next week, Winston. Either Gynnyfyr or I will be in touch before then, though."

"Wait..." I heard myself stopping her—but wished that I could stop myself instead. "Do you want a ride? I can drive you... I can drive. I'm a good driver."

She smiled. "I'm sure you are. I'm good. Thanks. See you soon." I watched her walk away. She never turned back to look at me. So much for Heathcliff. So much for Charles Bukowski.

CHAPTER ELEVEN
Better Sick (or Disabled) than Stupid

Iris had been almost invisible when she shadowed me at the rec centre. She wasn't shy exactly—it seemed she preferred to pass underneath the radar of other people's notice. She was subtle in her words and movements, as though she was always watching but was rarely observed herself. That wasn't the case with Gynnyfyr. Her personality entered every room like a tidal wave and filled up all the empty spaces. When Gynnyfyr realized that she could work out for free at the rec centre while being paid to accompany me on my shifts, Iris never came with me to work again. Gynnyfyr immediately began her own routine. She spent time on a bike watching TV and reading magazines and then spent most of the rest of my shift hanging around the free weights and chatting up the guys who were working out. By some scheduling miracle, in the first two weeks that Gynnyfyr came to work with me, my shifts never coincided with Iqbal's, but this good fortune could not possibly last. My boss, though astonishingly preoccupied with himself, paid

158

attention to all the women who came to the gym and was bound to talk to her. I needed Gynnyfyr onside.

"Would you mind if we didn't tell my work that you are my aide?" I said to Gynnyfyr as we walked into the rec centre. "I mean, you're here already. I just don't want to be treated differently than before."

Gynnyfyr reached up and patted me on the shoulder. "Fine. But, listen, I'm not pretending to be your girlfriend. That almost got me fired."

"No, no lies. That isn't what—"

"Plus, that would get in the way of my plans." Gynnyfyr stopped walking and leaned in conspiratorially. "You know that blond guy who uses the bench press a lot?"

"There is more than one blond guy who uses the bench press."

"You know, the guy I pointed out to you on your last shift."

"There is more than one blond guy that uses the bench press who you pointed out to me on my last shift."

"The really hot one."

That didn't help me much.

"He wears a red bandana while working out."

"You mean Cory?"

"Do I?" Gynnyfyr batted her eyelashes up at me. "Does he have a girlfriend? Is he seeing anyone?"

"How should I know?"

Gynnyfyr threw up her hands in disgust. "Ugh. You are useless."

"Why would I know that? I barely know the guy. Why don't you just ask him?"

"Don't be retarded. A girl can't just go up to a guy she likes and ask him if he has a girlfriend."

"Why not?" Guys have to do that sort of thing all the time. I mean, I don't. But other guys do. Theoretically.

"Because, Winston," she explained very slowly, "that would be so embarrassing. What if he said yes? Then what would I say? 'Good for you'? Geez. Think it through."

"Fifty-fifty chance he says, 'No', though."

Gynnyfyr rolled her eyes. "He looks like Captain America. No. Not fifty-fifty. Not even close to fifty-fifty." She fanned herself. "Did you see him in that movie when he emerged from that old-timey Easy-Bake Oven? Nice work, Chris Evans!"

"Huh?"

"Never mind," Gynnyfyr said and began biting at the skin around her fingernail as though it was some sort of compulsion. "Ugh! I hate her already!"

"Who?"

"His girlfriend. She's probably some skinny nightmare who bosses him around and doesn't let him get a word in edgewise."

"Cory isn't really that talkative. That'd probably be okay."

Gynnyfyr glared at me. "Or, worse, she's one of those homey types who makes handmade soap or some bullshit. Probably doesn't even have a single tat like she's Ivory, Queen of the Soap."

"Huh?"

She dismissed me with a wave of her hand. We entered the gym and I buzzed Gynnyfyr through without signing her in.

"Listen," Gynnyfyr said, peering around at the rows of machines for a sign of Cory as though she were scanning for her prey. "If he shows up, you need to warn me so that I can go freshen up."

"Freshen up" is a weird term that girls use. If I were going to "freshen," I would need to have a shower and put on a new T-shirt.

"Here's what we're going to do: If he comes in, I need you to give me a signal. But don't do something stupid like yelling to me that he is here. Just, you know, casually walk over and let me know. And! Oh, perfect! Find out if he has a girlfriend. You can ask and it won't be weird."

"Why wouldn't that be weird?"

"Because you already are weird. You can get away with it without damaging your reputation." Gynnyfyr was pleading now. Her hands were clasped in front of her chest and everything. "Please, Winston! Pretty please! I really want to date Chris Evans."

"Cory."

"You know what I mean."

"Barely."

"You're the best!" Gynnyfyr unzipped her hoodie, revealing a very cleavage-y Lycra top. "Seriously, I don't even know why you have an aide. For reelz."

I started to shrug—feeling awkward about the comment and wondering if merely failing to give an alternate interpretation of the situation was still akin to lying. My indecision resulted in a strange, jerky movement of my shoulders and a confused expression on my face. I suppose an ethicist or moralist or someone would say that lies of omission are still lies. But I wasn't really omitting anything. I told the truth. The problem was that once someone starts to look at you through a certain lens, it is very difficult to get them to look at you without it.

"Oh, never mind." Gynnyfyr turned away. "Just remember, heads-up when Bandana Boy gets here."

Gynnyfyr picked a stationary bike that allowed her a decent vantage point of the rec centre entrance. If Bandana Cory did make an appearance, she would know. She flipped through a magazine while spinning her legs around on a bike set to the easiest setting. I figured she had the situation covered and went about my duties, making sanitizing solution for the machines and doing basic maintenance. After the first hour, there was nothing much left to do besides man the desk. When I was a student, I had used the opportunity to study and the job had been ideal. More recently, I had done a lot of reading while sitting there buzzing students through. But my new situation made me self-conscious about my book selection, so, instead, I had brought nothing and I was bored out of my mind. I sat in the chair behind the check-in desk and watched as students and faculty arrived. Some—like the Olympic hopefuls—worked out with single-minded determination while others were really only there to chat and meet people.

I drummed my fingers on the counter and wished I had brought something to read.

"Save my machine for me?" Gynnyfyr approached the front desk. "I want to go get a snack."

I looked out at the rows of empty bikes. "I think it will be okay. Besides, you can't save machines. First-come, first-served."

"Not even for me? I'm not here to work out."

"Then it won't matter."

"No. What I mean is, I am not here to work out. I am here to work. If you want me to hang over your shoulder and watch your every move, then fine, I can do that. But I have a good view of you from over there. But if you want me to hover. I can hover. I mean, it is up to you, Winston. It is always up to my little friends."

That wouldn't do at all. Not with Iqbal coming in soon.

"Fine." I said—albeit a bit petulantly.

She gave me a sickly sweet smile and skipped out the door. "I'll be back soon-ish."

I nodded, watching her through the window as she disappeared into a crowd of students wearing Dinos sweats. I wandered over to the machine and threw a rag over the handle. No one would pick it now. Leave a jacket or a magazine, and someone would take it. That was clearly a sign of use and desirability. Leave something unusual, like a rag, and that machine would sit untouched until the offending point of difference was removed.

I returned to the desk in time to see Bandana Cory walk in ahead of Iqbal. He swiped in. I nodded at him. He looked nothing like Captain America—which, I suppose, meant that I looked nothing like Ryan Gosling. I glanced down the hallway to see if Gynnyfyr was anywhere in sight. She wouldn't like that she had missed him.

"Real nice, Win-win." Iqbal was staring at me.

"Huh?"

"I say, 'What up?' and you just look past me like I don't exist? I thought we were tight, yo. I was there for you, man."

"You left in the middle of my poem."

"I was letting you fly, little bird. Got to get used to your wings without Big Bird there, but that doesn't mean you should ignore your mama."

"Someone said that he looked like Captain America."

Iqbal got excited and peered around as Cory disappeared into the locker room. "Who?"

"Bandana Cory."

"Like who?"

"Captain America."

Iqbal was incredulous. "Captain America. *The* Captain America. Cap. Steve Rogers as Cap?"

"Is there another one?"

"Yes!"

"I don't care."

Iqbal looked momentarily deflated before he recovered his bravado. "Who said my man Cory looks like Captain America?"

I shuffled some papers on the desk. That was a tactical error. I hadn't meant to bring Gynnyfyr to Iqbal's attention at all. "They just left."

Iqbal stared thoughtfully at the men's locker room door. "Captain America in the movie, right? Chris Evans, right?"

"Yeah, I guess. I don't know." The last thing I wanted was to engage Iqbal on comic-book movies. I couldn't keep up and he had an encyclopedia of knowledge that he was dying to share.

"You have seen the movies, though."

"Some of them."

"Damn." Iqbal punched his fist into his open palm. "Damn, I wish some chick would compare me to Chris Evans. That dude is a stud, man."

"How do you know it was a girl?"

"What dude would compare another dude to an actor? Have you seen how cut he got for Captain America?" Iqbal's face fell from the heights of excitement to the depths of gloom. "I'm going to do a workout. Cover for me, huh?"

"Working toward Captain America?"

"Nah, that's for you white-bread boys. I'll be Pak Man!"

"You should maybe google that before you land on a name."

Iqbal headed to the locker room. He paused for a moment in front of the door and then kicked it open with a mighty kick. The heavy door puffed open about halfway—lazily, like a bed sheet on a laundry line blown by a slight breeze. Not exactly Captain America. Nonetheless, Iqbal gave a laugh that was full of bravado and then flung the door the rest of the way open as he entered the locker room.

Gynnyfyr returned a short while later and spotted Bandana Cory through the window before she even entered the rec centre.

"Winston!" She punched my shoulder. "He's here. Why didn't you tell me?" She was practically hissing at me.

"You went for food!"

"You should have texted me!"

"You said you'd be right back."

"I wanted. Time. To. Freshen. I could have been composing myself. Preparing for the scene! For the interaction." She threw up her arms in a dramatic fashion. "Now I am all flustered! I can't speak to him now."

"Why? Just go say hello."

"I can't just go talk to him!" Gynnyfyr was talking louder now and I saw a couple of girls on stationary bikes take notice. "A girl can't just go up and talk to a guy without some pretense. Otherwise he'd know that I was interested. You really are slow."

"Isn't that the point? You are interested."

"But he can't know that. Otherwise he has all the power. I have to play hard to get."

One of the girls on the stationary bikes leaned over to her friend and said something conspiratorially. When she caught me watching her, she quickly averted her eyes and started peddling with renewed intensity. She probably agreed that I was slow.

"Guys do it," I said.

"Not really." Her nostrils were flaring so that the stud diamond in her nose moved in and out almost hypnotically. She was really angry with me but I couldn't understand why. In moments like those I could easily believe the doctors' diagnosis. Nothing Gynnyfyr said made any sense to me at all.

"You have to fix this." Her arms were crossed so tightly it seemed she might crush herself. Her chest was threatening to spill out from her top like over-risen bread dough.

"How?"

"Get him to come talk to me."

"What?"

"You can do it."

"What would I say?"

"Whatever guys say."

I wondered whether I actually liked Gynnyfyr very much.

"Go on." She gestured toward Cory, who was making funny faces as he did lat pulldowns. "Get moving. And don't say anything about me or you'll pay for it."

I walked stupidly toward the weight equipment. Cory's eyes were squeezed shut as he finished his reps. His face was red and the red bandana darkened with sweat.

"Hey, Cory," I said. I didn't know what else to say. He opened his eyes and let the weights fall the last few inches into place.

"S'up?"

"Long time since I've seen you here." It was the first thing that popped into my head.

"Didn't I see you last week?"

"Oh, right. I'm losing it."

Cory wiped down the seat with a towel and moved to the chin-up bar. "Actually, I've been wanting to ask you what program you're doing. Did you just finish a cutting phase?"

"A cutting phase?"

"You dropped all that weight, trimmed all your body fat. Are you onto the bulking phase now? What program are you following?"

My mind conjured up the endless supply of strawberry SlimFast shakes that I had consumed and I felt a little queasy. "Kind of. It was sort of an accident."

"You're not sick, are you?" Cory said.

"No, just poor."

"I hear you, man. My student loan covers nothing. It looks like it worked in your favour, though; you could bulk pure muscle now."

"Yeah—" Gynnyfyr was glaring at me from across the room.

"So you don't have a program, though? Nutrition is key."

"You mean just eat, like, chicken breast and egg whites and work out a lot?"

Cory laughed. "Kinda. I've got some good tricks if you are interested."

"Totally," I said absently. How I was supposed to get him to go talk to Gynnyfyr without mentioning her?

"Listen," Cory said as he began to pound out his chin-ups. "I've got to design some fitness and nutrition programs for one of my kinese classes. Would you be interested?"

"Yeah, totally." I wasn't really, but I didn't know how to keep the conversation going otherwise.

"That's awesome. Thanks, man! I'll get to work designing you a nutrition program. Cutting is the worst part." He dropped back to the ground and wiped his face with his towel. "We could easily put thirty pounds of muscle on your frame." He held up his fist for me to pound it. "Now I just need a girl to design for and I am set."

Sometimes a conversation can take you right where you need it to go.

"Funny you should mention that," I said, suddenly feeling my conscience burn in a way it didn't when I signed up for Dignity. "I was just talking to a girl over there who was interested in starting a fitness and nutrition program. You should go talk to her." I pointed to Gynnyfyr, who at that moment was pursing her lips and looking at herself in the mirror.

"I saw you talking to her earlier," Cory said slowly. "She seemed a little nuts."

"Oh, she is," I said pleasantly. "But that solves your problem, doesn't it?"

"I guess."

"I've got to get back to work. Let me know when my plan is ready."

I returned to my station at the desk, tracking Cory out of the corner of my eye. His indecision showed on his face. I watched as he looked over at Gynnyfyr, who was studiously ignoring him pretending to read a magazine. He reached up to the chin-up bar and pulled himself up for another set. Gynnyfyr, for all her pretending not to notice him, looked over at me, her eyebrows raised menacingly. She mouthed something emphatically but I couldn't discern a single word. I looked back at Cory, who was in the middle of a set of chin-ups. Now Gynnyfyr was gesturing wildly toward me and Cory with her head.

"Give it a minute," I said it out loud over the din of the rec centre. Gynnyfyr looked both enraged and mortified and continued mouthing something at me again in her exaggerated pantomime.

I squinted trying to figure out what it was.

"You ... Are ... Dead."

What a psycho. I could go to Hell for putting a nice kid like Cory in her path. Didn't Dignity Begins at Home do any background checks whatsoever? If not on their clients, at least on the staff? I began shuffling the papers on the desk together so that I didn't have to pay attention to her. I was here to work, after all. I jammed the papers together as my conscience got the better of me. I needed to tell Cory to stay as far away from her as possible. It was my duty as part of the brotherhood of bros.

Too late. Cory was purposefully walking over to where Gynnyfyr was bobbing away on one of the ellipticals. She took out her headphones and smiled wide. He pointed at me behind the desk, and he looked surprised to find me staring at them. I waved stupidly. Gynnyfyr said something but the noise of the gym covered their conversation. If body language is anything to go by, she was more into it than he was.

"That was perfect!" She exclaimed to me after Cory had left the rec centre. "You are a genius, Winston! A true genius!"

I feel guilty all the time now.

CHAPTER TWELVE

Seconds aren't Epic

Michael's face was blotched with red and the fringe of his hair was plastered to his forehead like seaweed stranded on the shore. Both boys had an aura of dampness about them as they ran at me after their dismissal by their sensei.

"Did you see that? Did you see my headstand? I held it for—like—five minutes!"

"Five minutes?" Bret scoffed. "More like five seconds."

"It was way longer than seconds! You don't know!" Michael retorted indignantly as he shoved his older brother.

"You don't know anything. You can barely count." Bret elbowed Michael back sharply in the ribs.

"I saw it, Mikey," I said, hoping to derail their argument. "It was epic."

"See! Uncle Winston said it was epic. Seconds aren't epic. Sensei Drew said it was minutes!"

Bret cuffed Michael on the back of his head. "Whatever. It still wasn't as long as me. Did you see my headstand, Uncle Winston?"

"I did. It was also pretty cool. Nobody can stand on their heads quite like you guys." I pushed open the heavy glass door of the martial arts studio as a flood of crisp air rushed indoors. "You guys got all your stuff?"

Jeremy had dropped his kids off at their class and left me with precise instructions to pick them up promptly at a quarter to one.

"Twelve forty-five sharp," he'd repeated for the third time in three minutes. "If you're even ten minutes late, they'll charge me ten bucks a kid."

"Highway robbery," I said. "But what's that to you, Mercedes-Benz?"

"I'm serious, Winston. Please don't screw this up for once. Just be where you're supposed to be."

"I already said that I'll be there."

"It's important—" My brother's voice continued in the phone as though he hadn't heard me. "The boys need consistency. They need the psychological and emotional reassurance of their caregivers showing up when they say they will—"

"'Caregivers'?" I laughed. "You could have said 'family.' It's the same amount of wind."

Jeremy had sighed heavily into the microphone of his phone so that it sounded like a gale force wind in my ear. "Everything is a joke with you but none of it is ever funny."

"How about 'Thanks for helping us out of this scheduling jam, Winston. You're a stand-up guy and a prince among men'?"

"Twelve forty-five sharp," he said again and hung up.

He needn't have worried since I had already had a long text exchange with Beth about just how much it would mean to the boys if I showed up early and watched their class, which is how I ended up sitting in an uncomfortable metal chair around the edge of the mat while the boys did headstands and dive rolls for an hour.

The sweaty faces of my nephews looked up at me blankly until finally Bret asked, "What stuff?"

"I don't know—your gear, coats? Did you just come in your *gis*?" Both boys were wearing oversized white pants and a belted white jacket that criss-crossed and ballooned out over their narrow chests like overstuffed envelopes.

"We've got our coats," Michael answered. "Are we going to your house now?"

"Yep, are you guys hungry?"

"I'm starving! Can we get pizza?" Michael asked. "But only have ham and cheese on it?"

"Sure. I've got a frozen one at home and Iris will be showing up soon." I unlocked the car door.

"Who's Iris?" Bret asked. "Is she your girlfriend?"

"No. She's just a friend," I answered as I pulled my gym bag out of the back seat and tossed it into the trunk. I really needed to do some laundry.

"Do you have a girlfriend?"

"No."

"How come? How come you're not married like all the other adults?"

"Bad luck?"

"My mom says there is no such thing as luck and Dad says you have to work hard to make your own luck—" Michael explained helpfully.

"—which doesn't exist," I finished for him.

"Huh?" Michael looked up at me, confused.

"Never mind. Get in."

The boys jostled each other momentarily as they fought over who would be first to get into the car until Bret won due to his size advantage. "You know, there is another door," I said as I closed the back door and they settled into their respective spots.

"I'm going to be like you," Michael said as I got into the driver's seat. "I'm not going to get married ever, either."

"Whoa, whoa, whoa—who said anything about me never getting married? You think I'm too old?" This question didn't seem to register with Michael, who was now kicking the back of my seat. "Why don't you want to get married?" I asked.

He shrugged. "Lara said she was going to marry Isaac Kirk. I don't want to marry anyone else."

"Who's Lara? A girl at school?" I turned to look at him over my shoulder.

Michael nodded and looked out the window with a melancholy air that was almost comical.

"Well, you've still got some years to convince her to choose you instead. Marriage isn't legal in this country until you're eighteen. Or—maybe someone else will catch your fancy."

"Like Iris?" Bret asked, clearly mocking me. Sometimes that kid sounds like he could have had a role in *The Mighty Ducks*.

I raised my eyebrows at him. "Maybe."

"You want to marry her!"

"I barely know her." I put the key in the ignition and the engine turned over. "None of this talk once she gets there, okay?"

"I thought you said that she was your friend."

"What are you—the prosecutor?"

"What's a prosecutor?"

"A pain in the caboose."

"You mean, 'ass.'"

"Hey—watch your mouth or you'll be sucking on a bar of Dove all afternoon instead of eating a pizza with only ham and cheese on it." I put the car in gear and navigated out the parking stall. "The last thing I need is for my brother to think that I was teaching you bad words; then it'll be my head on the platter."

Bret shrugged. "My dad called you an—" He paused momentarily while he took my threat of washing his mouth out with soap seriously. "—that."

"I bet he did, but that doesn't mean that you can say it."

"That's not fair."

"Fact of life. Get used to it early."

"That's stupid." Bret crossed his arms indignantly, which made his white jacket balloon out around his neck. "It's stupid that adults do the stuff that they punish kids for."

I signalled to change lanes. "It's not stupid. The word you're looking for is 'hypocritical.' But it isn't really. It just looks that way."

"You're just saying that because you're an adult," he said from somewhere within the voluminous folds of his *gi*.

"Uncle Winston isn't an adult," Michael interjected. "You're not an adult until you get married."

"It certainly feels that way," I muttered. "The reason why your parents might wash your mouth out with soap for using a bad word that you heard them use is because—theoretically—as adults, they are choosing to bear the consequences of using that kind of language, but as a kid you aren't really able to make that decision."

"But if I get punished, then I do. That's a consequence," Bret protested.

"Only to a limited degree. You're getting a punishment that is meant to correct you. You don't even know what kind of consequences you might face from using that language. If your dad says it, he's choosing to do it knowingly, but if you use it, you're doing it ignorantly. It's not the same thing."

"What kind of consequences?"

"People might end up thinking you don't have any manners, or that you're being disrespectful and you won't end up getting a job. Or maybe some girl you like hears it and then thinks that you're a creep and then she doesn't want to give you a chance. That kind of thing. There are consequences to your behaviour that you never know about, but that doesn't mean that they didn't happen."

Bret looked as though he was mulling it over—or maybe not. I don't really know how to read kids very well.

"Did you make my dad suck on a bar of soap for calling you that?"

I shook my head. "Your grandma did, though, when he was a kid."

"Really!?"

I glanced at them in the rear-view mirror. Their eyes shone with excitement at the idea that Grandma had washed out their father's mouth with soap for swearing.

"Grandma takes no prisoners." I pulled the car out onto the road and headed toward my new digs in Bowness. "Your dad choked, though; he threw up after—like—thirty seconds of Irish Spring."

The boys howled with laughter. I laughed, too.

"Did you ever get your mouth washed out with soap?" Bret asked when he could speak again.

"Once," I said. That memory was slightly less funny.

"For swearing? What did you say?"

"You'd like to know, wouldn't you? But I'm not that stupid. Ol' Uncle Winston still has a few synapses firing. I will tell you one thing, though. I took it like a man. I never puked."

"Come on! Tell us! Tell us what you said! We won't tell!"

"Pfft," I snorted. "You two are about as trustworthy as pirates. A couple of errant knaves. A pair of scoundrels, if ever I saw them."

"You talk weird," Bret said, clearly disappointed.

"I don't mind being a scoundrel. That's what Han Solo is. Princess Leia said so," Michael said.

"That's true. August company."

"Did you say 'ass'?" Bret asked.

"Hey! You are cruising for pain, Palmolive."

"Just tell me! Was it the 's' word? The 'b' word? The—"

"Before you go through the alphabet, let me tell you, it wasn't any of those words." I looked back at my oldest nephew in the rear-view mirror. A perplexed look was on his face as his lips moved silently—clearly running through every bad word he'd ever heard. Fortunately, it didn't take too long.

"There are a lot of bad things you can say that aren't necessarily bad words. What I said was bad, but none of the words were bad by themselves. You can ask Grandma about it, if you want."

"Grandma won't tell me," Bret answered sullenly. "She never tells anyone anything."

"She says enough," I said as I turned the car onto my street. The sunlight on the snow was momentarily blinding. "Besides, you'd probably just go and say it to get a reaction. I hear that's the kind of thing that little punks like you like to pull."

The boys raised their voices in a chorus of objections as I pulled up in front of the house, the car sliding a few inches on a sheet of ice on the road.

"Come on!"

"Just tell us! We promise we won't tell."

"Maybe some other time," I conceded. "If it looks like you aren't turning into serial killers."

The boys groaned as they threw open the car door and spilled onto the sidewalk.

"Watch out, it's a skating rink."

"Watch me slide!" Bret took a few steps and slid a foot or two down the walk.

Soon both boys were sliding down the sidewalk. I locked the car door and looked up just in time to see Bret lose his footing and wipe out on the lawn.

"You okay?" I asked, peering over him as he lay flat on the ground.

Bret nodded. "Who's that?"

I followed his gaze across to the neighbouring house. A man—my neighbour, I guess—was dragging a table from his driveway toward the steps of his front porch.

"Wait here," I said to the boys and walked across the yellowed grass of our adjoining lawns, which was still strewn with islands of half-melted, half-frozen snow.

"Can I give you a hand with that?"

The man didn't acknowledge having heard me but continued to drag the centre pedestal of the table from his garage toward the front steps.

"Do you need some help?" I said again, louder this time. The man looked up at me for only the briefest of seconds before he moved around to the other side of the unusual table in acceptance of my offer. I took my place opposite him and simultaneously we hoisted the table and carried it up the steps. It was wider than the door, but he backed into the doorway forcefully until the edge of the oval top jammed on the door frame.

"I think—" I said, straining to pull it back toward me so that we could turn it onto its side. "I think we're going to have to get it in sideways, sir."

The man ignored me and yanked the table toward himself again, bashing it on the door frame.

"Sir? It's not going to fit that way. Do you mind if we try my idea?"

179

He dropped his side suddenly and stood there looking at the ground.

"I'm just going to tip it so that this side," I said, patting the smooth top, "goes toward the ground. Then we'll lift it again and see if we can angle it through the door."

The man was still staring at the ground, but his left hand was nervously playing with the fourth button of his red flannel shirt.

"Okay, so I'm just tipping it down—" I strained to keep the heavy tabletop from crashing down on the cement porch as the weight from the pedestal counter balanced unsteadily. "Now, if you can pick up your side, we'll carry it in."

My neighbour let go of his button and swiftly picked up his end of the table, startling me with his strength as the weight in my hands lifted. He backed up blindly, navigating the table with speed through his small living room and into the dining room. My eyes adjusted slowly to the dimness of the house after the bright sunlight outside.

"This is some table," I said as looked at it for the first time as we lifted it back into its upright position. The pedestal was shaped like the trunk of a tree and ornately carved with scrolling vines and flowers while the tabletop itself was a misshapen oval inlaid with turquoise that filled the irregularities of the wood grain.

"This is incredible." I ran my fingertips over the table. There wasn't the slightest ridge; it had been sanded and varnished until it was like glass. "I've never seen anything like this. Where did you even find something like this?"

I watched him shuffle the table back and forth several inches trying to get the placement exactly right. "Oh, wow, you made this, didn't you?"

My neighbour continued his trend of ignoring my questions, but I knew it was the truth. "Well, that's awesome. You're really talented," I said, trying to make it normal that I was in this guy's house and talking to him, despite the fact that he clearly didn't want me to be there. "I'm Winston, by the way. I just moved into the yellow house next door a few weeks ago."

The man didn't say anything or acknowledge that I had, either; he continued to jimmy the oak table back and forth.

"What's your name?" I waited for him to answer until it became abundantly clear that he wasn't going to. I looked around. There were no chairs to go with the table. "Is there anything else you need a hand with? Chairs, or something?"

In the dim gloom of his house, I barely made out the slightest shake of his head.

"No? Okay," I said, my sense of foolishness in this scenario finally reaching its apex. "Well, it was nice meeting you...neighbour. Be sure to come get me if you need help carrying anything."

I turned to leave and was almost at the door when I felt him grab my arm. He motioned for me to wait and then turned and shuffled down the hallway. As I waited, I glanced around the dim room and was startled to discover that the curtain that covered the picture window in the front room was alive. A thick, living wall of leaves glowed green in front of the window. The veil was made up entirely of the tendrils of numerous plants that sat on a shelf over the window. The light that managed to come through the foliage dappled the floor.

"This is incredible," I called out to him before I remembered that he probably wouldn't answer. "How long did it take you to grow these plants?" Some of the vines were starting to snake out across the living room floor. "Your house is really cool."

The man returned as I was looking through a small gap in the leaves to see that the boys were still sliding on the front sidewalk.

He didn't answer but held out his hand to me. I looked down to see two G.I. Joes. He pulled back the vines to peer out his front window, where I could see Iris had joined Bret and Michael on the sidewalk.

"For them?" I asked.

The man nodded.

"Are you sure? That's really not necessary. I'm your neighbour. You can get me to help you anytime."

He grabbed my hand as though it pained him to do it, and shoved the action figures into it. Then he sat down adroitly on his couch with his gaze fixed on the floor. His left hand found the fourth button on his shirt again.

"You sure you don't want to give these to them yourself?" I asked uselessly. He shook his head forcefully and his fingers began to twist on the button more frantically than before.

"Okay," I said, wishing that Iris was in here rather than sliding down the sidewalk with the boys. What good is a social aide if she's not around to provide actual social guidance in an emergency situation? "If you change your mind and want these back, I'm—I'm just next door."

I looked at the action figures in my hand. "My nephews are really going to like these. Thanks, man."

I watched him fiddle with the button on his shirt for a moment longer before I said, "See you around, sir."

CHAPTER THIRTEEN

My Friend, Benedict Arnold

Dignity Begins at Home improved my social life—I mean, in a weird way where women were paid by the government to spend time with me in order to work on my social and professional development. Gynnyfyr claimed the professional skills part. She liked working out for free at the rec centre while I was on shift. She spent most of her time chatting up the young guys who came to lift. She was happy to keep her distance from me and I was more than happy to continue in that arrangement. If the gym was relatively empty and she was bored, she would sometimes steal my chair at the sign-in desk and talk to me about things like what it must be like to be married to Kanye West, or whether I thought Ed Sheeran would be interested in a slightly more mature woman.

"He has red hair. I have red hair. I'm just saying, that's not exactly a coincidence. I'm just saying."

If Iqbal happened to be on shift, Gynnyfyr would pick a recumbent bike and leaf through the glossy pages of a magazine while letting her feet spin around lazily on the easiest setting. Within a couple of weeks, I got used to the arrangement and forgot to feel apprehensive when she was around.

Iris was another matter.

Iris. It is an archaic name—like Winston—and I started taking special care with her name before I even realized it. It was old-fashioned. Iris and Winston. Winston and Iris. It was like we were a Chinese couple who had adopted Western names without knowing which ones had receded with the ebbing waves of nomenclature trends. I began to think about our names as one half of a whole thing. It happened accidentally. You can see how I might get confused because all we did was hang out, run errands and go for outings. We went to the library. We went for coffee. She briefly met my parents. We went to Calgary's tourist attractions. We went grocery shopping together on Sunday afternoons. Once I followed her in my car to the mechanic's so that she could drop hers off in order to get the brakes done. I was the one who noticed that she needed to replace them. Anyone who saw us would have thought that we were together; like a couple who went out and did things together because we liked being together.

We went out but we weren't a couple. We weren't a couple because she was paid to accompany me on the basis that she believed I was mentally incapacitated. I mean, it wasn't like she was Julia Roberts in *Pretty Woman* or something sleazy like that. There was just no 'we.' There was just her job. Sometimes I wondered if she ever thought about how it looked from the outside, but I never asked. I didn't want anything to disrupt the pleasant ease of our interactions, which felt both natural and exciting.

She laughed at my jokes and had this distracting way of looking at me sidelong as a smile crept across her features. What hope did I have?

Iris did surreptitious little safety checks around my house. The first thing she did every time she came in was check the stove. She showed me where to light the pilot on the furnace. I knew where it was already, but I let her show me because her trying to find it was adorable and winning. She made sure I knew how to stop an overflowing toilet. She reminded me to lock all the doors at night. It was in these moments that I was the most uncomfortable. I oscillated between pretending I didn't already know what she was talking about and protesting myself capable because I felt guilty for lying.

"I know," I said during one of her afternoon visits when she told me that it was a good idea to rinse the dishes before putting them in the dishwasher. "My mom taught me that."

Iris smiled broadly, revealing her slightly uneven teeth. "Were you living with your parents up until you got this house?"

"No. I had a basement suite," I said, momentarily grateful for that soul-killing dive and its place in my history.

Iris finished loading the plates from our lunch into the dishwasher and moved to collect her keys and purse. We were on our way to meet up with my friend Robbie for a coffee. Regular social interaction was one of the "goals" that Iris was working on with me and she'd been bugging me for a week to set up something with a friend. Coffee with Robbie was not my idea of a nice way to spend an afternoon, but I had few options. I had initially asked Sam but she flat out refused to "participate in this despicable charade."

"Unless—" Sam had let the word hang over me like the guillotine blade ready to fall. "—you want me to explain to this poor misguided woman that you're a welfare cheat. Then sure! Let's all get a coffee. Heck, bring her along to help paint on Saturday. Let's all have a chat."

Sam had the crazy eye when she said it, so I demurred. That only left Robbie. I don't know when I lost touch with all my friends, exactly, but I couldn't help but marvel over the fact that the one I was left with was Robbie Marchuk—of all people.

"I am impressed that you were able to get into the program if you were already living on your own," Iris said.

"I hadn't been there very long." I pulled her coat from the closet and held it for her as she put it on.

"Who were your aides before you got on with Dignity? I've worked with a couple of these agencies. I feel like I know everyone."

"I didn't have any aides."

"You were okay on your own?"

"Well…" I paused, trying to think of what would be the best response to that. Technically—or depending on your point of view—I hadn't really been okay on my own.

"Your parents did everything."

I didn't know what to say to that, either, so I just held open the front door for her to pass through.

"So many parents struggle to carry such a big burden; I'm just impressed yours managed without respite workers."

"Listen, Iris," I said, surprising myself with a sudden impulse toward clarity. "I've never needed respite workers before at all. I don't really need any of this. I don't have special needs. That's not me." I felt as though I was on a rollercoaster that was slipping over the drop-off: slightly sick, but increasingly weightless. It felt good. I'd told the truth. I'd come clean.

"'Special needs' just means that additional support is helpful. The level of support varies a lot. It isn't a judgment, Winston. At least, not a negative one."

"Sure, but I don't even know why I am in this program. I'm not—you know—I don't fit." Iris was clearly a smart woman. Surely, she could see what I was getting at.

She just smiled and reached out to squeeze my hand. "I'm glad that you got in. Don't worry about it."

I reacted involuntarily, not because I didn't want her to grab my hand but because suddenly Sam's prediction about regret was echoing around my brain and I felt uncomfortable.

"Sorry," she said softly as she withdrew her fingers. "I forget that not everyone likes to be touched." Iris unlocked the doors to her '03 Civic—now equipped with functional brakes—and walked purposefully to the driver's side. I tried to think of something to say to mitigate what had just happened, to explain everything, but Iris changed the subject. "What do you like at Starbucks?"

"Doesn't matter—coffee—whatever." I felt doubly sick. She thought that I recoiled at her touch, when really I recoiled because I'm a lying jackass. She also thinks I'm special needs.

"Not a fancy-drink guy?" Her tone was still upbeat as she turned the key in the ignition.

"Not really."

I had just told Iris the truth but it hadn't mattered. She thought I belonged in the program. She spent hours on end with me and had seen me do all kinds of things and still thought I legitimately belonged in the program. There was no question in her mind about whether we looked like a couple out and about. To her, we did not. I felt hollow thinking about it. But maybe— maybe—Iris hadn't been a respite aide for a very long time. Maybe she didn't have enough experience to make a discerning judgement on my situation. Maybe this was all relatively new to her. Maybe. I clung to the thought desperately.

The Civic jumped forward as Iris gunned the engine, tearing away from the curb like we were the police on a call. I closed my eyes against the brilliant glare of the sunlight and the death-defying attitude with which Iris drove, changing lanes at right angles. I wished I could think about anything else.

"'Special needs' just means that additional support is helpful."

I guess I did need additional support. Hadn't I liked living with my parents? For the most part, I had. Had I been coping on my own? Not really. Figuratively speaking, I had been barely able to keep my head above water, never mind the actual water problems.

"I usually get a mocha," Iris said, speeding past all the cars around us.

"I like chocolate, too."

Good grief, maybe I was a special needs case and had never noticed it until now. Sure, I had applied for the program. I had gone to the specialist out of exhaustion and frustration and because I owed it to Sam. I hadn't really believed it. I just—I don't know—it was just a gambit; I was just wondering what would happen if I did apply. It was like buying a lottery ticket. I never expected to win. Then there had just been something comical about getting in and getting a house and aides and whatnot.

"What's not to like?" Iris answered cheerfully. When Gynnyfyr was around, Iris was subdued, as though her colleague took up all the oxygen in the room. She was different when it was just her and me. Iris came alive like the gentle unfolding of petals from a delicate flower.

"How long have you been an aide?" I asked as the car lazily drifted into the adjoining lane. The car beside us honked in warning. Iris didn't seem to notice.

"Almost ten years." She clucked her tongue in disbelief. "It sounds crazy that it has been that long."

"Have you always worked with the same person?" I asked, my last hope deflating fast.

"No—I've probably worked with at least a dozen. Some longer than others, but quite a few over the years."

"A dozen—wow. That's a lot. Did you always want to do this kind of work?" I asked, trying to distract myself from the realization that I was probably actually special needs.

She laughed. "No. I started out doing this part-time while I was in school and then——" Her words trailed off. I waited a moment for her to continue.

"——And then?"

"Sorry——I just kept doing it."

"What were you in school for?"

"I was training to be a nurse."

"What happened?"

She sighed heavily before she answered. "I had some issues that disrupted my studies. I didn't end up going back because——I just didn't."

We rode in silence for a few minutes as she slipped in and out of traffic as though she were being timed.

"It is really bright out." Iris said, glancing in my direction after a while. "We should get you some sunglasses." She tapped the clock on the dash with her index finger. "We're a bit early to meet your friend. We've got time to run into the Winners."

"Sure," I said. "I used to have some. I don't know what happened to them."

"Well, you definitely need them in this city." Iris pulled into a parking space at the outdoor mall. "Plus, you have blue eyes."

"What does that have to do with it?"

"Blue-eyed people are especially prone to cataracts," Iris said. "Particularly in Calgary, where the sun is always glinting off the snow. We don't have as much pigment to protect us."

"I did not know that."

"Do you ever wish that you had gone back and finished your nursing program?" I asked as we walked into the department store.

"Sometimes," she said as she led the way to the sunglasses. "But then I wonder if it was the right thing for me anyway."

"Why?"

"Just having to deal with certain things—people dying on you—I don't know if I would have always handled that very well. Here we go." She stopped in front of a rack of glasses.

"These are women's sunglasses," I said, looking at the abundance of rhinestone-studded frames. I glanced around at the scarves and hats and the adjacent jewelry counter. This was definitely the women's section.

"I guess I've never noticed whether or not they have men's sunglasses here." Iris flagged down a passing clerk, who directed us to the opposite side of the store for men's accessories—which really is a stupid term. The only thing men have accessories for is murder.

"I assume you'd get used to that after a while," I said, scanning the bank of men's sunglasses without really seeing them.

"That's what I was afraid of," she said matter-of-factly. "What about these? They're only $9.99." Iris held up a pair of sunglasses with white plastic frames and black lenses. She handed them to me.

"Sure." I turned to walk to the till.

"Wait," she said, laughing. "You have to try them on."

I put the frames on, trying to see myself in the inadequate mirror while trying to keep the stiff cardboard price tag from jabbing me in the eye. The security lock kept the sunglasses from sitting normally on my face. "These are $99.99, not $9.99," I said, looking at the tag in the mirror.

"Definitely not, then." Iris held out her hand for the sunglasses. "Besides, they make you look like a——" She stopped short of completing her simile and added instead, "Let's just say Gynnyfyr would love you in them."

I handed them back to her. "Good thing you stopped me."

Iris examined all the sunglasses, assessing each pair with a level of care that I could never match. She mumbled to herself as she examined and discarded several.

"These are nice—but they're $79.99. Pass on those. These are okay. Try these."

I mechanically put on a pair of sunglasses almost identical to the last pair that I had. Expecting a vote of approval, I turned to face her.

"You look like a bug. What is it about these stores that make everything seem like crap? Who recommends these prices?" She continued to paw through the rack, looking back at me periodically as though she was reminding herself what I looked like.

"What about these?" She handed me a pair of aviators.

I put them on and turned to face her. She smiled. "Pretty slick, Slick. And they are only twenty bucks."

Iris asked the clerk at the till to cut the tags off of them for me. My blue eyes now shielded by UV-rated plastic, we emerged back into the blinding light of Calgary's winter months and wandered down the sidewalk, where blue-tinged salt was strewn like some pragmatist's fairy dust. It crunched and scraped under the soles of our shoes.

"So, if you've never had an aide before," Iris began as we headed over to the coffee shop, "how do you like it?"

"It's a bit weird," I answered.

"How so?"

"It just is. What if you suddenly had Gynnyfyr job-shadowing you?"

"Does she do a good job?"

"I guess," I said, shrugging. "But I don't need the help."

"Well—" Iris paused as I opened the door to the bookstore for her. "We can certainly re-evaluate your level of support, though I would hate for you to lose your funding if we determined that you weren't eligible for the program."

"That's possible?"

"Dignity Begins at Home is brand new. I don't know what the procedure would be for that sort of thing; maybe there isn't one yet, but it makes sense that it should be possible."

"I wonder if my neighbour has aides."

"The guy you helped with the table the other day?"

I nodded. "He could probably use some help."

"Maybe he's in the Dignity program or something like it," Iris said.

"I doubt it. His plants look like they've been growing there for a long time."

We entered the bookstore and made our way through the shelves to the back, where the coffee shop was located.

"Should we wait for your friend before we order?"

"Nah, otherwise he'll just get me to pay for his."

"Better grab one of those," she said and gestured toward one of the few remaining empty tables. "I'll get in line."

I handed her some cash for the drinks and Iris joined the substantial line of people waiting to order while I cleared a detritus of broken stir sticks and torn cup sleeves from the closest table and sat down.

Robbie Marchuk arrived in Madame Goudreau's second-grade class a month after the first day of school wearing a grey matching sweatsuit and carrying a *Star Wars*-themed lunch box. The box was made of orange plastic and served as his passport to social success as we boys crowded around him at lunch to discuss the picture of the TIE fighter attacking an X-wing fighter. We became friends based on geographical convenience and a mutual love of building structurally unsound jumps for our BMX bikes. These points of intersection were the entire basis of our friendship. Robbie was a persnickety kid who serviced his BMX with a near-daily application of WD-40, going through several cans a season at least; whereas I never had any use for WD-40, except as a makeshift flamethrower.

We've kept in touch over the years, more through Robbie's efforts than mine. He prides himself on maintaining a vast network of social connections of which I am merely one far-flung outpost. He drifts in and out of town every now and then and calls me to meet him for a beer. The last time was at least a year and a half ago, and he was aerated on the topic of Indigenous land rights. We argued—as we always do—and he walked out leaving me with the bill for his gluten-free beer.

I glanced back at Iris, who hadn't made any forward progress in line, as Robbie threw himself into the chair opposite me. For a guy who is always on the move and lives out of a camper van, he's a pretty snappy dresser. He wears those tight jeans and carries a man bag. It looked to me like he might be using that old WD-40 to do his hair these days. It was coiffed in an undulating wave that looked like it belonged in a gay men's magazine, not a camper van.

"So, to what do I owe the honour?" Robbie asked.

"What do you mean?"

"You never call me."

"That's because you're always off making movies in Tucson or someplace. I can't keep track."

"It was Albuquerque and that was ages ago. I've been in Madagascar for the last six months. I'm back while I'm waiting for my crowdfunding to come in. Have you donated yet? I sent you the link."

"Of course not."

"Jackass. We're working on getting some indie festivals to screen it and then hopefully a distributor will pick it up. It's important stuff. Not that I expect someone like you to care. How've you been? What have you been up to? You're a piss-poor friend," he said, smiling broadly. "You look different. Have you aged a hundred years since I last saw you?"

"Thanks a lot."

"You're welcome. Hey, how's Sam doing?"

"She's fine."

"Yeah? Married? What's she doing?"

"She's not married. Dating some guy in the Peace Corps—or something equally silly."

"I can count on you to sabotage that. One of these days, the stars are going to align for me and her, and it's gonna happen."

"Just like an end-of-days kind of thing." I looked back to the coffee bar to see Iris pick up the drinks and head in our direction.

"Robbie," I said, standing up as she approached. "This is Iris. She's my—" She was my *what*, exactly? Why hadn't I thought about how I was going to handle this introduction ahead of time?

Iris handed me my coffee and extended her hand warmly. "Hi, I work with Winston."

Robbie shook her hand enthusiastically "Robbie Marchuk. I've been trying to teach this loser a conscience since the beginning of time. He needs a lot of help."

"Nice to meet you," she said. "Can I get you a drink?"

"Aren't you a sweetie," he said, smiling at Iris like she was supposed to take him seriously in those tight jeans. "I'd love a green tea. Large. Two tea bags."

Iris nodded and returned to the line.

"Are you seriously letting her buy your drink?"

"Why not? She offered." Robbie crossed his leg so that his pant leg rode up, exposing some vibrantly patterned socks.

"Because you're a dude."

"I'm a feminist. I wouldn't insult her by presuming that she couldn't pay on the basis that she's a woman."

"That's not why you don't let her pay. It's not an assumption that she can't afford it on the basis that she's a woman."

"Sure it is," he said firmly.

"You don't even know her. You let strangers pay for you?"

Robbie shrugged. "Why not? Girls buy me drinks all the time. Besides, green tea is cheap. Is your girlfriend so cheap she can't swing a couple of tea bags?"

"She's not my girlfriend."

"Yeah, you brought your co-worker to meet me."

Iris returned to the table and set down Robbie's tea. "I'm just going to browse some of the books for a few minutes. You guys enjoy your visit."

"Why don't you join us?" Robbie asked. "I'd love to hear what Winston is working on these days. High achievers are always interesting to follow."

Iris looked momentarily perplexed before changing the subject. "So, what do you do, Robbie?"

"I'm an activist and a filmmaker."

"What kind of films do you make?"

"My mandate—my mission—is to raise awareness," Robbie answered. "Particularly about environmental causes," he added after a moment. "I'm Gaia's town crier."

"I see," Iris said as she took a seat—somewhat reluctantly, I thought.

"Yeah, like documentaries on how we're desecrating the planet. I'm in the process of editing one together right now."

"Uplifting," I said, taking a gulp of my coffee.

"The world isn't all sunshine and unicorns, Winston," Robbie said. "It's full of corruption and betrayal. We're decimating the planet, man. The people with power are doing terrible things to the people without it."

"Decimating? Are you sure? Because that really doesn't sound that bad. That's one-tenth."

I could see I was getting under his skin because he shifted his attention to Iris. "So—Iris—what's a nice girl like you doing hanging around with this asshole?"

Iris smiled in a guarded way. "The government pays me to keep an eye on him."

"Money well spent," Robbie answered.

"Why do you hang around with him?" she asked with what I interpreted to be mock innocence.

"Oh, I'm just a creature of habit, and Winston and I go way back. Once upon a time we used to like hanging out together."

"Yeah, but the line of before and after is pretty starkly drawn," I said. "It's only my sweet and merciful nature that accepted you back after that performance of squealing betrayal."

Robbie laughed. "That was all you, bro. The bomb was all you. You admitted it."

"I beg your pardon," Iris said. "What bomb?"

My blow-up with Robbie occurred in the summer between the eighth and ninth grade and left us estranged, grounded and bored for the rest of the summer. It was the familiar juxtaposition between frantic excitement and unrelenting boredom that characterizes youth. The breakdown revealed the fissures in our friendship, and though we made peace on the first day of school at Vincent Massey Junior High four weeks later, our relationship never really recovered its former sheen. The summer was hot, and the sun seemed brighter in the dry heat of sapphire-blue skies punctuated by the billows of storybook clouds that yielded no rain. Throughout the month of July we passed the tread of our bikes all over the city, exploring deep into the Weaselhead Flats, some 237 hectares of wetland that joins the city's reservoir to the out-of-bounds land of the Tsuu T'ina Nation. We followed Calgary streets to their end and beyond, visiting the surrounding towns of Cochrane and Chestermere. We brought salami-and-cheese sandwiches and cans of no-name cola that grew warm in our backpacks until we popped their tabs when our stomachs began to rumble and the sweat of the ride dripped down our spines and blotted on our No Fear T-shirts. It was during one of these repasts of sour cream and onion chips and sandwiches and warm pop that we hatched a plan to overnight in the Weaselhead—No Camping Allowed—whilst lying to our parents that we were at the other's house. We had ditched our bikes on the edge of the trail and wandered deeper into the trees looking for shade at high noon. Finding a larger spruce amid the dense and scrubby birch trees and willows, we sat down to eat our lunch and spied a tent in a small clearing through the trees.

It had never occurred to us until we saw that bedraggled tent that we might camp in the middle of Glenmore Park's Weaselhead. The fact that it just wasn't done—that it wasn't allowed—ignited a fire in our teenage brains. There would be nothing cooler than staying out all night in the Weaselhead, where wild animals followed the woods and water into the middle of the city. We would have such a story to tell come September to our friends who went other places in the summertime. We plotted for the upcoming Friday night, because Friday was the night for sleepovers.

We made our plans—as much as the consequence-adverse brains of teenage boys make such things—involving imaginative details and anticipated, unlikely outcomes such as an attack from bad guys, all the while ignoring essentials like food and water and appropriate shelter. I was exultant as I snuck into Jeremy's room to steal the nightstick that he had bought at the Army Surplus so that we would have a defence against other illegal dwellers in the Weaselhead at night. After ditching our unsuspecting families, we arrived at the park and made a small campfire on the smooth, white stones on the shore of the Elbow River and felt both wild and free. I don't remember what we talked about as we stared into the flames. Robbie had an intense crush on Sam in those days, which made me supremely uncomfortable, so it's possible he spent a good portion of the evening badgering me to persuade Sam to be his first girlfriend. Or maybe we just talked about how we would have such a cool story to tell to our respective kids when we grew up. Whatever it was, it was shattered and forgotten in light of finding the bomb.

No kidding. We found a bomb. "Unexploded ordnance," as the Department of National Defence called it. Robbie came across it first thing Saturday morning when he wandered away from our makeshift camp to pee. The night had been somewhat uncomfortable in our indoor sleeping bags from Canadian Tire. When the bright sun gave us licence to rise, decamp and be on our way to find a more abundant breakfast than the remaining can of Pringles from the night before, Robbie stormed out of the tent with the statement that camping in the Weaselhead had been the worst idea I had ever had.

"It's not my fault you didn't remember to bring a foamy," I muttered, chaffed by his sour mood after what had been one of the most exciting ideas I had ever cooked up. He left the tent flap wide open when he departed and a swarm of mosquitos entered in his place. I remember that as clearly as what followed with the bomb. I was fuming and swatting at insects that were dead set on buzzing in my ear as he rushed back to the tent.

"Winston!" Robbie shouted from a distance and then I heard him crash through the brush and shoved his head in the tent. "You gotta see what I found!"

I followed him back through the trees to an honest-to-goodness bomb.

"Can you believe this?" Robbie squatted down next to it and tried to push the thorny branches that covered its nose out of the way.

I shook my head in disbelief.

"It's a bomb, right?" he said, excitement brimming in his words.

"It looks like it."

It was a rusted and faded mortar with stabilizing fins. It looked like the kind of thing you saw in war movies dropping out B-52s over Germany or something, and yet there it was, half-buried in the dirt and tangled in the briars of a wild-rose bush in Calgary of all places.

"We should bring it back."

This. This was the point of contention that brought about our estrangement. Whose suggestion was it? Robbie claims it was mine. I thought it was his. But truth be told, even if we hadn't gotten busted in the biggest trouble we'd ever found ourselves in, we probably would have fallen out in greed over our treasure, anyway. When we arrived back at my house with a literal unexploded bomb, another kind of bomb of a less literal variety went off in my father's head. The idea that the shell might still be dangerous never crossed our fool minds. It was just a cool relic from a bygone era. We didn't know why it was there. We figured it was a dud or maybe a prop. Honestly, we didn't think about it all that much. We didn't think about it as we dug it out of the ground. We didn't think about it as we traded its incredible weight back and forth on the ride home. We didn't think about it being dangerous. We just thought, *We found a bomb! Cool!*

When my generally placid father exploded with adrenalin and fury as Robbie and I unpacked our prize onto his lovingly tended front lawn, the accusations and Soviet-style squealing began in earnest. The police were called, the neighbours evacuated and the bomb disposed of by the bomb squad. When the Department of National Defence began their investigation, the real fallout began. Robbie said it had been my idea to bring the bomb home, my idea to camp in the Weaselhead in the first place. I called him a stool pigeon and hissed with every ounce of contempt I could muster that he had betrayed the code of friendship. We were neither of us supposed to talk. Friends were supposed to stand together. We were supposed to have each other's back, but he withered under my father's (and very shortly thereafter, his father's) ire like tender green shoots caught by a frost. His willingness to let me bear the full weight of the punishment that was inevitably to come left me feeling cold and it ignited a slow burn of fury that I fed for the rest of the summer (and actually, much longer, if I'm honest) with thoughts comparing Robbie to all the turncoat characters of fiction. He was Benedict Arnold to my America. He was Edmund Pevensie to my Peter, Susan and Lucy. Brutus to my Julius Caesar. Scar to my Mufasa. He was like the annoying red-haired guy in *Dead Poets Society* who sold out Robin Williams. I stopped short of saying he was Judas Iscariot to my Jesus because even my fifteen-year-old self could see that would be taking it a bit too far.

My parents were mad about me bringing the bomb home because it was so clearly a stupid thing to do. My mom ranted for days about what was—or wasn't—going on in my brain. My dad's disbelief was almost harder to bear. There was one small upside to the whole debacle, though: Dad started explaining to me how explosives and guns worked because he believed my ignorance was fuelling a dangerous lack of judgment.

What I really got in trouble for was lying about being at Robbie's house when I was illegally camping in the Weaselhead. That was why I ended up being grounded for the rest of the summer. That was why I had to do the dishes every night until 1997.

I fumed with all the surplus energy and disaffection my teenage self could muster and directed my enraged thoughts at Robbie, at my parents and at the former Sarcee artillery range where Canada's troops were trained for both World Wars. I exhausted myself with anger and finally decided to reconcile with Robbie despite his traitorous betrayal. After all—I conceded quite charitably when I did not want to be angry anymore—the fire had revealed more unpleasant things about him than it had about me. It is like those moments of danger in movies that demonstrate who amongst the characters is heroic and who is a coward. Robbie had been revealed as a coward who would sell me out to save himself. I imagined as I sought him out at his locker and extended my hand that he would be happy for the mercy that allowed him to save face.

"I'm sorry about what happened with the bomb," I said. "At least we got a good story out of it."

Robbie had slammed the door to his locker and I could see immediately that his appetite for anger was greater than mine. "Yeah, well, because of that stupid stunt, my parents said I won't be getting the dirt bike I wanted from my cousins. So your apology doesn't really do shit for me."

"Then I probably saved your life. You can't ride for shit."

"And weirdly enough, we're still friends—kinda," I said, finishing the tale to Iris's wide-eyed amazement. I assumed she was impressed by our reckless stupidity but then I remembered that she believes I'm mentally-deficient so I guess the story played. I don't know what Robbie's excuse is though.

But really, that has always been the case anyway.

CHAPTER FOURTEEN

I Love the Smell of Chlorine in the Morning

The lights over the Olympic-sized pool sputtered and popped as they flickered to life in a rudimentary display of electricity, as though lightning had just struck the University of Calgary and that elemental force had travelled through crude conductors until it was powering the buildings of the Kinesiology Complex like Dr. Frankenstein's monster. At four in the morning the campus felt like a great slumbering giant. I can count on one hand the number of times that I had arrived at work so early. Rona, the manager of the aquatic centre, had called me at eleven last night, begging me to cover her opening shift since her daughter, Tam, had gone into premature labour and "no one on my team is answering their phone!"

"Sure, Rona. I can do that."

"Really? Winston, you're a lifesaver. All you have to do is turn on the lights and have it ready for lane swim by 5:30 because the regulars do show up right before six.

They want to be swimming at six. I know it isn't strict protocol, but I like to accommodate them when we can."

"Ready by 5:30. Got it."

"I mean, it isn't a huge deal if you open right at six, but it would be better if you were ready before that. Like, doors open at ten to six. But ready by 5:30. Jess and Trina are scheduled to come in at six, so they can take care of the rest of the morning duties. I've left each of them, like, six messages so they'll know something is up. I'll text them to say that you are opening the doors but that they—"

"Okay."

"Thanks, Winston. I don't know what I would've done without you. You're a hero."

"That's me: big hero. Unlocking doors. Turning on lights—I hope everything goes well with Tam."

I'd worked at the aquatic centre lifeguarding years before, but the requirements were stringent and I didn't feel like getting my CPR lifesaving recertification every ten minutes as the aquatic centre regs seemed to demand. Rona had been irritated with me over it, likely because she was tired of having to schedule sixteen-year-old lifeguards who were flaky about showing up for their shifts. She was one of those responsible, organized types who would never be caught without an active certification in a lifesaving manoeuvre. Tam's premature labour had thrown her schedule out the window and left her in a frenzy of worry and discarded plans. Some people just long for order and predictability but I'm not one of them. The fact that I know exactly what tomorrow will look like depresses me. It was part of the reason that I had arrived far earlier than was necessary. I'd spent the night tossing and periodically punching my pillow into an elusively comfortable shape. When I was wide awake at four and staring at the shadows cast by the streetlight on the ceiling, I got up and headed to the pool to swim laps, which I hadn't done since I finished my geology degree.

I changed into my suit, leaving my clothes strewn over the bench in the change room. My trunks didn't fit as well as they used to. The ancient knot I had tied in the waist was embarrassingly loose. I picked at it until I was able to untangle the chlorine-hardened strings and retie them tighter. It looked like my poverty diet had reduced my waist by at least two inches. I paused in front of the mirror to take inventory of the changes. I wasn't quite as skinny as I had been a couple of weeks ago, but I didn't recognize myself. I looked like Matt Damon in that movie where he played that gay serial killer. There were corners and indentations in my arms and torso with which I wasn't familiar.

"I should be hitting the weights, not doing cardio."

The sound of my voice startled me in the emptiness of the locker room. I felt silly and exposed examining myself in the mirror. There wasn't a soul on earth who was even thinking about me, but still I felt self-conscious, like maybe God was wondering why I was staring at myself in the mirror. No, worse—like God knew why but I didn't. He was lifting His proverbial eyebrow at my new life; I didn't want to think about what God might be thinking of me. I left the locker room purposefully and walked to the edge of the water. The tile floor was dry under the soles of my feet. The cavernous room was like a tomb of memories resurrected by humidity and the smell

209

of chlorine. Dad driving us all to the pool on dark winter mornings. Nat trying to sleep in the car during the five-minute drive to the pool. Jeremy complaining that the teacher hadn't timed him properly on front crawl and that he had better not get held back. Eventually Jeremy had decided hockey was more his speed and quit once he obtained his bronze medallion certification. Nat and I had continued to competitive swimming. She excelled at the butterfly and her coaches always commented on her exceptional technique, but my sister was indifferent to her accidental success and preferred to pursue piano instead, lending creditability to the notion that people rarely value the things that come for nothing. I liked the front crawl and did okay in the freestyle events. I never had trouble with nerves because I had never really cared where I placed.

Red and gold pendants were strung over the motionless blue water, reminiscent of those long-ago swim meets. My dad in the bleachers reading a book while the competitors swung their arms and hopped in place at the edge of the pool to warm up. Whistle blasts and coaches' voices echoing over the water as the swimmers sliced their rhythmic path through the water.

I wandered over to the green lifeguard chair, climbed into its curved seat and looked out over the still, illuminated water. The lanes stretched out like endless possibility and the minute-counter wound its disciplined spin around the gigantic face of the clock like it, too, was a competitive swimmer in one of the longer events. Maybe I should get my recertification again. I wondered if being part of Dignity would disqualify me. People probably didn't want to be lifeguarded by someone who needed an aide to stand by. Maybe I would talk to Iris about it. I climbed down from the lifeguard tower and stood up on the starting block. My body remembered the crouched start position and I watched the clock zero before I dove out into the middle lane.

Stroke. Stroke. Breathe. I fought against over-rolling as I turned to take a gulp of air. My hiatus from the pool had robbed me of much of my former strength. I used to be a machine at this but every muscle felt weak and foreign to me. I had been strong in the water.

Stroke. Stroke. Breathe.

Stroke, stroke, breathe. I was going to fix this. I was going to get back to where I had been. My arms propelled me through the water and the old coaching comments ran through my mind. Hand like a paddle, underwater arm technique is more important than what is seen above. I reached the opposite end feeling tired but turned and pushed myself off the wall to continue back over the distance already travelled. I wondered if Iris liked to swim.

Stroke, stroke, breathe. I didn't really want to think about her. I didn't want to like her too much. I didn't want to feel that melancholy emptiness that comes from hoping for things that won't come true. I focused on my breathing. I struggled to meet my old lung capacity. I used to breathe every four strokes. There was no way I could do that now. I would work up to it. I was going to come here every morning to swim. I was going to regain my former strength. I reached the end of the pool and flipped onto my back and began another length. I looked at the light dancing on the ceiling. No wonder rich people always installed their own pools. There was something almost spiritual or transcendent to this. I was moving through difficulty. I was getting stronger. I was going somewhere. Maybe Rona would let me take on some shifts here again and I could come early every morning.

I swam for nearly an hour. I was so exhausted by 5 a.m. that I had trouble dragging myself out of the water. I showered and mopped up the water I had dripped on the pool deck and in the locker room. I had the doors open at quarter to six when the first early-morning swimmers arrived for their workout. By the time Trina and Jess arrived, all my muscles felt languid and my stomach rumbled at its cavernous emptiness. It was only starting to get light out when I walked back to my car. I inhaled the crisp morning air, feeling more cheerful than I had felt in a long time.

I glanced at my watch. Sam would be expecting me within the hour. I'd promised to help her to paint today. She was transforming some room at the Friendly Horizons office into a nursery for the kids to play in while their moms were at some desperately needed parenting classes or something. That was the sort of thing that she did with her free time. She probably paid for the paint out of her own money, too. I'd volunteered to help her because I hated for her to be a sucker all by herself.

"Are you doing this to make some kind of political point?" Sam asked as she pried the lid off of a can, revealing thick mint-green paint.

"About what?" I yawned widely. My sleepless night and early-morning swim were beginning to take their toll. I looked around the small room. "This isn't going to take very long."

Sam stood up and handed me a paintbrush. "I hope not. I want to get some of the artwork hung while you're here. I bought these adorable little animal prints from a local artist at a craft market and got some white frames to put them in—I think it's going to be super cute."

I nodded as another yawn threatened to swallow the room.

"Seriously, though, are you trying to make some kind of point about charities being ripe for fraud or something?"

"Are you accusing me of defrauding the government?" I dipped the brush into the paint can and carefully wiped the excess on the interior edge of the can.

"You bet your ass, I am."

"Sam, I'm offended. I had two doctors—one of whom was possibly over the age of thirty—think I was eligible for my dignity to begin at home."

"I can't decide whether I think you actually believe this garbage diagnosis—which is troubling—or if you are just happy to steal from the Canadian people."

"The Canadian People are involved? This is serious." I lay down on the floor and began to cut in along the baseboard. There was something satisfying about seeing the mint-green paint cover the taupe of the wall in a fresh rectangular line.

"Can you just tell me which it is, please?"

"Honestly, Sam, I don't know." I reloaded my brush with paint and continued the satisfying line of fresh paint along the bottom of the wall.

"Don't pretend. How could you not know?" Sam said as she started cutting in along the door frame.

"I'm not pretending. Every time I think I get some clarity, something happens that makes me question it all over again. It's not like I want it to be true. Do you think that it makes me feel good to know that when I told the truth about myself to two different doctors that they both thought I was retarded?"

"Don't say 'retarded.'"

"If I am it, I can say it."

"You aren't, and it's a pejorative term."

"Any adjective that describes a negative attribute eventually becomes a pejorative term. How many words is political correctness going to blackball before we realize that?"

"That statement alone proves you aren't mentally disabled."

"Please don't use that term; it's a pejorative. We are all able."

"So, this is a political statement on your part."

"What I'm telling you is that when outside people look at the facts of your life and impartially come to the conclusion that you are not able to manage on your own, it rocks your confidence a bit. You start to look at it from their perspective and wonder if maybe they have the missing piece—the reason why nothing ever worked out—and then you try and make the best of it."

"But it's a lie!" Sam turned and gestured at me emphatically with her paintbrush. "It's a misunderstanding. It's them looking at a small snapshot of your life and drawing conclusions based on a misinterpretation."

"Is it?"

"You know it is."

"I *don't* know. I was myself. I told the truth. This is the conclusion that two medical professionals gave me."

"Doctors can be wrong. You spent—what—at most an hour with them? They can get it wrong. They can misdiagnose. They're just people. Why would you let strangers tell you who you are?"

"It wasn't just the doctors." I felt a strange, sick feeling in the pit of my stomach as I thought of how Iris had no difficulty with my diagnosis.

"I never once believed this," Sam said defiantly

"Everyone else does."

"Now you're just feeling sorry for yourself."

"Geez. Can we talk about something else?"

"What about Jeremy?"

"What about him?"

"I doubt he believes it. Jeremy has always been hard on you. Have you ever stopped to ask why?"

"I've never cared why."

Sam sighed and I felt so tired I wanted to lay my head on the table.

"He expects a lot from you. He sees your potential. I think he feels frustrated because so many things came easy to you and he had to work really hard for them."

"What are you even talking about? Jeremy's got the wife and kids. Jeremy's got the career and income stability. He's the one who has made it. Ask him."

"Your problem is that you think that there is only one way of making it. That an outlier is somehow a mistake. Did you ever stop to think that maybe you were made for different things than Jeremy was?"

"I don't want to be the outlier. I want those things, too."

"Fine, work for them, then. I'm just putting forward the idea that perhaps you were made for other things. Things that—on the surface, to outsiders—look so foreign that they come to all the wrong conclusions about them. They see your unconventional life and think 'retard' because you don't fit their expectations. But that doesn't mean that they are right. You know that they aren't."

"It isn't a political stunt."

"Then what is it?"

I sighed; the elation I had felt while swimming had fled for the horizon. "Look, I'm as much a believer in the burden to work hard being on the individual as I ever was."

"Then what the hell?" Sam almost kicked over her Tim Hortons coffee cup when she retrieved more paint.

"At a certain point, Sam, I just—I think I have to accept that I'm not as capable—or something."

"That just isn't true."

"It's like with swimming. I can swim. I can learn it and go through the motions and enjoy it. But I wasn't competitive enough to succeed. I don't have that drive."

"Not being competitive is not the same as having a developmental disability."

"Maybe it isn't a developmental disability. Maybe it is more social. I don't know. The doctors don't even know. They agree it is something, though."

"You're being too easy on yourself."

"How is this easy? What kind of future does a guy like me have? Think I'm getting married? Think I'm going to be a father?"

"Yes," Sam was practically shouting. "Yes. If you wanted to, you could be."

"Some catch I'd be. We can't all be your guy from the Corps."

Sam rolled her eyes. "He's not perfect, either."

"Why the hell isn't he here painting and getting the lecture? When's he going to come to town?"

"Soon. But that's not what we're talking about."

"No, you ambushed me here with this conversation."

"I *ambushed* you? Are you kidding me? I'm here telling you that you've got potential, that you're smart— that you aren't retarded—and you think that I've ambushed you? Poor Winston! Poor guy!"

I shook my head and took a swig of my own coffee, which was quickly growing cold. "It's not that simple, Sam."

"Look, just be careful what you believe because you feel sorry for yourself—okay?"

"And you be careful what you believe just because you feel sorry for others."

"Fine."

"Fine."

Good times. We spent the next forty-five minutes in a tense state of détente, neither of us speaking as we both made remarkable progress in outlining the small room with a mint-green border. After a while, Sam played some music on her phone to cover over the silence.

"Did you ever play theatre sports?" I asked, after we had started to roll the walls and it was clear that Sam wasn't going to talk about something else.

"I didn't take drama."

"Well," I said, "there are a couple of different improv games that you spend a lot of time playing. There's one game where the audience calls out situations and characters and it is up to the actors to bring those things—which usually have nothing to do with one another—together. And the scene usually ends up being funny because the actors know who they are and what they are doing."

"Okay, so?"

"So—that's a game that works because everyone knows who they are and what they are doing. But there is another game called Freeze Frame where the actors start with whatever idea is in their head and then someone from the audience will call out 'Freeze' and then go take the place of one of the actors and start a completely different scene."

Sam stopped rolling and looked at me quizzically. "Why are you telling me this?"

"Because most of the time Freeze Frame sucked. Kids would want to be the centre of attention, so they would call out 'Freeze' but then they would blank. Usually, they would then just start going through the motions of daily life because they didn't know who they were supposed to be or what they were supposed to be doing. They had no identity. They had no purpose."

Sam narrowed her eyes. "Are you saying that you are going through the motions?"

"I don't know. I don't know what I'm doing and—more disturbing—I don't really know what I think about who I am since all of this began."

Sam looked at me for a long moment before she bent down to reload the roller with paint. When she did finally speak, her voice was quiet and the fire that had characterized the earlier part of our conversation was gone.

"That's just not true, Winston. You may not know what you are doing right now, but I don't believe for a second that you don't know who you are."

I sighed and finished rolling the wall with paint. First, Iris; now, Sam. I don't know what you're supposed to do when you tell people the truth and they choose to believe something else instead.

CHAPTER FIFTEEN

Curds and Whey

"Winston, wait up!"

It was Monday. I was leaving work at two in the afternoon when I heard a familiar voice call my name. I turned to see Cory—Bandana Cory, object of Gynnyfyr's carnal attraction—crossing the parking lot toward me. "You got a minute?"

"Sure."

Cory jogged the short distance between us. "Would it still work if I designed that fitness plan for you?"

I had forgotten about that. "Whatever you need."

"That's great. That really helps me out. I'll do the food plan for you, too."

"Okay."

Cory squinted at me. "I'll do the initial assessment and then we need to meet to work out six days a week. Can you do that?"

I would basically be spending all of my time at the rec centre but it was better than doing nothing and feeling depressed. "Sure."

"Awesome. Thanks so much, dude. Do evenings work for you? Like, around nine? Starting tomorrow?"

"To work out? Probably. Does that work for you?" I asked unnecessarily because it obviously did.

"Yeah, I'm free." He scanned me up and down unapologetically. "Look, man, if it is all the same to you, do you mind if I set your goals?"

"What do you have in mind?"

"I want to pack your frame with muscle but also work on your agility and endurance. See, I want to be a celebrity trainer and nutritionist, and I need to be able to demonstrate that I can transform people into superheroes in a short amount of time. But it will be totally gruelling, so if you're not totally committed to the idea, I'd rather set smaller goals for my project."

"How gruelling?"

"You're going to want to kill me, but you'll be too tired to hatch the plan and too sore to carry it out."

"Great. Sign me up."

His face lit up. "Really? You're game?"

I shrugged. "Why not?"

"This is awesome." He held up his fist for me to pound it. "I'll have your nutrition plan with me tomorrow night. That really is half the battle. You've got to stick to it."

"It just so happens that I'm great at sticking to unvaried food plans."

"That part isn't bad. If anything, it just seems like a lot of food. It's all about hitting your macros."

"What are macros?"

"Macronutrients. Carbs, protein, fat—I'll explain everything tomorrow. What kind of workout are you doing these days?"

"Not much. Sometimes I'll go for runs; haven't done that in a couple of months, though. I just started swimming laps before work. I used to swim a lot."

"I see that. Swimming is good cardio, but you'll have to be careful not to overdo it. I'll build it into your program if you still want to do it."

"I want to keep swimming."

"That's cool. Also, I'll be documenting your progress on social media for my project and also as part of my portfolio. Is that a problem?"

"Uh—"

"Just like progress pics and whatnot. I can pixelate out your face if that is a problem."

"I don't care one way or another."

"Cool," he said, grinning. "I'm gonna make you an Instagram star."

The following night I walked into the weight area of the rec centre to find Cory already waiting. He smiled when he saw me and seemed to bounce on his feet, radiating a kind of kinetic energy that made me slightly nervous.

"We're going to kill it tonight, dude."

"As long as you don't kill me," I answered warily.

"You'll wish I had tomorrow morning when you feel a thousand years old." He laughed fiendishly as he unzipped his backpack and pulled out—Mary Poppins style—a stack of papers, calipers, a measuring tape, his iPad, a digital food scale and a gigantic, black plastic canister containing, what I hoped, was protein powder for the next several months.

"No lamp?" I asked.

"Not unless you want to start tanning, too."

"I'm good."

"First things, first. Let's get your weight and measurements. Then, I'll run through the food and workout plan for this week." I stood still as Cory meticulously recorded every measurement and my current weight into his iPad. He then handed me a stack of papers.

I thumbed through the pages dumbly. "This is for this week?"

"Yeah. I'll be updating dynamic nutrition and tailoring it to where you are at each week."

"You know," I said, my gaze sliding over the minutiae of instructions, "when you write someone a single-spaced, double-sided, multi-paged message, it is a cry for psychotropic intervention. Or at least that's what my ex-girlfriend told me."

"You're one of those moony guys, huh? Don't worry, by the time I'm through with you, your ex-girlfriend will be writing you the letters."

"That would be something," I said thoughtfully and tapped my hand against my eating orders. "So, what's the deal?"

"Your grocery list is first. After we're done here, you're going to need to go to the grocery store and pick up any of the stuff that you don't already have. Nutrition starts tomorrow morning. Seriously, no exceptions to any of this. If you have questions about anything, just text me. I don't care what time it is. I don't want to find out you were binge-eating corn dogs at two in the morning because you weren't sure if they were on the list. News flash: they aren't. Which reminds me, no drugs at all. Is that going to be a problem?"

"No midnight toking. Got it."

Cory looked at me earnestly. "Seriously, dude. No judgment if you are into that or whatever, but it just won't fly with my program."

"Turns out, I'm really judgmental about that so it won't be a problem." First Jeremy, now Cory. Does everyone just assume I'm a pothead?

"Good—we're golden," Cory said. "Let's hit the weights. We've got to figure out what your baseline strength is and then I'll know how much to push you each week."

What followed was a terrible abuse; and like everything that kind of sucks in my life, I did it to myself. Cory ran me through a punishing weight routine focusing only on my chest, back and abs and by the time we left when the rec centre closed at 10:30, I wasn't sure if I was going to be sick or if I was just sore. My face felt as though it were on fire and I relished the cold night air as we walked to the parking lot.

"Remember," Cory called out to as he unlocked his car, "you've got to hit the grocery store tonight. Otherwise, you won't have the right stuff for breakfast. No exceptions or substitutions!" He waved as he got into his car and I leaned my face against the cool metal of the roof of my car, letting the heat from the workout dissipate. I heard a car pull up beside me.

"I don't want to see you anymore," I said to Cory without looking up.

He laughed that same gleeful laugh that would soon come to characterize my workouts with him.

"Don't forget to set your timers."

I began meeting Cory every night at nine and we would work out until the gym closed. He was methodical and unyielding. There was no detail too minute for him to care about, no acceptance of nutritional grey areas or sloppy technique.

"Are you using the scale? Accuracy in reporting is key. People think that they can look like action stars by eyeballing it. Sorry, gang, it just doesn't work that way. Every gram counts."

"I'm weighing everything. I counted out twenty-one almonds this morning. It's obsessive, but I'm doing it."

"Who says it is obsessive?" Cory asked innocently, as he spotted me at the bench press.

"Sane people," I answered breathlessly. There was a giant barbell in my hands threatening to crush my throat. I wasn't about to explain the strange looks Iris had been giving me since I started weighing out chicken breast, dry curd and spinach.

"Don't listen to them," Cory answered earnestly. "It is crazy how many people try and discourage others from working out and following the nutrition. Don't let the naysayers get to you. Get new friends."

"Don't—" I dropped the bar back into place on the rack. "—worry. No one really cares that much about what I am doing." I sat up slowly, feeling as though I was going to vomit. My chest felt like jelly. I stood up unsteadily and followed Cory to the incline bench. He picked up some dumbbells and sat back on the bench, showed me the precise technique for the chest fly and then traded places with me.

"Are you kidding?" The weight of the dumbbells threatened to pull me off the bench.

"I know. Aim for four reps, then we'll drop it down 20 percent. Pound them out," Cory said as I struggled to bring the weights up to the starting position.

"Don't be a punk," he said dismissively as I strained to maintain the proper form throughout the movement. "I wouldn't have given you those if I didn't know for sure you could do it."

"That's a—mighty big—comfort," I grunted. I was only on my second rep. Four seemed impossibly far away.

"I think I am going to take some psych courses next semester as my options," Cory said as he walked over to the rack of free weights. "Seriously, people have got weird issues around food and fitness."

I had no extra air with which to answer this statement. Sweat was running off my burning face into my ear, where, I assume, it was evaporating immediately.

Cory continued, "I think people need the whole package overhauled. It isn't just getting to look a certain way. It is about dealing with your shit. Your self-image baggage. Some guys only work their upper body and they take creatine and other chemical garbage. Others just do cardio because they are marathoners or whatever. But—I promise you—nine times out of ten, you ask someone to change up his eating and he loses his mind." He paused for a moment as he watched my technique. "Your knuckles should face each other at the top. Think of it like hugging a tree trunk. There."

I focused on the movement, trying to maintain what he had adjusted.

"Girls are even worse. Holy cow, they are crazy."

I just nodded.

"Your friend, Gynnyfyr? Bat-shit crazy. No offence, man."

"I wouldn't exactly call her my friend," I gasped. I was almost at the impossible fourth rep. "More like an acquaintance I have no control over."

"She's impossible. We talked about what her goals were and how to get there and I made her up a whole plan—food, workout, everything—but she won't do it. She shows up for the workout drinking a mega-sized Frappuccino. When I told her she couldn't drink that stuff and look like Jennifer Lopez—" Cory threw up his hands in air quotes. "—her 'body idol,' she burst into tears and called me a 'Nazi asshole.'"

"She's only half-wrong," I said, setting the weights down to rest and wiping the sweat off my face with my shirt. "She just wants to hook up with you. That's probably the only reason she agreed."

Cory looked like I had spit in his face. "Not going to happen," he said, handing me my water bottle. "You need to stay hydrated."

"She told me as much before you asked to do her fitness plan." My arms felt like dead weights at my side. "I felt bad about it before I knew you very well, but for some unknown reason I'm okay with it now."

"It's not too smart to provoke the guy who controls your food and workouts."

"There's been some suggestion lately that I'm not that bright. But what's the matter? She's not your type?" I asked as I sat up to take the water from him.

"I have trouble believing she's anyone's type."

"Not everyone is so picky." I unscrewed the cap on the bottle, took a big swig and nearly choked as water ran down my chin and onto my shirt.

"Small sips." Cory looked at me sideways. "Sorry—are you—is she someone you…?"

I snorted at the thought. "I just meant that a lot of guys don't care."

"See, but that's the same kind of garbage mindset I'm talking about. Getting involved with chicks like her is like taking creatine. You think it makes you look like a stud, but the next thing you know, the anabolic steroids you're taking have given you high-pitched girly voice and you're being treated for the clap."

Cory returned the dumbbells I had just been using to the rack and selected two slightly smaller ones for my next set. I set the empty water bottle aside and took the weights from him.

"Six reps this time," he said. "Most people lose because they don't anticipate what their choices will mean in the long run. They eat mindlessly, they sit on their asses for hours on end, they don't think about who they surround themselves with—bad-company-corrupts-good-character kind of stuff."

"Is that from the Bible?" I said, as I started to count out my reps. The lighter weights soon felt just as heavy as the last set.

Cory looked momentarily sheepish. "Possibly—probably. My grandma used to say it all the time."

"Gynnyfyr is bad company."

"And I'm good character, so you can see that I am in a no-win situation. I'm going to have to play nice if I want to get my project done." Cory eyed my last few reps. "Good. Stop there. Next chest day I'm upping the weight and dropping the reps. You didn't premix your protein before you got here, did you?" Cory said as he typed something into the iPad.

I shook my head as I sat up and set the weights on the floor. "I know better than to disobey my diet orders." I walked unsteadily to the water fountain to refill my water bottle. "About Gynnyfyr, though: if she can tell you aren't interested in her, she probably won't bother doing the work for you. But it doesn't sound like she was doing it anyway, so the outcome will probably be the same."

Cory looked up at the ceiling in frustration. "How am I going to get my project finished?"

"Feigning interest in her for the sake of your grade would be a colossal mistake. Better to fail the course. A guy like you must have some other female friends you could ask."

Cory exhaled loudly. "Not really."

"Maybe just start randomly approaching women who are working out and ask if they want to be trained for free."

"That would make me the creepiest guy on campus. They'd be holding Take Back the Night vigils against me."

I walked to my gym bag, pulled out my shaker cup with the scoop of whey protein I had added before I came and walked to the water fountain. "Yeah, probably."

The alarm on my phone sounded for the fifth time. I stifled a self-pitying groan as I shifted on the couch. The thought of more food made me feel vaguely nauseous but Cory's nutritional program was non-negotiable.

"You make it or break it in the kitchen, dude. Don't self-sabotage."

I stood to my feet with difficulty. Everything was on fire. I was seizing up like the Tin Man caught in the rain. My new workout regime had uncovered a weird click in my shoulder that I had never heard before. I staggered unsteadily to the fridge and pulled out a container of plain, cooked chicken breast with distaste. Still feeling overfull from my dinner, I reached into the clammy container with my fingers and weighed out my evening snack. I referred again to the already dog-eared food plan for this week. Forty-two hundred calories a day would have seemed like a dream when I was subsisting on SlimFast and bagels, but this was merely a different form of restriction. I was still a slave to my diet. Cory's plan wasn't quite as unvarying as my poverty subsistence diet, but it wasn't that far off. I scanned the chart of meals and reset my alarm for my last protein shake of the day. Cory had given me the first tub of protein powder because he wanted me to get started on the food plan right away, but it was quickly disappearing as I consumed nearly five protein shakes a day, not to mention the pre-workout supplement that made my palms itchy and my ears feel hot.

"That's just the beta-alanine. Learn to love it."

Two weeks into the program I still spent all of my thoughts on when I had to eat and what it was going to be. I shelved everything else. I wasn't thinking about Dignity. I wasn't thinking about the fact that my family— and more importantly, Iris—all thought I was some sort of Rain Man idiot savant. Frankly, it was a relief to have a project to distract me. I was working toward something. I scrupulously followed Cory's plan and didn't let myself think about anything else, not even my trebled grocery costs. I just asked Iqbal for a few more shifts and told Rona to call me if she needed coverage at the aquatic centre.

"What's with all the chicken?" Iris asked on Sunday afternoon as she watched me pile packs of air-chilled skinless, boneless chicken breast into the grocery cart.

"I'm a guinea pig for a friend of mine. He has to design a fitness program for his class."

Iris peered into my cart, raising her eyebrows at the three value packs of discounted chicken breast and the tubs of dry curd. "That must get kind of expensive for you, though? Is this just for this week? What is he trying to turn you into? Superman?"

"It's just for a little while." I began to push the cart down the aisle toward the freezers. I still needed spinach—so much spinach.

"So, he just came up with a diet for you?"

"Workouts, too. He needs this to graduate. He asked Gynnyfyr if she would be willing to be the female test subject, but it hasn't been working."

Iris rolled her eyes. "I could have told you that."

"Do you know any women who would be interested in being trained for free? Gynnyfyr has kind of left him in a jam."

"I could have told you that, too. Actually, I'm kind of amazed she ever agreed in the first place."

"She thinks Cory looks like Captain America."

"Ah—that would do it," Iris said, snapping her fingers. "You're beeping."

I pulled my phone from my pocket and shut off the alarm. "I need to drink a protein shake."

"You have alarms for this?"

"It's all about nutrient timing—so Cory says. And the macros. It's all about hitting those, too, and the workouts. Look—it's all about a lot of things. It's basically a full-time job keeping track of it all," I said as I found the frozen spinach. The door on the freezer case resisted momentarily until the suction broke. The little boxes felt like icy bricks as I piled six of them into the cart so that they spilled out over the copious yams that were shredding the thin plastic bags I had loaded them into.

"You wouldn't want to do a workout program with him, would you? He's a nice guy. He just needs some help."

Iris raised her eyebrows and perused my groceries. "I think I'll pass. Thanks, though."

"Okay—I just need some bread and then I'm good to go," I said, scanning the list that Cory had compiled for me. We wandered down the aisle back to the bakery section as I tried to ignore the pastries and chocolate long johns that seemed to sing to me from behind the pristine case.

"White Wonder Bread? Really?" Iris asked in disbelief as I reached for the brightly coloured bag.

"That's what's on the list. I don't make the rules. Nor do I question them. It just means extra push-ups."

"I would think you'd be eating whole-grain, nutty pumpernickel. Not Wonder Bread."

"It's my pre-workout fuel. I'm supposed to eat a slice before the workout to fuel my performance."

"I guess that's why they call it Wonder Bread."

I paid for the groceries and we returned to Iris's car. I had taken to bringing my shaker cup and protein powder with me everywhere I went since I was always about to drink another one anyway. I set the cup and groceries on the hood of Iris's Civic and opened the jug of skim milk I had just bought to mix with the vanilla powder. The cheap shaker cup I had warped in the dishwasher dribbled under the lid when I shook the cup. Licking the excess off the cup, I tried again to snap the lid into place.

"That milk better not spill in my car," Iris said as she buckled her seat belt.

"Can you take this for a sec?" I handed her my drink as I positioned the milk jug between my feet on the floor. "There. Steady as a rock."

Iris peered into my inadequately mixed protein shake. "This is incredibly unappetizing. How do you stand it?"

"It's better with a banana blended in, but they don't appear on the food plan every day. Cory says they are too high in sugar to have all the time." I took the cup from her and she put the keys in the ignition. "That little explanation cost me twenty push-ups the other night."

Iris looked at me like I was crazy. How was it that she seemed to grow more attractive every time I saw her?

"Don't try to dissuade me or he won't let me hang out with you anymore," I said lightly. "Besides, I've had worse. I used to drink diet shakes for breakfast before I got into the Dignity program."

"Why?" Iris shook her head in disbelief, turned on the car and shoulder-checked before she began backing out of the stall.

"I was broke and it was cheap. Trust me, this is a million times better."

Iris guided the car out of the parking lot and onto the street and stopped at a red light to leave the shopping centre.

"Cory says that food reveals people."

"Cory says a lot of things," Iris said cheerfully.

I took another swig. These were getting to be a bit tiresome. I wondered if I should get another flavour so that I could alternate. I made a mental note to clear that with Cory tonight. The light turned green and the car lurched suddenly forward. The drink spilled down my chin.

Iris looked over. "Sorry."

I wiped the protein shake off my face with the cuff of my sleeve. "You drive like Picasso paints."

"What on earth does that mean?"

"It's a compliment."

Iris laughed. "It doesn't sound like it. Sounds like you think my driving is awful."

"Picasso is one of the masters. It works. It makes a kind of sense even though it makes no sense. It's all right angles and stops. It is skilful, even if you don't really want to look at it."

She laughed as she accelerated, merging her small car into a small space in the thick line of traffic on Glenmore Trail. "Thanks a lot. My driving is skilled but ugly."

"Beauty is in the eye of the beholder?" I braced the milk jug with my feet. It hadn't shifted but I wanted her to see that I was being conscientious about not spilling four litres of milk in her car.

She laughed. "I feel like that statement is only true within a very narrow range."

I realized that I liked making her laugh and so I tried to think of something else funny to say, but Iris spoke first.

"You remember that I'm going to be away next week? So Gynnyfyr is going to cover my shifts next week."

That was a bummer. I looked forward to spending time with Iris. Iris, who was skilfully—albeit aggressively—navigating through the heavy traffic. Brake lights illuminated suddenly in front of us.

"Where are you going?" I asked as she slowed down.

"Out to Kelowna."

"Visiting someone?"

"My dad and his wife and kids live out there. They've been asking me to come out for a while." Every trace of mirth that had been in Iris's eyes disappeared and her expression became serious—and sad. "So—I'm trying," she said.

"Trying is good," I said—stupidly.

"You have a good relationship with your family?"

I shrugged—except for the whole, they-all-believe-I'm-mentally-handicapped thing. But instead I said, "Pretty good, yeah."

"That's really nice." Iris sighed and smiled at me with a weariness that I had never seen on her face before.

"Yeah, I'm lucky," I said.

"Yeah." Iris sped up and changed lanes again, more for something to do—it looked like—than because it was necessary.

"Are you okay?" I asked.

"I'm—I'm actually terrified."

"What? Why? What are they like?"

Iris inhaled deeply and I could see she was trying to regain control of herself. I looked down at the shaker cup in my hand. I needed to drink it in the next few minutes or I would be off schedule, but I just held it and waited for her to say something.

"I just really don't want to go back there. I was—I was a pretty miserable person there. Miserable, and miserable to be around. I'm afraid that when I go back, I'll just be in it all again." She smiled thinly at me as though that would lighten the atmosphere. "Sorry. I don't mean to get all heavy all of a sudden. It's just all been on my mind and I feel like I'm on a raft that's headed for a big emotional waterfall."

"I don't mind you talking about it—" I said. "—if you want to tell me."

Iris bit her lip as though she was considering it. I took a swig of my shake and looked out the window.

"My dad was a pastor when I was a kid," she began tentatively. "It wasn't a huge church but it was big enough: a few hundred people, maybe. I was always really proud of him. I remember watching him at a funeral and the way that he spoke to people so kindly and always knew what to say. How people loved to talk to him. How they would cling to him. He used to bring my brother and me to the church with him during the week while he was working. We'd play in the gym or do our homework outside his office while he met with different people, and they always seemed to leave lighter than when they'd come. He was really funny, too. You kind of remind me of him in some ways. He could always make people laugh. He was a good man."

I noted the past tense with a growing sense of unease.

"He—he messed up, though," she continued. "My mom was having a lot of issues. Mental health stuff; depression, I guess. She was hospitalized for a while. I didn't really know what was going on. He was trying to hold it all together but then he sort of lost it, too. I was thirteen—my brother Reese was fifteen—when we found out from some other kids that our dad had been fired from the church for having an affair with some woman. Neither of us believed it, until he told us it was true."

"Oh, man."

"The thing is, Dad going off the rails turned into this weird licence for everyone else to go crazy, too. My mom divorced him in this bitter rage and then went from boyfriend to loser boyfriend. I never knew where she found them. But it was like all the values that we'd been raised with up to that point were thrown out the window.

She'd move the latest guy in with us and then call the cops when she wanted him to leave. Some of them were real winners, you know? I spent all of my time in my room with the door locked. Reese couldn't stand it; he took off and went to live with Dad after a year."

"How come you didn't go, too?"

"I blamed my dad for everything falling apart. Besides, someone had to take care of Mom. I couldn't abandon her, even though I hated her a lot of the time—I hated everyone, though. All the boyfriends. My mom for being the way she was; she'd been depressed or whatever before with Dad, but on her own she was crazy. I was mad at Reese for leaving me all alone. I hated Dad for letting this happen. I hated God for not protecting us at all."

"That's brutal."

"I think my dad must have felt like he was trying to hold back the tide," Iris said. "He was better at it than me, though. I couldn't stop her from doing anything bad and I couldn't make her do anything good."

"Did you ever see your dad?"

"On the weekends. He used to beg me to come live with him. He remarried and had two more kids with Martina. He got to start over. New sane wife. Sweet new kids. Whole shiny new family. Reese and I were just these leftovers."

"What's your stepmother like?" I asked after a while.

"She's nice," she said dejectedly as she brushed the hair from her cheek. "She really is. She was as welcoming as she could possibly be, but it didn't matter. Everything was ruined and she was just this benign intruder on my broken family. Reese took to her okay. Everyone seemed to be able to start over but me."

"Was she the woman that—?"

My question was cut short as the shoulder strap of my seat belt pulled tight across my chest. Iris hit the Civic's brakes hard as red lights suddenly illuminated the line of cars ahead of us. "Sorry," she said. "No. That woman was long gone."

The line of traffic began to move again as we glided past the incoming merge lanes from Crowchild Trail. I rotated my cup in my hands methodically. I didn't feel like drinking it anymore.

"It's just hard to go back," Iris said as she gripped the steering wheel tightly.

"I get that," I said, as I watched cars from four different lanes braiding in and out in a complicated choreography. "This is a bad weave zone."

"Yeah," Iris agreed absently. She was either concentrating on navigating through the heavy traffic or lost in her own thoughts. "I don't understand what this guy is—" Iris shrieked as a green sedan seemed to come out of nowhere at speed and cut sharply across the front of the vehicle, nearly clipping Iris's car. Reflexively, she pulled the wheel hard to the right, sending us into the adjacent lane to avoid the green sedan. My shaker cup went flying out of my hand, hitting both the passenger window and the dash. The lid exploded as protein shake showered over us and Iris over-corrected again, weaving back into the other lane in a flurry of horns and adrenalin.

Her hands clenched the wheel as we proceeded over the causeway. "Oh, God—Oh, God!"

"There is a pullout just by the exit to 14 Street. You can stop there," I said, wiping the shake off my face with the arm of my shirt.

She changed lanes to the exit and pulled over to where we skidded to a stop in a pile of road salt and gravel. The rush of air from cars passing us shook the little Civic.

"Are you okay?"

"Oh, oh, oh——" Iris was covering her mouth with her hands and shaking.

"Hey, it's okay. It's okay," I said, trying to put together the jumble of images that had just happened before my eyes. "You're okay. That wasn't your fault." Streams of protein shake were running down the inside of her windshield.

"I just about got us killed." Tears were beginning to pool in her eyes. "I was distracted and I just about killed you." She was crying now. "I just about killed you."

"Not even close. That was 100 percent the other guy's fault."

She wiped at her eyes with the back of her hands, unaware of the spatter of protein shake that had landed on her cheek.

"If you hadn't done what you did, he would have hit us."

Iris squeezed her eyes shut. "That was so scary," she said quietly. "If anyone had been in the lane beside us—I didn't know—I didn't see that it was empty. I could have killed you and someone else. I can't—I don't think I want to drive anymore." She clenched her hands into fists as though to keep them from shaking.

"Okay," I said, unbuckling my seat belt. "I'll trade places with you. Slide over. Don't get out on that side." Iris manoeuvred herself across the emergency brake and cupholder into the passenger seat while I waited for a break in the traffic so I could open the driver's side door safely. When I got back into the car a moment or two later, Iris was still trying to pull herself together.

"Okay," I said, "I'll drive for a little while but then you've got to take over. You can't let that spook you. Back on the horse."

"That could have been so bad, Winston," she murmured, looking out the passenger side window.

I craned my neck to watch for another break in the traffic. "'Could have been,'" I repeated as a wide gap opened and I eased Iris's car smoothly back onto the road. "I guarantee the idiot who caused all of that isn't beating himself up. Probably a stolen car or something like that. You reacted. You did exactly what needed to be done."

Iris exhaled loudly and looked over at me. "I don't even know how I did that."

"Seriously, Picasso. You saved us. That was practically your *Guernica* back there. Besides," I said, gesturing to my empty shaker cup on the floor at her feet, "I don't know what you're crying about. I'm the one who's going to have to log missing his mid-afternoon protein shake. Cory isn't going to make you do push-ups until you puke."

Iris laughed and wiped her eyes with the back of her hand. "You're a nice guy, Winston."

"'Nice'? What a terrible thing to say to someone."

"I stand by it," she answered.

CHAPTER SIXTEEN
Constant(ly) Comment(ing)

"Yay! You're home," my sister exclaimed as I opened the door to find her yet again standing on my doorstep laden with another laundry basket. This one was clearly new and contained a stack of primly folded chocolate-brown towels tied with a wide yellow ribbon.

"I brought you a housewarming present. Towels. Brown is masculine, right? I love white; you can bleach it. But Joel said, 'No guy is going to bleach his towels.' So I got you brown."

She handed me the laundry basket and walked past me into the house. "This is really nice, Winston."

"Thanks," I said as I looked down at the towels and wondered why the truth got me nowhere and the lie got me an abundance of towels. My sister kicked off her shoes and wandered through the house, opening doors and commenting positively on various things that I didn't know existed, like "finials," whatever the hell those were.

"Where are the kids?" I asked after she'd seen and complimented something about every room in the Dignity house. "I'm not used to seeing you without a baby carrier anymore."

"Joel's got them. They were all watching *Sleeping Beauty* when I left. It's Joel's favourite of the princess cartoons. He says it's one of the only ones where the prince actually does anything."

I stared down at the laundry basket with the brown towels and the cheerful yellow bow that I was still, for some unknown reason, carrying around and felt a disturbing rise of emotion. I clamped down on it immediately. Guys who cry over towels deserve every bit of censure that the world can levy at them. I replayed what my sister had just said in my mind to understand its meaning. "I guess those princes are pretty much empty suits."

"I never noticed it until he pointed it out after having watched them all over and over. Joel's afraid that it'll subconsciously train the girls to be fine with empty, selfish guys who have no impulse for heroism."

"Are you worried about that?"

My sister smiled and leaned against my counter. "I am the most laid-back person in our family. I worry about very little." Natalie glanced around my kitchen. "Got any tea? Coffee? I need to make the most of my moments of escape. Joel suggested that I go shopping or something, but I wanted to see my baby brother."

"What would you like?" I grabbed the kettle and took it to the tap to fill it with water.

"Tea, if you've got any."

"Mom brought me some Constant Comment when I moved in."

"Great." Natalie settled herself onto my couch, folding her limbs underneath her like a bird tucking its wings away.

"Is there much opportunity for masculine heroism these days?" I asked because it was the sort of question that my sister would enjoy musing over. It could occupy Nat for a good long while. I plugged in the kettle and took two china mugs out of the cupboard. Iris had urged me to buy them at a garage sale because "tea tastes better out of china." She'd clucked her tongue dismissively at the presence of a solitary and ancient CFCN mug that I had inherited from my parents.

Nat looked thoughtful for a moment before answering my question. "I think so, yes."

I snorted involuntarily. "You're more optimistic than me."

"Why is that, do you think?" Nat asked, her eyes looking unnaturally green and piercing.

"Why is what?" I asked.

"Where did your optimism go?"

"I traded it for a place to live," I said, rapping my knuckles against the countertop. "You really think that you're the most laid-back person in our family?"

"In our family or in mine?"

"I count them as one in the same," I said, as the kettle started to rumble. "I've only got the one."

Nat laughed cheerfully. "Between me and Joel and the kids, I definitely am. The kids lose by a landslide. Everything is a disaster."

"Joel doesn't strike me as uptight."

"Caring deeply about things doesn't make someone uptight."

I thought about that as I opened and closed several empty cupboards in search of the tea. It was hiding behind the canisters of protein powder. I picked up the brand-new box of tea and scraped my fingernails uselessly over the cellophane looking for a way in.

"Here, give it to me. I've got nails," Nat said, her hand outstretched.

The kettle clicked off and I methodically filled the mugs and then opened the fridge door to retrieve the milk.

"Can I ask you something?" I said, not waiting for my sister to answer. "Do you ever regret not continuing on with swimming? Or not doing the modelling thing? Or stopping with piano when you got married?"

Nat looked momentarily surprised before she took a tentative sip of the steaming liquid. "Modelling? Absolutely not. Besides, that was just someone's suggestion. It wasn't like I passed up on some million-dollar contract."

"Nobody starts out with a million-dollar contract," I said, like I knew or understood how that industry operated.

"That never appealed to me," Natalie said. "Having a bunch of people look at you, decide your worth based on lighting and camera angles, and tell you what to wear and how to act—no, thank you. Besides, I think those women lead pretty unhappy lives, for all their money and opportunities. I read an article the other day where this former model was claiming that her agency basically acted like her pimp. She ended up in this Saudi guy's harem."

"Where do you find this stuff?" What my sister found to read never ceased to amaze me. It wasn't that it wasn't interesting; it's just—where?

"I know," Nat said. "It's revolting. So, no, even without knowing that sort of thing happens, it did not appeal to me. I don't need the whole world offering their opinion on what I look like. That's a nightmare."

"What about the swimming?"

"Swimming is fine, but I preferred the piano."

"How did you know that?" How had my sister figured everything out and not told me? How had we been part of the same family?

Nat's expression was one of sympathetic amusement. "How did I know that I preferred the piano?"

"Yeah, you were equally good at the butterfly. How did you choose?"

Natalie picked up her mug and blew the steam away while she thought about my question. "I guess—it was the way that I felt when I played, versus when I was swimming. Swimming just felt like a workout. It was challenging and it had its accompanying feeling of success when I would win. But, to me, it didn't reveal anything true."

"What do you mean, 'true'?"

Natalie took a ladylike sip of her tea. "Something about sitting down at the keyboard and seeing the notes on the page and connecting those notes from my eyes to my hands to the black and white keys; and that those keys were hammers striking strings in the instrument and that all of that was making something so beautiful. Something that only exists in the moment that it is being played. It was expressing something true; it was telling a story and when I was playing, I was part of it. I felt like I was touching real beauty. Not beauty like the world sees in a magazine, but something bigger, something transcendent." My sister's eyes were suddenly glistening. "I need to play more," she said softly.

I took a swig of my tea and wondered if I had ever felt that way about anything in my whole life.

"Do you think getting married derailed all of that? Your piano career?"

Natalie laughed unexpectedly. "I think Jeremy feels bad about all that now."

"You *are* more optimistic than me."

"Marrying Joel is my favourite thing I ever did. I didn't have to sacrifice music for it. I can feel that way anytime I sit down and play."

I drained the rest of my cup while my sister stared thoughtfully into hers.

"Nat, do you think I'm mentally—"

My sister cut me off. "No."

"You don't think I deserve to be in the Dignity program?" Hope fluttered faintly in my chest.

"No."

"Do you think I'm a bad person for signing up?"

Natalie drained the rest of her mug and walked over to put it into the dishwasher. "I think—sometimes—you have to eliminate even the most ludicrous possibilities so that you can find out what is true. I think you're going through a process of elimination."

"But I was accepted into the program. Doctors—"

My sister cut me off with a flutter of her hand. "No one needs the whole world offering their opinions.

247

It's too much. Just look for the truth and follow that." Natalie looked earnestly at me for a moment before she glanced at the watch on her wrist. "I better get going. I still need to get some groceries."

My sister stood up and collected her coat from the kitchen chair where she had dumped it. I followed her to the front door and waited as she pulled on her shoes.

"I love you, Winston," she said as she threw her arms around me for a brief hug before she opened the door, letting in a flood of cold air. "We all do."

Nat walked down the steps into the front yard and then turned around to look up at me. "You'll want to wash and dry those towels before you use them; otherwise, they won't absorb at all."

I walked Natalie to her car, the cold of the frozen pavement seeping through my socks. I waved as she drove away. It all seemed to clear now. How had I ever thought that this was a good idea? I wasn't handicapped. I had been hungry. I had been frustrated. Those aren't the same. Sam had been right. I did regret everything to do with Dignity.

Well. Almost everything. I didn't regret meeting Iris, but what good did knowing Iris do me if she thought that I was either handicapped or the kind of despicable fraud who lied about being handicapped to enrich himself? A flicker of movement caught my eye and I glanced to see the curtain of foliage swaying in my neighbour's window. He would be in there right now. He was being a decent guy who cared for living things and gave toys to children. He wasn't pretending anything. He was just being himself. Maybe he needed more help and didn't have it; and here I was with all this extra help and I didn't need it. Despite the cold air, my face burned with shame and I looked at the ground as I walked back up the steps to my front door.

I had to get out of this. Maybe if I just explained everything to Iris, that it was all a big misunderstanding, that I hadn't been eating enough and my parents moved and my house flooded and I got into that fight and was all misshapen, and that doctors had misunderstood, too. Maybe she would understand that it wasn't that bad.

I yanked open the front door. I would do it right now. I would call her and explain everything. I would tell her exactly what had happened and how I needed to get out of the Dignity house so that someone like my nice, nameless neighbour could get the help he deserved, instead of undeserving me. I picked up my cell phone off the counter where I had left it and called Iris. My heartbeat seemed to be pounding in my ears. The first ring seemed to raise my blood pressure a notch further.

"Don't punk out," I whispered as it rang again.

If only there were a way to do this and not lose Iris. The phone rang a third time. That was really up to her, though, I thought. She would be the one to decide what she thought of me. Anything that I did, short of telling her the absolute and complete truth, would just be another manipulation. It would be me signing up for Dignity all over again. The phone rang a fourth time in my ear and it occurred to me for the first time that I might not be able to talk to her right now while my courage to do the right thing was up. There was a click on the other end of the line and then Iris's voice instructing me to leave a message so that she could "get right back to me."

"Hey, Iris, it's Winston. Sorry to bug you while you're out there with your dad—Shit—" I said, remembering why she was away in the first place. "Sorry—I—shouldn't have bothered you while you were out there. I hope it's going okay and that you're doing alright. I—I just needed to talk to you about something. It's pretty important but—you know—not like an emergency you need to worry about. Don't let it interrupt your time with your family." I could feel sweat appearing on my forehead. *Just get off the stupid phone, already.* "Anyway. No rush. But call me when it's not inconvenient, okay? If you can. Okay. Hope it's going okay for you. Bye."

I hit the End button and tossed my phone back onto the counter. It used to be a mercy that an answering machine would cut you off and prevent you from leaving long, rambling messages on women's phones.

Now that I had decided to tell Iris the truth, I didn't know what to do with myself until I could do that. I checked my phone to make sure that the volume was turned all the way up so that I wouldn't miss her call. I cooked up some chicken and yams for my dinner and found myself drumming my fingers against the counter waiting for her to call. I needed to talk to someone. Get an outsider's perspective. I was going to work out with Cory at nine but that was still several hours away. I picked up my phone again. Sam. I could talk to Sam.

I was startled to see a text from Jeremy waiting to be opened. What had that come?

Beth's mom fell and needed to go to the ER for an X-ray. Can u pick up the boys at school at 3:15?

I glanced at the clock on the oven. It was almost three o'clock now. Bret and Michael's school was halfway across the city from me. It was going to be tight to get there on time. *Leaving from Bowness now. Might be a few minutes late.*

His reply was almost instantaneous.

Gr8. I'll tell them to wait on the playground for you.

I grabbed my keys and shoved my phone in my coat pocket as I headed for the car. It was good to have a task to occupy me while I waited for Iris's call. I dialled Sam's number as I waited for the car to warm up. She answered on the second ring.

"So—you were right," I began as I switched over to speakerphone and set the phone in the cupholder. "Turns out I'm not really retarded. So, that's kind of a drag."

Sam paused for a moment before she said, "Truth hurts, huh?"

"So, what do I do now? How do I get out of this?"

I put the car in gear and pulled away from the curb.

"You tell whoever you have to tell and you move out of that house," she said.

"I just left Iris a message. She's out of town for another few days. I told her it was important that she call me back when she could. Sounded like a rambling idiot."

"That's good."

"It's good that I sounded like an idiot?"

"It's good that you are doing the right thing." I waited for her to continue, but she didn't—which is strange because Sam always has more to say rather than less.

"That's it?" I asked after a long pause. "Where are you? Why do you sound funny?"

"I'm—Just a second." Sam paused and the line muffled as though she had covered the microphone with her hand.

"Sam?"

"I'm here."

"So, what do you think I should do now? I'm going crazy waiting for her to call me back. What if she hates me?"

"What if who hates you?" I could hear Sam's confusion in her voice. "Your aide? What do you care? Besides, that's the least of your worries. What if the government fines you? What if you get charged by the police? What if the story hits the news and you become public enemy number one?"

"You're a mighty big comfort," I said, as I joined a line of cars waiting to merge onto Sarcee Trail.

"I told you that this was a bad idea from the beginning!"

"Yeah—you're a genius. Can you put that substantial intellect toward helping me instead of crowing about your prescience?"

"Wait—Why are you worried about your aide hating you?" There we go. She was clueing in; slower than usual, I might add.

"Um." I let the sound hang there suspended in time and space between us.

"Oh. Wow."

"Yeah."

My cousin burst out laughing. It wasn't a mean laugh, but she was clearly enjoying herself at my expense.

"So, are you asking what you should do about that?" she asked once she caught her breath. "Are you asking me how you get to keep the girl?"

"If you've got any ideas, I want to hear them."

Sam snorted. "If she thinks that you're her client, she doesn't think of you in that way as it is. It isn't a matter of keeping the girl. You don't have the girl."

"You said that, not me."

"So, what are you asking?"

"Is there a way to salvage it?"

"Why are you asking me? How would I know?"

"Because you help people who screw up their lives through their own shitty choices," I said, glancing at the clock. It was already 3:15 p.m. and I was still a few minutes from the boys' school. "Or do you only perform that service for foolish women? No help for your dumbass cousin? How do I avoid the consequences of my own behaviour here?"

"The only thing you can do is tell her the truth. Wow. I really hope she does forgive you because I want to meet this woman who made you realize you're a liar and a fraud. Aww. It's like *As Good as It Gets*." Sam's tone was teasing. "She makes you want to be a better man."

"When do we get to the part of the conversation where you say helpful things? Because I'll be at Bret and Michael's school soon."

"You've just got to ride it out and see what happens."

"That's it? You give advice for a living, and that's it?"

"I'm in a good mood today. You're getting my best stuff."

"Thanks for nothing," I said, even though I was feeling unexpectedly light-hearted. "Why are you in such a good mood, anyway? That's not like you."

"Thanks, a lot—" Sam hesitated for a second before she continued. "I wanted to tell you in person, but I'll tell you now. I picked up Kai at the airport this morning and—"

"Who's Kai?"

"Kai. My boyfriend, Kai."

"The Peace Corps fraud?" I said. "I thought his name was Kyle."

"You should listen when other people talk, you jackass. It's Kai and he's not in the Peace Corps."

"Of course he isn't. That's such a make-believe thing to say on a dating profile."

"Says the man who pretended to be handicapped to get free housing from the government," Sam answered dismissively. "You know the old saying 'People who live in Dignity houses shouldn't throw stones'?"

"Very funny."

"I thought so," Sam said cheerfully. "Anyway— when I picked him up at the airport this morning, he got down on one knee in the arrivals hall and—" Sam trailed off expectantly.

"What—? Peace Corps proposed? This is the first time he saw you and he proposed?"

"It was the *Marine* Corps, not the Peace Corps. Seriously, do you hear anything I tell you?" In the background I heard male laughter.

"What did you say?" I pulled up to the curb in front of the playing field of the school and put the car in park.

"I said yes!" Sam's voice jumped an octave higher than usual.

"Whoa, that's—that's big. That's big news." Sam had already agreed to marry some guy and I had never even met him. "Congratulations, Sam. When can I meet him?"

"Your mom invited us to a picnic on Saturday afternoon with everyone at Shouldice."

I turned the ignition off. My hands were chilled through from the steering wheel. "It's only the end of March. Still kind of cold out for a picnic, isn't it?" I scanned the school grounds for my nephews but didn't see them.

"We'll be freezing by the river and it's all your fault," Sam said cheerfully.

"How is it my fault?"

"We could have still been at your parents house if you hadn't forced them to sell it in order to launch you."

Huh. I guess it was kind of my fault.

"Okay, I'll look forward to that then," I said. "Look, I've just arrived at the boys' school and I've got to go find them. I'll talk to you soon. Congratulations, again."

I locked the car door and tried to shake off the feeling of being adrift. I had counted on Sam to help me come up with a plan. She usually knew how to phrase things so that they didn't sound so bad. She had this way of setting the tone of a situation and then other people followed suit. If she was optimistic, then others were, too. If she was negative, it was almost impossible to overcome. She would have found a way for me to tell Iris the truth without it sounding so bad. But she was too ecstatic in her own happiness to have much interest in my situation, and given the circumstances, that's how it should be.

My steps crunched softly in the frozen grass. Jeremy had said that the boys would be waiting on the playground, but the school seemed mostly deserted but for a few children beginning their trek home. I pulled my sleeve up so that I could see my watch. It was 3:35 p.m. The clock in the car must be slow. Where were the boys?

Suddenly, I heard coughing and a flash of royal blue caught my eye on the playground. There were two boys sitting under the climbing structure. Both of my nephews were huddled under the apparatus like they were in some secret club.

"You guys hiding?" I called out.

Bret and Michael both turned at the sound of my voice. "Uncle Winston!" they said in unison with a strange overexcited tone in their voices that I recognized as trying to hide something. They both looked guilty and the acrid smell of smoke hung in the air under the climbing structure.

"Were you guys smoking?"

"No!" they answered in perfect unison again.

"Oh." I bent down to duck under the slide. "Why does it smell like smoke, then?"

Bret answered quickly. "There was a teenager out here smoking. He just left before you got here."

"Funny," I said, looking back to where my car was parked a hundred metres away. "I didn't see anyone as I was walking over here."

Michael jumped in. "Right before you came, he ran inside."

"Inside the elementary school?"

"Yep. He ran super fast." Michael tried to look solemn, but only succeeded in looking guiltier. Bret shoved him and told him to shut up.

"Hmm," I said, stalling for time. I had no idea what was required of me in this situation. I looked around. "Must have been really fast. Why would a teenager run really fast into the elementary school?" I asked.

"He—he—," Bret was stalling, trying to think up a good cover. "He had to go to the bathroom. He said he had to go really bad."

The smouldering remnant of a hand-rolled cigarette lay in the dirt. "He just left it on the ground?" I asked, stubbing it out with the toe of my shoe.

"He was in a big hurry."

"Really?"

Bret nodded vigorously. "He had to go."

"Yep," Michael chimed in helpfully. "It was dinnertime."

"Pretty early dinner," I mused, looking back and forth between my nephews' faces, wondering how Jeremy would handle the news of his sons smoking. They would probably have to move schools. "So, does this really fast, incontinent teenager with the early supper hour smoke here often? Or was this his first time?" I asked.

Bret hung his head as shame washed over his features. "It was the first time," he answered quietly.

"That's good," I said. "Don't want to develop a habit."

Bret kept his eyes trained on his shoes and didn't say anything. Michael followed his example.

"Let's get going, huh?" I said. "My back is killing me from being hunched over under here." I followed them out from under the climbing structure and we walked to back to the car in silence.

"Uncle Winston?" Michael asked tentatively as we neared it.

"Yeah?"

"Are you retarded? Dad says that you're lying. My mom believes you are, though!"

"Shut up." Bret shoved his little brother again. "Are you going to tell my dad? About the cigarette?"

I looked down at my shoes. They were stained with road salt. "Well—"

"We promise we won't ever do it again!" Bret said.

"We didn't even like it."

"Where did you get it?"

"Found a pack by the garbage." Bret handed me a flattened and weathered half-empty pack of rolling papers.

"How did you light it?"

Bret reached into the pocket of his blue ski jacket and took out an equally weathered lighter. I held out my hand to take it from him. "I found it on the side of the road." The lighter was almost empty. The clear pink plastic was scratched and dirty.

"You know," I said, "there are better things to do with lighters than light cigarettes."

258

"Like what?"

"If you smoke cigarettes, you just have to stand around outside in the cold looking silly. It's a good thing I caught you. Otherwise, you wouldn't know, and you'd just look like goobers huddled by the doorways."

"Goobers?" Michael said suspiciously. "What's that?"

"A peanut. A yokel. Jimmy Carter. Don't they teach you anything at school?"

Michael shook his head definitively. "No. My teacher is so dumb. She wouldn't know what a goober was."

"Hey, respect for elders even if you don't like them. Win the argument, instead."

"What else can do you with a lighter?" Bret asked, uninterested in his younger brother's assessment of the state of education and nervous that his career as an arsonist might never get off the ground.

"You can make a face, but you have to be careful what you do it on." I scanned the ground for something that might work. The school grounds were empty. Except for a lonely scarf tied to the chain-link fence, there wasn't a scrap of anything anywhere.

"How do you get it to make a face?" Michael asked.

"How old are you guys? Maybe you aren't old enough to know this yet."

"Ten," Bret answered quickly.

"I'm eight," Michael said. "I'm old enough, right?"

"Probably," I answered. "Has your dad never showed you this? He was the one who showed me."

"Mom says fire kills people and if we play with it, we'll die," Michael answered solemnly.

"It does do that," I said. "That's why you need to know what you are doing and be careful. Fire is serious stuff. Very little margin for error."

"It wasn't a real cigarette," Michael confessed.

"What was it?"

"Bret made it out of stuff from the pencil sharpener."

"Shut up!" Bret's face flushed pink. "It looked the same."

I smiled as I considered that the curled tendrils of orange HB pencil shavings were reminiscent of the twisted tobacco leaves in cigarettes. "I guess it does."

"Are you going to tell my dad?" Bret's voice wobbled.

"Did you burn yourself?"

Bret didn't answer and I watched as his eyes threatened to fill with tears against his struggling will. Slowly, he nodded.

"Let's see."

My nephew held out his hand somewhat reluctantly. The skin on his fingers was pink and angry.

"You'll be alright. Just put your fingers in the snow or run them under cold water. It will stop hurting soon." That didn't seem to comfort him much, so I decided to change tactics. "Or maybe you'll lose the hand—end up living the dissolute life of a pirate with a hook for a hand. No one will ever be able to give you a high-five again. Next thing you know, you'll be populating the ghost stories Grandma used to tell us when we were camping about the Man with the Hook."

Both of my nephews grinned with excitement. This is what boys need. They need another guy to look at their burnt hand or their open wound and say, "That's no big deal." We need someone to tell us to toughen up. It is the dismissiveness of masculinity toward personal pain that is helpful. It tells us that we're men. I wondered vaguely, if someone had told me that my pain was no big deal—that it would turn into a cool scar one day—would I have avoided this stupid situation with the Dignity Program? If the guys who were my friends had just told me to suck it up and stop feeling sorry for myself, then maybe I would have chosen to be happy with the Beltline Basement Lair. Then maybe I would have just handled the stale bagels and strawberry SlimFasts with humour. Maybe I would have seen it through with Cassandra. Who knows? But then I wondered who could have told me. Most of my friends were women. Jeremy had tried, but he'd squandered all his capital with me a long time before that—sometime between the broken nose and the broken arm. It's a drag, really, when you realize your detractors are probably right, but because they were your detractors, you didn't listen and so instead you chose to be the idiotic grasshopper who sang all frigging summer.

Michael laughed hysterically at the notion that his older brother might lose his hand.

"Grandma tells ghost stories?" Bret asked with a look of awe.

"She used to—sometimes—when we'd go camping."

"Were they scary?" Bret asked, his expression full of doubt at the notion that the grandma who bought him

Bible story comic books also told bone-chillingly freaky ghost stories to her own children.

"The scariest. She stopped when your dad threw up because he was so scared." I flicked the pink lighter a couple of times, but it only sparked and didn't ignite. "I'll show you guys how to make the face next time. This lighter isn't up to the task. Besides, you need your fingers working properly to do it."

Both boys moaned with disappointment as I opened the car door for them.

"Your dad's going to be showing up at my house to pick you up soon. If we aren't there, he's going to suspect all kinds of shenanigans."

The boys buckled themselves in dejectedly as the memory of their malfeasance intruded on their thoughts.

"Is smoking really bad? Is Dad going to be really mad?"

I got into the driver's seat as I thought about what to say. "It's really bad for you. Makes you sick."

"How come some people do it, then? Why is it allowed at all?"

Michael looked stricken. "Are we going to die?"

I turned around and smiled faintly. "From pencil shavings? Not on your first try. But I wouldn't push it. That isn't really the worst part."

"What's the worst part?" Bret asked.

"Be careful of anything that makes you lie," I said, turning back around and starting the car. "Something I'm learning, too. And it doesn't get easier, it gets harder."

"Uncle Winston?"

I turned to look back at Bret. My nephew looked at me sombrely and then tilted his head to the side like a Labrador puppy. "I'm sorry I lied."

I looked from Bret to Michael—who was also nodding solemnly. I smiled as a warmth crept over my chest.

"Me, too, pal."

CHAPTER SEVENTEEN
Jingle Keys

"I thought Iris was back today," I said as I held the door leading into the Kinesiology Complex for Gynnyfyr.

"I got a text last night saying that she wasn't coming in today and I had to do it or cancel."

"She sick?"

Gynnyfyr screwed up her features into a picture of exaggerated sympathy. "Don't fret, Lite Brite. Family emergency or something. No big D. She'll be back before you know it."

"Family emergency," I repeated slowly. That explained why she hadn't called me back yet. I hoped she was okay.

"Of course she has a family, *mon petit imbecile*," Gynnyfyr answered cheerfully. "What, do you think we arise from our cryo chambers just before our shifts?"

"Possibly a coffin, in your case."

That notion seemed to charm Gynnyfyr. "I am a little Elvira, Mistress of the Dark, aren't I? Only hotter, though. That lady mullet was fugly." Gynnyfyr flipped her hair off her shoulders as she continued, "Of course Iris has family. As do I, bee tee dub, in case you were wondering, but I noticed you don't seem as concerned."

"If you're married, you shouldn't be hitting on all the guys at the gym," I answered, deliberately misunderstanding her because, well, I can; and I didn't want her sniffing around my feelings about Iris. "You should be faithful to your husband."

"I'm not married, doofus. I meant that I've got parents." Gynnyfyr tossed her hair again in what was beginning to look like a practised affectation. "I'm too young to settle down. Too free. I mean, if I met the right guy, I'd want him to propose because being engaged would be pretty cool. But I don't want to be married. Yet. I plan on getting married when I am twenty-nine. Maybe twenty-eight. No, definitely twenty-nine. Then, we'll spend three years travelling and stuff and then I'll have my first kid at thirty-two—that is, if I have kids. But if I do, the first one is coming at thirty-two."

"Why thirty-two?"

"Because then I'll have my second at thirty-four and get my boobs done at thirty-five so they won't be droopy."

I was sorry I asked. "You do know that being engaged is just declaring your intention to marry?"

"Maybe it was a long time ago, Father Time. Nowadays it means you don't want to break up and you get a ring to prove it. I want a big-ass diamond. A pink one. Like the yellow one that Ben Affleck gave to JLo, but pink. There are pink ones. Want to see a picture? It's from Tiffany's." She threw out her arm to stop me in the hallway and pulled out her phone, jabbing it several times so that her weirdly thick, blood-red nails tapped loudly on the screen. "There." She held out her phone.

"Twenty-nine thousand dollars." I whistled in disbelief and pulled the phone out of her hand to look closer.

"I know, right?"

I thought it looked kind of fake. "What if your dream lover can't afford it?"

"Duh, that's what he has a credit card for," she said as she took her phone back from me and we proceeded to the rec centre doors. Gynnyfyr waited expectantly for me to swipe her in.

"A sound financial principle at work."

She made a face at me and disappeared into the women's locker room. I nodded at a couple of guys I knew at the free weights and went to change for my shift. Women want a ring for thirty grand? Gynnyfyr probably wasn't a reliable control group for female expectations but maybe she just expressed what other women knew to conceal. I hadn't spent thirty grand on Cassandra. Not even close. Maybe that was the problem. Maybe I just hadn't been all in. I threw my jacket into my locker and was pulling on a U of C Recreation shirt when Iqbal swaggered into the room.

"Winnie the Pooh Bear!" He enunciated each word as though he were announcing the winner of a contest. "My brother! Have I got great news for you."

I turned to face him as I closed my locker door. "What's up?"

Iqbal's usual bravado was in full swing. "'What's up'?' That's no way to meet your destiny. That's no way to jump in with both hands open!"

"That doesn't make any sense."

"You don't make any sense, Wing-a-ding-ding. I'm the good news police. I'm the guy behind the curtain who is going to make all of your PG-rated dreams come true. Follow the yellow brick road to all the midgets, big guy. Hey, did anyone ever tell you that you kinda look like Captain Kirk? You're like The Shat, but not as cool as The Shat. Have you seen his Twitter? That old white dude is lit."

I sighed heavily—like Great Dane–heavily. "So what should I be jumping into with both hands?"

Iqbal laughed. "Did you know that a drunken munchkin committed suicide on the set of *The Wizard of Oz*?"

"Why is that funny?"

"It's crazy that they left it in the movie, yo. Think it through, Wincest."

"They did not leave a suicide in a movie. Think it through."

"I saw it with my own two corneas, Anne of Windy Poplars. You can see him swinging in the trees. He hung himself because he was in love with a midget woman. She spurned him for a key grip. Hell hath no fury, man."

"Are you sure it wasn't one of the flying monkeys?"

"You're mocking me, Winadequate, but it is true. Ha! Winadequate! That's one of my best so far. Ten points to Gryffindor!"

I left the locker room and Iqbal followed me out to the check-in desk. "What was it you were going to tell me?"

"Oh, yeah! Good-news gospel, my friend!"

"Aren't you a Muslim?"

"What?"

"Never mind." This could go on all day.

"The good news, my friend, is that I have put you forward for a promotion."

"What do you mean? What promotion?"

"There is only one job for you to climb into, Winterfell. My job."

"You want me to take your job?" I said. "What about you?"

"I'm moving up in this world, Win Tin Tin. I didn't just get a job, like some slack-ass loser. I got me a career. No more wiping ass sweat off the machines."

"You never did that."

Iqbal shrugged. "I'm the manager, Winster-the-Spinster. I can't be doing the menial tasks. Besides, this is a very strange response to my telling you that you will be the new manager. Where's the exultation? Where's the hallelujah chorus? Where's my parade of triumph? You ought to be greeting me like Elizabeth Taylor. Damn, she was hot until she became friends with Michael Jackson. Where's the gratitude, huh? Where's your attitude of gratitude? Have a purpose-driven life, Windows '94."

"I'm just surprised since you fired me a couple of months ago."

"That was then! This is now! I live in the present! Be in the moment! No, be in the future. Stop living in the past. You were a loser then. Losers lose. Now you're all jacked."

"Thanks."

"There," Iqbal said, still slightly mystified. "That's more like it. That's a normal response. You are going to be the manager! You need to get excited. You're like a limp noodle."

"Winston can't possibly be a manager."

I whipped around to see Gynnyfyr standing behind me. Up close her inadequate allotment of spandex seemed almost obscene.

"Well, well, well—who do we have here?" Iqbal looked at her with exaggerated interest.

"I'm Gynnyfyr. I'm his aide." She extended her hand to Iqbal in a professional manner that belied her attire.

"His aide." Iqbal took her hand hesitantly while looking at me in confusion. "What does that mean? Winston doesn't need an aide. Why would Winston need an aide? You a general, Winnebago? You leading a war that you need an aide-de-camp? Why didn't you ask me? No offence, but I don't think lululemon here has the balls for the job because I will follow you once more unto the breach, el capitano. You are The Shat. What is it? You don't trust brown people? You think I'm a terrorist?"

In the innumerable ways that the artifice of my deception could have come crashing down, I never contemplated this way. The jig was up.

Gynnyfyr smiled too widely. "I am here to help him with his job. To make sure that he doesn't make some mega mistake."

"What is she talking about?" Iqbal asked me. "Do you even know her?"

"You can talk directly to me. I'm the responsible adult here," Gynnyfyr said.

"Okay, crazy naked lady," Iqbal said with some latent professional tone emerging. "I'm talking to my employee here."

Gynnyfyr smiled a sickly sweet smile at me. "Tell him, Winston. Tell him the truth. He really should have been properly informed the whole time."

Time seemed to slow down and speed up. Both of them were right. Iqbal was right that I didn't need an aide. Gynnyfyr was technically correct in saying that she was my assigned aide. The room seemed to grow tighter around me as my brain stalled on producing what I could possibly say that would smooth this all out until I could explain everything to Iris.

Gynnyfyr signed with a phony beatific air. "Winston recently became a participant in the Dignity Begins at Home program for adults with disabilities. I am his aide."

Her words seemed to hang in the air above me like some horrible banner. Then Iqbal burst out laughing and looked around the gym expectantly.

"Where is he?" he asked with excitement. "Where are you, Ashton? Cuz I know that I am being punk'd here!"

"Tell him." Gynnyfyr turned to me expectantly. "Tell him the truth, Winston."

"Ashton?" Iqbal was going about the room in an exaggerated manner, peering under the workout benches and around the various exercise equipment. "Where are you, man? Where are your cameras?"

"Iqbal——" He was drawing more and more attention from the people working out.

I could tell that Gynnyfyr's patience was wearing threadbare. She turned on her heel and marched to the locker room in a huff.

"Iqbal."

"Where are you, Ashton?" Iqbal grabbed the shoulder of a guy working out and spun him around to see his face. "Is that you? No? I know that you are here somewhere."

I tried desperately to think of something to say—to explain—but my mind was paralyzed and I could only watch mutely as everything unfolded in front of me.

Gynnyfyr emerged from the women's locker room with a sweater and her identification. "Ashton Kutcher isn't here, moron," she said. "Look at my ID. I'm telling you the truth, even if Winston won't confirm it because he is embarrassed."

Iqbal stopped to look at her card. He peered at it closely for what seemed like forever. Whatever embarrassment I had felt before was nothing to the heat that surged up my neck and into my face as every person in the gym looked on in amazement. They had removed their headphones. They weren't listening to their own music. Everyone was paying attention to me.

"I don't believe this," Iqbal said. "Winston. What the hell, man? Are you a retard, or what?"

Gynnyfyr looked exultant. "Tell the truth, Winston. There is nothing to be ashamed of."

The way that she said it—I just knew that she was trying to humiliate me. "She is who she says she is."

Iqbal—seemingly for the first time in his life—was struck dumb. Then he stammered quietly, "I didn't mean 'retard.'"

I shrugged. Honestly, who cares?

"Well, you probably can't be the manager then," he said slowly.

"He most certainly can't be the manager. Firstly, it is beyond him. Secondly, he can only earn five-hundred dollars a week or he is out of the program."

"Five hundo is nothing," Iqbal said.

"He gets a free house," she retorted. "I think the government can decide what is enough money."

"You trust the government to decide?" Iqbal said incredulously. "Lady, you might need the aide."

"Can you keep your voices down?" I said weakly.

"Seriously?" Iqbal whistled in amazement. "A free house. Maui Wowee. That is something, Winstant Gratification." He turned to look back at Gynnyfyr. "But he has to spend all his time with you?"

Gynnyfyr didn't seem to sense the dig. "I am one of his aides. He has another, as well. Iris takes him grocery shopping. He's very dependent."

Iqbal seemed to be revving like an engine warming up. "Lucky him. Lucky guy. He's like the fountain of all lucky charms."

Gynnyfyr narrowed her eyes and crossed her arms.

"Still. It seems kind of a high price to pay."

"He can't take the job."

Iqbal turned to me. "How long have you been *I Am Sam*-ing it, Win-baby-Win? Wait. Is this some blog stunt? You writing a book? 'My year with Madame Medusa, the bad lady from *The Rescuers*?'"

"A couple of months," I said. "But it is all a big mistake. I'm not mentally handicapped. It's all a big misunderstanding."

Iqbal burst out laughing. "This is the best thing I have ever heard. It must be my birthday." He turned to Gynnyfyr. "Whose idea was this? I've known this guy for years. He's not handicapped. Unmotivated, sure. That's what I always tell him on his employee review. Not retarded. You should see the books this guy reads." Iqbal held up his hand to measure out several inches. "They're this thick. How many mentally challenged clients do you have that read books on Mao that are that big?"

A flicker of doubt crossed Gynnyfyr's face—but she recovered herself quickly. "You don't know anything about it. He was diagnosed by a doctor, genius. You think that you know better than the professionals? Better than me? Better than the doctors who recommended him for this program? I don't care how many books on cats he's read."

Iqbal roared with laughter. "You've never heard of a misdiagnosis? You aren't God, lady. You guys are all wrong on this one."

"I'm not going to stand here and argue with you about it."

"Have a seat if you need a rest." Iqbal gestured to one of the nearby recumbent bicycles. "By all means."

"We're leaving. Get your stuff," she practically hissed at me. Suddenly Iqbal's identification of her as

Medusa in that ancient Disney film was comically apropos. I should have been thinking about how to handle the present disaster, but all I could think about was that cartoon villain standing over the hole in the ground and shrieking at little orphan Penny, "Bring me the Devil's Eye!"

"Did you hear me?"

"I heard you. My shift isn't over."

"Your job is over," she said, somewhat viciously.

"No, *Of Mice and Men* here has a job as long as he wants it," Iqbal said, wiping tears from the corners of his eyes. "Besides, if I let him leave with you, you might blow poor Lenny's head off. Can't have that."

Gynnyfyr collided with the doors of the rec centre like a cartoon character bursting through a brick wall. The sight of her leaving my life for good made me adventitiously elated, despite the fact that I knew she was probably dialling Iris's number as she hit the parking lot. I still hadn't spoken to Iris. I still hadn't explained anything to her and now it would look like I only revealed it because I'd been caught. Iris would think I was a despicable human being and she was also going to have to manage the inevitable fallout with Dignity. She probably going to be called on to explain why she hadn't noticed I was a fraud. What if Dignity blamed her and she lost her job? What if she couldn't find another one and ended up like Fantine in *Les Misérables*, desperate and sick? Would I be able to transform myself into Monsieur le Mayor in time to help? I needed to find a way to give the house back immediately and without Iris's help. I needed to get off the government's mentally handicapped list—if such a thing exists. I needed to think of a way through the mess that I had made, but my thoughts were thick and cold and all I could do was imagine what disappointment looked like when written across Iris's pale features.

I finished off the rest of my shift in this paralytic brain fog and then worked out with Cory in the same mechanical state. Cory didn't seem to notice, only commenting once that he "liked my single-mindedness. It's like you've finally got your head in the game."

I nodded as beads of sweat rolled from my hairline to the tip of my nose and landed in perfect circles on the mat below my face as I completed the set of Spider-Man push-ups.

"You're a machine today. You beat most of your targets. I'm going to have to look at the math." I felt weak and gelatinous as I rolled over onto my back on the mat at the end of the set.

"Is that it?" I gasped.

"For today," Cory said as he made notes on his iPad. "We have to work out in the morning next week; I need my evenings to study."

I nodded.

"As soon as the rec centre opens? Six?"

"I guess."

"Good," Cory said as he stuck out his hand to help me up. "It's been ten weeks, man. Almost at the end of the road. I've got to update your photos and measurements. Tarps off."

I struggled to my feet and pulled my sweaty T-shirt off. "How much longer until we're done?"

"My project is due in a couple of weeks. We'll probably do your final photos in a week. Your progress is pretty epic, dude. You've got a lot of fans."

"Fans?" If there was one thing I was about to have none of, it was fans.

"My Instagram feed has been hopping since I took your week-six photos. I even had one guy ask me to train him after he saw you."

"That's great, Cory."

"I know. I'm super pumped. Thanks, man. I couldn't have done it without you. I thought I was sunk when Gynnyfyr flaked out on me, but you've more than made up the difference."

"Didn't you need a female example, too, though?"

"I was supposed to have both for the project, but I explained to my prof and she said it was okay. She said if my one profile was in-depth enough, she wouldn't penalize me. We've gone above and beyond the basics."

That was something. At least I had helped Cory out. I may be a total loser, but I wasn't a total user. I said goodbye to Cory and headed back to the Dignity house. I needed to think. I checked my phone again to make sure I hadn't missed a call or text from Iris. Nothing. It had been four hours since Gynnyfyr had found out the truth. Four hours was surely enough time for her to get a hold of Iris and tell her what had happened with Iqbal. Four hours. Geez. The cops could be at the Dignity house already, just waiting to arrest me. My fingers tightened on the steering wheel as I turned on to the empty street in Bowness. There were no cop cars. There were no circling red-and-blue lights. There were only a few vacant cars parked intermittently along the road.

I pulled up out front of the house. Would the cops stake out a guy who was accused of pretending to be handicapped in order to get free housing? I sat in my car with the engine off for a few minutes while I contemplated what to do. I glanced around in the fading afternoon light. The tactical team wasn't swarming. No one was here. Not even Gynnyfyr or Iris. The car grew cold as a plan began to form in my mind. It was sort of a plan. Sort of like seeing a cliff ahead and pushing down fully on the accelerator is a plan. I just needed to jump.

I flung open the car door and got out like I wasn't worried about being arrested. I even stood there nonchalantly for a moment and took a deep breath like a guy just enjoying the oncoming evening. The wind picked up forcefully as though it was trying to push me to take a step backward. I stood my ground and looked up at the indigo sky that was almost night. A handful of bold stars twinkled through the city lights. It was a beautiful night. If all the nights were like this, it wouldn't be so bad.

When I was a kid there was this thing that happened to the housing market in Calgary thanks to the National Energy Program tanking the provincial economy. Businesses went under and people lost their jobs and eventually the housing market crashed. People started walking away from their homes. They'd just leave because the value of their house was way less than the value of their mortgage and they couldn't afford to pay it. So, they left. Average people. Responsible types. Families. They mailed their house keys back to the banks that held their mortgages and walked away to lick their wounds and eventually try their luck again at some later time when the stress of such financial difficulty had grown more remote in memory. My dad worked three different jobs trying to stay afloat, one of which was doing insurance checks on all the empty houses on which the banks had foreclosed. One of my dad's old university friends killed himself by stepping off the LRT platform in front of an oncoming CTrain at rush hour because he had lost their family house and his finances were in ruins. After the funeral, Nat asked Dad why the man had died and all he said was, "It's an unhappy time."

Jingle Keys.

House keys rattling around in envelopes being returned to the bank as people defaulted on their mortgages. I was not the type to step in front of a train but I could mail my keys back to Dignity Begins at Home. I thought about composing a letter to explain my situation. I could write a sincere and evocative missive explaining that while I was an underachiever, while I'd had a run of bad luck compounded by a couple of misdiagnoses, I hadn't meant to deceive anyone. I could write eloquently (I imagined) about that watershed moment when I had realized that there had been a mistake. I could explain that I had no desire to defraud the government or the Canadian People, who were paying for this munificent program for the disadvantaged, or differently abled— whatever term was appropriate and suitably kind.

I entered the house and started throwing my clothes back into the suitcases I had so recently borrowed from my parents to move in. I tried not to think about Iris because I was afraid. I was afraid like when I was a kid and I'd wipe out skateboarding and I'd skin a knee or something. I would clamp my hand over it as though seeing the wound was the most painful part. I didn't think about Iris as I carried my stuff out to the car. I tried not to think about anyone, really. I looked around the house at all the furniture that wasn't mine. Most of the stuff in this house was given to me by the Dignity Begins at Home program. It wouldn't take me very long to move out. That was something, anyway.

The clock on the microwave proclaimed it a quarter past five when I started emptying the kitchen cupboards of my meagre collection of dishes. I wrapped the two china mugs in paper towels but piled the rest into a laundry basket. I stripped my bedding and threw it into a black garbage bag along with my towels. Room by room, I cleared out my possessions until every sign that I had lived here was removed. My clothes and oddments— groceries, books, dishes and the like—were all piled into my car. At seven thirty, I started cleaning. I am not a messy person as a rule, but I was determined to be fastidious. I scrubbed the bathtub and tile so that it was show-home clean. There was not a single room that I did not intend to leave perfect. I even vacuumed the lint out of the lint catcher in the dryer until it looked brand new again. Thankfully I had never hung any pictures so there were no holes in the walls to be repaired, because given the fury with which I attacked any sign of my presence there, I probably would have patched and repainted, too. There were no water spots in the stainless-steel sinks. There were no fingerprints on—well—anything.

I only paused in my work long enough to drink my protein shakes, which I had already carried out to my car and fixed in the front seat. I sat with the door open for a moment and chugged the shake and felt relief. I would be finished soon and then I would be free. Free from the omissions that made me a fraud. Free to do something different. I was contemplating what that might be when my phone buzzed and my heart raced in expectation of Iris's call. I felt both disappointment and relief as I read Robbie's message.

U free?

I stared at the screen for a moment, wondering just how free I was. Everything was basically done in the house. Vacuum tracks being the height of cleanliness to my way of thinking, I wanted to be sure to leave them in the living room carpet, but that was my last task.

Robbie sent another text before I had answered the first. *Need to talk.*

That was weird. Robbie and I liked to argue with one another, but we didn't talk. Not in a I-need-to-talk kind of way. He throws up loony notions about history and politics like skeet and I shoot them down in so many pieces of broken clay. Those are the sorts of things we talk about. Arm's-length things. We argue about the abstract. I stared at the phone a few moments longer. Part of me was interested in what was bothering him, but another, more selfish part of me wanted this to be my own moment. I wanted to leave vacuum tracks in the carpet while covering up my own footprints and then to stand at the threshold of the Dignity house and turn the lights off for the last time. I wanted to savour the moment as I accelerated toward the edge of the cliff into the unknown.

I didn't really want to argue with Robbie tonight. I didn't want to hear about whatever project he had in mind. I didn't want to roll my eyes at his choices. Normally, fine. But not tonight. Robbie sent a third text as though he could sense my indecision.

Come on, man.

I looked at my watch. It was just after ten. *I need an hour. Where?*

His reply was almost instantaneous. He texted the address of a pub not far from my parents' old place. I finished the rest of my shake and returned to the house to finish vacuuming. The house wasn't large and it didn't take very long but I made sure the tracks looked almost mathematical in their precision. Then I stood at the threshold. I turned off the lights for the last time. I could see the free fall approaching. I closed the door and made sure it was locked.

Here I go.

CHAPTER EIGHTEEN

Hobos and Bros

"I don't eat flesh."

The waitress, a petite but solid girl in her early twenties whose name tag read "Shields," looked bored as she rattled off a variety of vegetarian options in response to Robbie's declaration.

"Are the deep-fried pickles local?"

"They're from a big jar in the kitchen," she said.

"Fine. I'll have those. But you should talk to your management about using local produce."

She nodded indifferently and turned to me expectantly. "For you?"

"Chicken fingers. Extra chicken," I said as I handed her the menu. I knew Cory wouldn't approve of this little repast but it's the best I could do for pub food and I was starving from skipping dinner.

"Still committed to the wholesale destruction of the planet, I see," Robbie said, leaning back in his chair.

"When I can fit it in," I said lightly. "Besides, what do you think is going to happen to those foreign pickles, you sadist?"

He shrugged. "It's important to raise awareness. Did you see her face? Unconscious. Most people are unconscious."

"Is that what this is about? Consciousness-raising? Because I was actually busy."

He ignored my question. "You don't even care what happened to those chickens that you're responsible for slaughtering. I have a documentary I'll lend you about it."

"I'm good. You think YouTube videos are well sourced."

"Unfortunately, I think you would watch it and still eat meat, which makes you the worst kind of person. You don't think your choices matter."

"It isn't that. I just don't care. What you think is a big deal, I don't think is a deal at all."

"How can you not care? You live on this planet."

"I find environmentalists shrill and unconvincing, not to mention unapologetically authoritarian."

"You're just trying to annoy me." He took a swig from his drink. "So, what degree are you working on now? Bodybuilding? You look like you ate the Hulk."

"Nothing. I'm not taking anything now."

"Except steroids."

"Possibly in the chicken, I suppose."

"You're despicable. Neanderthals like you have to be forced to do the right thing."

"Your fascistic tendencies would be more troubling to me if I didn't think you looked so anemic.

When my chicken fingers get here, help yourself to some protein. I'm generous that way."

"My values don't just melt away in the presence of your overgrown physique." Robbie looked me over critically. "There should be a food tax on your kind. Instead of a luxury tax, we should have a douche-bag tax."

"No need to be jealous. I know a guy who can get you ripped, too. He'd probably appreciate the vegetarian challenge, come to think of it."

"The last thing I would want to do is spend time with the kind of person who thinks that is a good idea."

"I grant you, Cory probably hasn't thought it through from the chicken's point of view. But he'd be a captive audience—longer than a waitress, at any rate. And he's nicer than me, so you might make some headway."

"That's your best argument yet. That's how the world changes, by making people aware. And then, if they don't listen, we—"

"—Hold a gun to their head?"

"We legislate it. Otherwise, between Big Business and idiots like you, the whole planet is going to die in an overpopulated cesspool."

I leaned back in my chair, lacing my fingers together behind my head. "I think it is the apocalyptic scenarios that endear the environmental movement to me the most."

"I'm serious."

"Undoubtedly. I know how you feel about all the things. Overpopulation. Global warming. Global cooling, and the hole in the ozone, which is why I rejoice every time there is an election and you are out of town and unable to vote."

The waitress appeared with our food, set down our plates briskly and turned on her heel. She had forgotten the ketchup.

"Whatever happened to that, by the way?" I asked, digging into my unadorned chicken fingers.

"With what?"

"The hole in the ozone. Nobody worries about that anymore."

"It's still there." Robbie made a face and pushed his chair back from the table, whether it was about the chink in the ozone or his unappetizing pickles, I couldn't say.

"I read somewhere that it is closing. I thought you'd be all over such good news."

Robbie didn't seem to have heard me. He picked up one of his deep-fried pickles and stared at it for a moment like he didn't know what it was before he set it down again.

"So, listen—I've been sleeping with this girl," Robbie said, "and it's made me think, made me realize that, as a society, we've advanced really far, right? Like you said, we're closing the hole in the ozone. Humans are in control."

"I wouldn't say that."

"Of some things we are, though," Robbie said it so earnestly that I wondered where this was going.

"Of very few things, maybe," I conceded. "What are you referring to?"

Robbie downed some of his beer with a shrug as his features rearranged themselves into their usual cynicism. "Like, overpopulation. We know how to control it."

"What, with death squads?"

"No—at the source."

"Robbie. I'm impressed. I never took you for the abstinence type." I raised my arm to get the waitress's attention but thanks to Robbie she was studiously ignoring our table.

"Don't be stupid," he sneered. "Abortion. Contraceptives. Accidental pregnancies are a thing of the past."

"For a second there, I thought this was going to be a serious discussion. Why is it that all environmental arguments eventually end with the conclusion that the planet would be better off without people?"

"Because it would. It would function in perfect balance. It is humanity that throws everything out of whack."

"You don't know that. You have no idea what the planet would look like without people. What would have happened, what wouldn't have—there is no way of knowing."

"We're the freaks. The outliers. The monkey wrench in the machinery. We're the one factor that ruins everything for every other species. An evolutionary accident."

"If we're all accidents, then there is no such thing as 'ruining' anything. For something to get ruined, there would have had to have been a plan," I said dismissively, while scanning nearby tables for a bottle of Heinz. Even toddlers don't like their chicken fingers plain.

"Accidents are just things that happen whose net effect is worse than it would be if they hadn't happened. Accidents need fixing."

I spotted a bottle of ketchup on a table that had yet to be cleared and stood up to retrieve it. Sometimes you have to take matters into your own hands. "Are we back to the death squads so soon?"

"I'm just saying that there are accidents—like humanity—and then there are 'accidents.' Things that people claim are outside their control but really aren't."

"Such as what?"

"So, this girl—Kelly—she's not my girlfriend. It's not serious—"

"What would it look like if it were?" I unscrewed the cap of the Heinz bottle and turned it upside down. The ketchup stubbornly refused to budge.

He looked perplexed. "What do you mean?"

"You're sleeping with her, but it isn't serious. What would it look like if it was?" I thumped the end of the glass bottle with my palm to get the sauce moving.

"We don't have anything in common, anything to talk about. Anyway, she ends up pregnant—"

I looked up at Robbie as a flood of ketchup spilled onto my plate. "'Ends up'? That's pretty much cause and effect, my friend. I'm sorry that public education failed you so completely but that is the endgame of the activity."

"In this day and age?" he protested. "It shouldn't have happened at all."

"Did she want to get pregnant?"

Robbie pulled at his hair in exasperation. "Not that I knew. But she doesn't want to get an abortion; so, it makes me think she did it on purpose. Or she was just really incompetent with the birth control."

Robbie's plate of pickles was neglected and growing more unappetizing by the moment. "I can't be a dad, man." He leaned in across the table. "Kelly and I don't have any of the same views. We can't carry on a conversation, let alone be parents."

"You managed enough communication to get this far."

"That's different. I can't be a father. I've got a calling. I can't be tied up like that."

"A calling?"

"Yeah—I've got to—you know, raise awareness and change people's behaviour. I don't even believe people should be having children. Have you been to Asia? There aren't enough resources for us all."

"Are you seriously talking about the environment being your calling instead of taking care of the human being you've fathered?"

"I'm saying that it should never have happened."

"Humanity or your child?"

"Micro and macro version of the same accident," Robbie said. "I told her I wasn't interested in being involved. I think she should get rid of it. If she wants to go ahead, that's her deal. I'm not going to be a part of it. I've been upfront."

"You must be on your way out of town, then."

"Why would I be?"

"Because you're abandoning the girl you got in trouble. I thought lighting out of town was part of the act."

"Hey—if she's dumb enough to keep sleeping with me, that's her problem. I'm not responsible for that. She's an adult."

"That's pretty—" I struggled to find the right word. "—misleading."

"Why? I've told her I'm not participating."

"You are participating. You're saying one thing but doing the exact opposite. You don't think having sex with her sends the message that you're planning on sticking around?"

"It has never meant that."

"Are you sure she knows that?"

He shrugged with what can only be described as defensive indifference. "That's not my problem. I shouldn't have to spell everything out."

"Because maybe if you did, she might harness her vestigial self-respect and not sleep with you anymore?"

"You're supposed to be my friend here. Not hers."

"I am being your friend," I said. "So, just to clarify, sex isn't connected to pregnancy and children, and it isn't connected to love or commitment, either."

"It doesn't have to be. That's just society's norms. It's just an impulse. A biological imperative."

"Right, but, even from a biological perspective, it's really only about procreation. Doesn't your kid need a dad?"

"Kelly is attractive. Some other guy—some good guy—will step up eventually."

"Who are these good guys, I wonder?"

Robbie tried to lighten the mood. "You're not busy these days, right? You're wholesome. You could."

I snorted. "Let's imagine that hypothetically I'd be interested in such a role. Why would you want me to? You disagree with everything I say. Why would you want me to raise your child to think like me? I mean, in terms of your 'calling,' wouldn't you be raising awareness and changing the behaviour of that individual child?"

"You always think too small. One other person isn't enough. I need to have a wider impact than just on one kid. Than just on a family. That's why I told her she should terminate—I mean, whatever, it's her body, her choice—but I wasn't going to be tied down by it. I'm not going to live that small life."

"The life you have now is so much bigger? You drive around in a VW camper van with no connections and a dislike for people—particularly, women, it seems."

"What are you talking about? I'm a Feminist," he said defensively.

"Why? The world would be better off without people, right? Certainly the women irresponsible enough to keep having babies are to blame. I get that you like to have sex with women, but you don't really care about them. You just use them."

If Robbie had been a bird, he would have had some seriously rumpled feathers. I could see he was getting ready to walk out. Our conversations often ended that way.

"I'm surprised you even wanted to talk to me about this, let alone have me raise your offspring for you." I mopped a chicken finger through the sea of ketchup on my plate. "What made you want to? Call me, I mean."

Robbie shook his head. The expression on his face was both sour and quasi-hostile.

"You got a chance here, Robbie," I said, feeling the irony that it was me who was going to give him this pep talk. Me, currently homeless, previously fraudulent Winston. "One chance to change your whole life and live greater than just looking out for yourself. I think you should take it."

"Live greater? Are you kidding me? It's a prison sentence." His voice was loud enough that some of the people at other tables looked over at us.

"You've got an invitation to be more than you are now. You have a kid; you have to grow. You have to be more. You have to meet his needs. Provide. Be better than who you are on your own. Think of someone else first. You're looking at it all wrong. You think you're being limited. You're being expanded—if you've got the stones to follow through. This is your ticket to being a man. Take it from me, they don't come around as often as you hope."

"Not everybody lives the same way. Not everybody wants to." Robbie sounded so sullen I could be forgiven for thinking I was talking to a thirteen-year-old version of my friend, not the thirty-three-year-old version.

"Do you think you could raise your kid the same way as someone else if you were trying to?"

A smile cracked his sullen expression against his efforts to stifle it. I could see I was having an unexpected impact on him. I felt a rising elation, but I couldn't tell if it was because I couldn't remember ever convincing Robbie of anything before, or if I was on a high because I had finally left Dignity behind.

Robbie leaned his elbows on the table and buried his hands in his hair. "What am I going to do, man? What am I going to do?"

I took a drink of water as I thought about how to answer. "What do you like about Kelly?" I asked. "How'd you meet her?"

"At Stampede last summer. She was protesting, too, so we went into the beer garden for a drink and then went back to her place."

"Sounds like you have something in common."

Robbie shrugged. "She's vegan—so that's something, I guess."

"And a protester," I said cheerily. "You love that."

"Yeah. She does really hate the oil industry—all Big Business, really."

I resisted the temptation to argue with Kelly by proxy.

"Yeah, she's alright. She just threw me for a loop with this baby thing. What the hell, right? It's like she abandoned her principles with this."

"Is that the problem? You thought she'd want an abortion and she doesn't?"

"Maybe," he said. "It's just like this whole thing got out of hand."

"I know that feeling," I said and finished off my last chicken finger. "The thing is, you don't want to be someone who goes through life unable to adapt to a new circumstance."

Robbie sighed heavily and ate one of his deep-fried pickles. "So, what do I do?"

"Sack up."

"What does that even mean, though?"

I looked at him expectantly but didn't answer.

"You think I should ask her if she wants to be my girlfriend? If we should, like, do this thing?" He had that strange, earnest expression again that made him look like he did when he was a kid.

"Thing is, buddy," I said, suppressing a smile and trying to match his earnestness, "it looks to me like you already want to."

Robbie didn't deny it but his earnest expression disappeared as he morosely tackled another pickle.

"So, what's all this she-isn't-really-my-girlfriend-and-how-come-she-isn't-getting-an-abortion stuff?"

He took his time chewing before he said, "What if she says no?"

"Give her the chance." I drained the rest of my water and wished I could order a beer.

Robbie sighed heavily. "What if it ends up being terrible? What if we're like my folks and that kid ends up—" His voice trailed off and he shook his head.

I waited for him to continue but he didn't.

"Ends up what?"

"What if he ends up lying in bed at night listening to his parents screaming at each other like I did? Turning up his Walkman so loud it makes his ears crackle because he's trying to drown out the awful shit that they say to each other? A kid can't leave. He's just caged."

Robbie picked up the last pickle on his plate and seemed to contemplate it. "What if we end up like them? It could be terrible."

I looked at my friend and felt a wave of compassion. "You're not guaranteed to fail just because your folks did," I said slowly, choosing my words carefully.

293

"It could be amazing, too. I'd hate to see you forego something good out of fear of what may or may not be."

Robbie set the deep-fried pickle back down without taking a bite.

"Look," I said. "The way I see it, is that we are in the stage of life that demands big moves. Grand gestures. We too old to allow ourselves to be anaesthetized any longer by the kind of flaky stuff that doesn't matter."

"My movies aren't flaky," he said irritably as though the window of earnestness that had been open briefly was quickly closing. "I'm proud of my body of work."

"That's fine, but it's not what I'm talking about. I'm saying you got a chance to be more. You've got an opportunity to strike out on a brand-new road. You said that it was all about changing one person's mind. This isn't one person. It's three—so far. You might change the world more through these people than you ever would have even if your documentaries are all great successes. You don't know what will be, but you have to make a choice anyway. Why not make the bold one? Why not bring the bomb home?"

He smiled at the remembrance. "Just like that."

"Just like that." I pushed my ketchup-filled plate away from me and leaned back in satisfaction. "I told you it would make a good story."

The alarm on my phone buzzed in my car's cupholder and woke me with a start. I blearily righted the driver's seat position and sat upright. Robbie and I had stayed at the pub until the music was turned off and the lights came on, then we stood around in the parking lot talking for another forty-five minutes. I blinked several times trying to clear the sleep from my brain. I was not as stiff as I thought I might be from sleeping in the driver's seat but gave an involuntary shudder as I reached into my pocket for my car keys. I started the engine and yawned several times in succession as I waited for the car to warm up. I had parked in the Walmart parking lot after leaving Robbie and set my alarm so that I would wake up in time for my workout with Cory. I put the car in gear and turned on to the empty street that would take me to the university. Two hours of sleep was not enough. I leaned my head back against the headrest as I drove through the mostly deserted city with everything I owned crammed tightly around me. I wondered where I had shoved my gym bag. I hoped I'd had the foresight to put it on top. I rubbed my eyes trying to clear the cloudiness from my brain. The thermometer on the dash declared it to be just above zero. It wasn't so bad, really, sleeping in the car. Sure, I was chilled through like those value packs of skinless, boneless chicken breast that I had lately been eating so much of, but it was manageable. If I'd had a decent blanket or sleeping bag, it would have been alright. Where was my good bag? I wondered. I had one rated for at least -10^{0}C. Someone had borrowed it a while back—Joel, maybe? Today was the day of the picnic at Shouldice to meet Sam's guy.

"Ask Nat about the sleeping bag," I said aloud to try to cement it into my mind and then yawned so wide I lost sight of the road for what felt like too long. Since packing last night, I had toyed with the idea of asking if I could stay with Nat and Joel until I found someplace else. But after spending the night in the car—or two and a half hours at any rate—a new notion was forming in my mind. I could shower at the rec centre. I could make my food for the week at either Nat's or my parents'. Winter was pretty much over and I could sleep in my car for a few days or a week or however long it was until I found something else. If I wanted to find something else, I thought.

I pulled into my regular parking lot spot and left the car idling with the heater on full blast. I was starting to warm up a little. Everything except for my feet and hands. I tucked my hands into my armpits and leaned against the headrest. Okay. One minute and then I had to get moving. I closed my eyes.

A sharp knock on the window caused me to jump and bang my knee on the steering wheel.

"Dude." I looked up to see Cory's perplexed face through the driver's side window. "You alright?"

I threw open the door.

"You looked dead."

"I got here a little early and fell back asleep."

Cory looked at me critically. "Were you partying last night? Not cool, bro. You're so close. No booze right now. You look like you've aged ten years since I saw you yesterday. I can't believe that you're willing to throw everything away in the last week. This is not the time to slack off. This is the time to leave everything on the field." Cory's wasn't yelling but his voice sure seemed to be echoing over the parking lot. "What are you thinking?"

"First off, I was up late. Secondly, I only drank water and I hit my macros yesterday. Thirdly, please, for the love of all that is good in this world, stop yelling."

Cory's disappointment with me evaporated almost instantaneously. "Good. Good. That's great," he said, and then added, "How's the shoulder? Still clicking?"

I rotated my shoulder in an exaggerated movement. "Seems okay. Little stiff."

"Sorry, man," Cory said. "I am just so pumped about this that I'm getting stress dreams about it going wrong."

"What, you dreamt that I was binge-eating or something?" I opened the trunk hatch and was relieved to see my gym bag sitting on top of a laundry basket full of books, rather than the other way around.

"Whoa." Cory whistled at the sight of my tightly packed car. "Everything okay, dude?"

I pulled out the bag and closed the hatch. "I just moved. I was up late and I'm exhausted."

Cory smiled fiendishly as we crossed the street separating the parking lot from the long cement sidewalk that led past the Olympic Torch into the Kinesiology Complex. "That's too bad. It's a forty-minute HIIT workout today."

"Oh, come on. Seriously? I hate those."

"Look on the bright side. It is intense, but short."

"You're a terrible motivator. The bright side is that this is over in a week."

"Didn't you ever learn not to attack your coach? I hold the power."

"You have the makings of a tyrant."

"Quit whining."

I'm not sure whether it was the lack of sleep or the intensity of the workout but halfway through his forty-minute HIIT circuit, I threw up. (Fortunately, I'm well aware of where the cleaning supplies are located.)

Cory gave me five minutes and a protein bar from his bag while lecturing me about not celebrating in the end zone but getting the ball across the goal line first like a real champion. Then I returned to complete the rest of the routine. By seven thirty, I was showered and walking back to my car when I checked my phone. The sight of Iris's name caused my heart to skip a beat.

CHAPTER NINETEEN
The Reckoning

This is so bad I can't even believe it.

Iris's text was time-stamped at 6:12 a.m. I stared at the words on the screen and wondered what—if anything—I should text back or if I could just light out of town and try to forget her existence in the manner of some no-good cowboy. I was all saddled up, so to speak. My thumb hovered over the keyboard as I tried to conjure up something—anything—to say that could mitigate her disappointment in me.

Yeah. I pressed the Send button with a sense that I was signalling my own executioner. "Yeah" was the best I could come up with. Friggin' useless three degrees.

I can't believe you did this to me.

I typed quickly. If minutes of contemplation only yielded a "yeah," I might as well send the first thought that entered my mind. I sent three messages in quick succession.

I'm sorry.
I didn't mean to.

What can I do?

Her reply was swift. *Come right now!!*

I stared at the screen with a mixture of dread and sorrow. This was it. This was the last obstacle to face in freeing myself from Dignity, but it was also the hardest one. I could almost bear the thought of never seeing Iris Naess again more than I could bear the reality of facing her. Was she angry? Was she disappointed? Was she—heartbroken? Not likely. I tried to shake reason into my head as another text with her address arrived, reiterating with multiple exclamation marks that I was to go there immediately.

!!!!

Right. I was on the verge of being heartbroken. She was pissed off.

I arrived outside Iris's apartment building to see her waiting on the steps. She was wearing a long, draping blue sweater that seemed inadequate for the crisp morning as she hugged herself tightly. Strands of her pale hair were falling around her unhappy face. I pulled into a parking spot next to where her car was parked and I got out slowly, my muscles already seizing up from the workout with Cory. I had a protein shake in hand because it was time for one and they were the easiest thing to make out of my car.

"You and your stupid protein," she said when she caught sight of me. "Do you have any idea of the nightmare that you've created for me?"

I looked down at my shoes. What possible defence could I offer? Besides, every time I had tried to explain myself it came off sounding so weak. I'd rather let Iris shoot me than feel that way in front of her, like I was trying to justify myself or hoping that she would offer me mercy or something.

"I'm sorry."

"It's like someone has died, Winston."

That struck me as a little melodramatic. I crossed my arms. "I think that's overstating it a little bit."

"Can't you smell it?" Her face was almost wild and desperation clung to her voice. "I can smell it on me all the time. It smells like death! Like decaying flesh! Like putrescence!" She grabbed at her sweater and tried to yank it up to my nose. "See? See!"

"Listen," I said, beginning to wonder if maybe all the people who work as aides are crazy. "I'm sorry, I didn't mean for any of this to happen."

Iris rolled her eyes. "Well, obviously, but what are you going to do about it? How are you going to fix this? There's no fixing this! I tried, but nothing works."

"I moved out of the house last night. I'm trying to make it right."

"I've bought all the sprays and the——" Confusion washed over her features, displacing her mania. "You moved out of——? Wait——what are you talking about?"

"What are you talking about?"

"My car." She strode over to her car and dramatically threw open the passenger door. "Take a whiff of that!"

I leaned into her Civic and almost threw up for the second time that morning. I gagged as I took several steps away from the car to get to clean air. My eyes began to water from the pungent fumes. "What the hell did you do?" I asked, coughing and burying my nose in the crook of my arm.

"What did *I* do? You mean, what did *you* do? You and your ridiculous He-Man shakes! You spilled it in my car when we almost got into that accident."

"When you almost got me killed, you mean?" I smiled behind my arm. "I cleaned that up. This is—this is something else."

"You wiped it up, but why does it smell like a dead body was stored in my car the whole time I was in Kelowna?"

I picked up the offending shake from where I had set it on the hood of my car. "This smells like cookies 'n' cream. I don't know what you do in your spare time, but I recommend that you turn yourself into the authorities and beg for leniency."

"Ha ha. I had to drive back from the airport Park and Jet lot in that smell. I pulled over to throw up on the side of the road, hanging out of the car because I still had my seat belt on. It was three degrees and I was driving down Deerfoot Trail with all my windows down and my eyes streaming and I still had to throw up! I've showered twice since then and I can still smell it. Here! Smell my hair. It smells like a corpse."

"I doubt that."

"Seriously!" She held out her hair for me to smell. I leaned away, not because I didn't want to smell her hair, but because I didn't want it to smell like cadaverine and putrescine when I did.

"Okay, okay. I believe you."

"It's hopeless."

I couldn't help but laugh. "It's not hopeless. I'll fix it."

Iris laughed, too, but said, "This isn't funny. I can't be throwing up every time I have to drive somewhere. I haven't thrown up since I was seventeen years old and got Norwalk! I threw up, Winston! A smell did that to me! A smell that you are responsible for! It's not funny."

"I'm sorry——" I said, trying to approach the car again to get a better look of what—if anything—there was to see of the protein-shake spill. "I'll take care of it."

"You can't. I tried."

"What do you mean?"

"I mean, you cleaned it up after it happened and it still smells like this. It's like my whole car is infested with maggots."

I raised an eyebrow and buried my nose in my elbow as I looked into the car. "I don't see any maggots."

"Microscopic maggots, then," she said, her eyes filled with a wild desperation that I admit I found charming. "Maggots that make that terrible smell."

"That's not how maggots work. If there were maggots, it wouldn't smell this bad because they'd be eating the decomposing protein."

She covered her face with her hands. "Don't talk about it. I'm already sick to my stomach. I don't think you should drink those things anymore. Smell the smell they make! It can't be good for you. You're probably suppurating on the inside."

"Now you're just getting hysterical," I said. "I'll deal with the fetid smell, fair maiden. Fret not thyself."

"I told you, I tried. On my way home from the airport I stopped at the twenty-four-hour Walmart and bought all of these hardcore upholstery cleaners. I've doused the car and it hasn't made one bit of difference. There's only one thing to be done. I've resigned myself to it."

"What's that?"

"Torch it."

"You're kidding."

She looked hilariously solemn. "I am not. But I need your help."

"We are not torching your car."

"We could—you could—just drive it to a deserted field and then we'll light it on fire. That smell has to be killed with fire. It's the only way to kill the microbes. Think about how nice smoke smells. Nice, woodsy smoke. I've been dreaming about it since I texted you."

"Iris—"

"Winston, don't you see? We have to burn it to the ground."

"Let me see if I've got this straight. I could drive it to a deserted field. We could light it on fire and then run to a minimum safe distance for when the tank of gas ignites?"

"It has to be a really deserted field. Think of somewhere."

I couldn't help but smile. "No—that's insane. I'm glad you texted me, though—to keep you from committing arson just to get rid of a bad smell."

"You're making jokes, but that isn't a smell. It's an aggressive act. It's basically a declaration of war on all that is good and right in the world."

"Okay, Napoleon. But here's what's going to happen: I'm going deal with it, but if everything I try still doesn't work, then we can look at implementing your nuclear option. Deal?"

"I guess so, but I think the time would be better spent looking for big, deserted fields. I don't know if I can ever feel good about that car again," she said as I handed her my car keys and enjoined her to follow me to the professional car cleaner service.

"I'll pay to get it steam-cleaned and then you can decide."

"I wasn't trying to get you to clean it."

"Of course you were. You said it was my fault."

"It *is* your fault. But I wasn't trying to get you to pay for it."

"You sent me a text at 6:12 in the morning."

"Which you took your sweet time responding to, I noted." Iris dug her car keys out of her pocket. "I was desperate. I had just driven to the Home Depot and it wasn't open yet. I threw up in their parking lot. I've used up two bottles of upholstery cleaner and I think it is actually worse. Now it smells like perfumed death."

"Just follow me in my car."

With the windows open and mouth-breathing to avoid tossing my cookies 'n' cream shake, I drove to a car-detailing service station that I knew Jeremy liked to use. I spoke to the service guy about what happened and if anything could be done and he stated—somewhat ominously—that he could deal with an actual decomposing body and that protein-shake overspray was not a problem, but it was going to cost me. Iris sat in my car while I made a deal with the guy. I saw she had moved over to the passenger seat and was holding the laundry basket of neatly folded brown towels on her lap.

"So, you really did move out," she said when I opened the door.

In the misunderstanding and trying to deal with the smell, I had momentarily forgotten that a reckoning was coming with Iris. I got into the driver's seat and pulled the door closed behind me but I didn't turn the engine on.

"Last night," I said.

"Why?"

"Haven't you spoken to Gynnyfyr?"

"Suppose you tell me what happened."

I took a deep breath. "I'm not handicapped, physically, or—or otherwise," I said. There—it was out. Everyone who I could possibly tell, I had told.

Her expression was unreadable. "How did you end up with Dignity?"

"A series of unfortunate events?"

"Nice try. Do better."

There in the parking lot of a place called Bubbles, I told her everything. I started from way back when I broke up with Cassandra because I just couldn't see being a husband. I told her about all my schooling. All my non-achieving. Jeremy. My parents. The Beltline Basement Lair. SlimFast and sour-smelling bagels. I told Iris about Sam and the misunderstanding with Dr. Yu and then the flood and the toilet towel, which suddenly didn't seem quite the indignity it had felt at the time. I told her about running into Cassandra and being in a fugue state during my visit with Dr. Mann. I told her about the forms for Dignity and how I thought maybe the diagnosis explained all my failures, how it was much less troubling to believe that I was sick than to accept that I'd just made one terrible judgment call after another.

Iris asked one or two questions during the course of my monologue, but for the most part she just sat there silently tracing the yellow ribbon around the towels with her fingertips while I talked. She didn't look angry. She didn't look anything.

I kept talking because I found her silence unnerving, but eventually I ran out of things to say and awkwardness stretched out between us like an overburdened elastic cord.

"For what it is worth—I am sorry."

Iris was looking through the dashboard into some unknown place and didn't seem to have heard me. After a few moments of silence, I said, "I guess that doesn't really change anything, though."

"I don't know," she said slowly, her pale blue eyes still staring into some faraway place. "Maybe it does."

"Are you mad at me?" I asked finally because we had been sitting in the car in the parking lot of Bubbles Car Wash and Detailing in silence for eight straight minutes. It didn't seem like she was going to say anything else.

Iris turned to look at me, her expression mystified. "Mad—? Why would I be mad?"

Sam had been mad. Gynnyfyr was mad. Dignity Begins at Home would likely be mad. "Everyone else is."

Iris sighed heavily, but her expression was unexpectedly bright. "You know, once I began to sort out which things were about me and which things weren't, it was such a relief. I'm not inclined to pick up offences just for the heck of it."

"Well—thanks," I said stupidly. In all my imaginings of the way that this would go down with Iris, I'd never imagined her taking the news in stride. I'd envisioned tears. I'd imagined rage. I'd pictured cold indifference. Never this. The woman was a total enigma to me.

"No problem," she said lightly. "I mean, no personal problem, but there might be some professional stickiness."

A ticker tape of newspaper headlines went through my mind: "*Man pretends to be mentally handicapped in order to defraud the Canadian People.*" "*Con man abusing housing program for the Disabled causes many handicapped Canadians to be out on the street.*" "*Man who pretended to be handicapped has been convicted of fraud and given a prison sentence.*" "*Man who pretended to be handicapped has died in prison as a result of inmate violence.*" And then simply: "*Good riddance.*"

I sighed heavily. "What do you think I should do?"

"Get out of town," she said, her face deadpan. "Change your name. Change your hair. Disappear." She smiled suddenly. "Just kidding. You were the one to tell us, so I think that should count in your favour. You say it was a misdiagnosis."

"It was," I said emphatically.

"I believe you."

"What about Gynnyfyr, though? Didn't she tell you what happened?" I asked.

Iris nodded. "She called me yesterday afternoon. She was pretty angry but she only said that your boss was a terrible person who had sexually harassed her and that she wasn't willing to go there anymore. She didn't say anything about you not being—" Iris paused while she tried to think of the right term for whatever I was or I wasn't. "—suitable for the program."

"She didn't believe it?" I said incredulously. "How is that even possible? Iqbal was a witness. He told her."

"I'm just telling you what she said to me. There was nothing about you being a fraud. I thought she was just annoyed that she had to take an extra shift."

"Is it me?" I said in exasperation. "Why is it that no matter what I tell people, they come to their own wrong conclusion anyway? No one ever seems to believe me."

"Maybe that felt too humiliating for them?" Iris suggested mildly. "I believe you. It never made much sense to me why you were in the program."

"But I asked you—I told you that I didn't think I should be in the Dignity house weeks ago and you said that you thought it was a good thing."

"There is always an adjustment period for people when they get any kind of diagnosis that will affect them for the rest of their life. You didn't seem like you needed that level of help, but I only saw you for a couple of hours at a time."

"I'm not—I didn't expect you to know—I'm not blaming you for anything," I said. "It's my fault. I know that. I'm the only one responsible for allowing this to happen. I should never have filled out the forms."

Iris smiled. It was a calm, steady expression as if nothing ever rocked her emotional equilibrium—well, except for the dead-body smell in her car this morning, but that was a unique moment.

"I logged that conversation in my shift notes, if that comforts you. I also logged the fact that you called me while I was away in Kelowna, in order to talk about this."

"You don't think that Dignity will want their pound of flesh?"

"Anything is possible. But it is a brand-new program and you've only been in it a couple of months. It always takes a while to work out the kinks in the system. If anything, you showed that their program parameters need tightening."

We sat there quietly for a while, each thinking our own thoughts. I wondered what the outcome would be. Would I end up in court proclaiming my own stupidity as a defence? Or would the whole thing just disappear in the bureaucratic bloat that is a government-funded program? The bright April sunlight streamed through the windshield, causing us to squint.

"Do you think I should offer to pay back the amount that was spent on me these last few months?"

"Would that make it alright?" It seemed like a loaded question but her face still had that serene expression. "Do you think that would make you feel better?"

"I would feel a little better," I said. "You know, penance and whatnot."

"Penance," she repeated thoughtfully. "Paying back the money might be a good exercise—a good thing for training your conscience—but forgiveness is more important than giving yourself a punishment so that you won't feel bad anymore. That doesn't work. I've tried. It only makes you feel more guilty because once you've completed your self-inflicted punishment, you realize it isn't enough. What you need is absolution. Take it from me."

"But then the taxpayer wouldn't be out any money."

"If that is the only thing that was wrong, then maybe you should try and pay it back."

"How do you mean? What else is there?" I asked.

She wasn't looking at me but watching the traffic go by as the sun bathed her in a glow of gold. She had that look again, the one that I had noticed the first time she and Gynnyfyr had showed up at the Dignity house. Like she was a sun-bleached woman in a Western, delicate in aspect but as hard as a blade of steel.

"It's such a gorgeous day," Iris said, tapping the passenger window with her knuckle. "We should be spending it outside."

I turned the car on. I wanted her to stay with me. I'd take her wherever she wanted to go. I'd drive to the end of the road with this marvellous creature beside me who continually astounded me with her reaction to things. She wasn't mad at me. She didn't even seem inconvenienced.

"I'm supposed to go to a family picnic today at Shouldice Park." I looked at the clock on the dashboard. "In an hour."

"Let's go," Iris said, "that is, if it's alright if I join you. Otherwise, you need to drive me home."

"I'd love for you to come along," I said, putting the car in gear. "That'd be great." We drove in silence for several minutes. I tried to sort out where she was trying to lead me. I felt as though I was only grasping the edges of something important but couldn't find my way in. I periodically stole glances at Iris, trying to anticipate what it was that she was thinking. I had expected she would hate me. Everyone else who knew me was pretty mad. But who was I to her, really? No one. Just some guy. Why should she get herself all worked up over what some strange idiot did?

"You're being pretty easy on me," I said after a while.

"You think so?" Iris smiled faintly and turned to look out the window, which was both intriguing and unsettling.

"I mean," I said, trying to draw her out, get her to explain what she meant when she'd said I should pay back the money if that was the only thing that was wrong, "I misled you. Not on purpose, but I'm still guilty of it."

"It was an honest mistake, Winston. I forgive you. It's done."

"Just like that?"

Iris raised a solitary eyebrow. "You want me to sit on it for a while first?"

"I'm just—I thought people always wanted time to process stuff before they made their decision about things. I'm just amazed. You amaze me."

"If I know I have to end up there, then what's the point of getting all offended first?" Iris asked. "Why would I want to get all worked up for nothing?"

Who was this woman? I pulled into the unpaved lot of the park and found a spot at the end of a row of cars. I turned the engine off. I wanted to tell Iris everything that I admired about her. How much I liked her. How it was more than just "like" and "admire," and the more she talked, the stronger the feeling became. To prevent myself from blurting it all out, instead I said, "So what does a person like you possibly need absolution for?"

Iris laughed at that, but not her usual free laugh that came from somewhere deep inside like joy bubbling out. There was a discordant note of cynicism that I had never heard from her before.

"Oh, just killed my mother is all," she said lightly. "So, keep that in mind before you get too attached." She threw open the car door and exited swiftly, closing the door behind her before I could respond.

I wasn't sure which statement arrested me more: the thing about her mom or the fact that she knew that I was falling for her. I unbuckled my seat belt slowly and got out of the car, locking the door behind me. Iris was standing about twenty feet away, staring down at the river. Last summer's overgrown grass was dead and lay folded over on itself and was slippery under my shoes as I approached her. She didn't turn to look at me.

"You certainly know how to make an exit," I said as I took my place beside her. She smiled faintly. Her eyes were bright, but she wasn't crying.

"I can forgive you for your mistake, Winston, because I needed forgiveness," she said, not looking up from the water. "It's easy. Even if you had done it on purpose but were truly sorry about it, I can forgive that.

313

Forgiving other people used to seem really hard, but it isn't anymore. Not after what I did."

I nodded, wondering if she was going to offer up the circumstances or if I was going to have to ask, and just how I was going to do that, if she didn't. Iris turned away from the water and I fell in step beside her as we followed the pedestrian path that ran along the Bow River.

"So, was it with an axe or—?"

Mercifully, Iris laughed and pressed in close to my side to let a dog walker pass. The air had a bite of cold but the sun was warm on our faces as we walked along. The smell of the thaw was in the chill air.

"The river has opened up," I said, changing the subject in case she really didn't want to tell me about her mom. "The ice is practically gone."

"I told you about how my folks divorced, right?" Iris said, side-stepping a patch of ice on a shady section of the path.

"Yeah."

"And my mom went from bad to worse in terms of her boyfriends?"

I nodded.

"My grade-twelve year she took up with Rudy. He was this—this creep. He hung around for my dad's child-support checks and then they'd go out partying. Or they'd stay in partying, which was actually worse."

"If his car was out front when I came home from school, I would climb in my bedroom window so that they wouldn't know I was there. They didn't think of me if I wasn't in front of them, so I would come in through the window and then be as quiet as I could be. When they would go out or pass out, I would sneak into the kitchen for some toast or whatever we happened to have on hand."

A cool wind wiped Iris's hair across her face. She looked up at me and smiled somewhat ruefully. "It's exhausting being angry all the time, but youth was on my side."

We rounded a bend in the pathway and the sun glistened on the open water of the river. What remained of the winter ice was piled on the banks like swept-up pieces of broken pottery.

"Three days before my last diploma exam, I studied at the school library until it closed. Rudy's maroon Cavalier was out front again when I got home. I could hear them arguing even before I got in my window. He was swearing at her—saying these horrible things—and she was screaming back. I hated them both so much. I would clench my teeth together so hard that I used to get these spasms in my jaw."

I tried to picture Iris angry—angry enough for jaw spasms—but couldn't.

"I tried to study for my exam but I could hear the terrible words that they were saying through my earplugs. The house seemed to shake, as though chaos was this monster that had grabbed a hold of it and was trying to tear it off the foundations."

"I'm surprised the neighbours didn't call the cops."

"They were the same kind of people," Iris said dismissively. "After a while, I heard Rudy storm out. He slammed the door and I heard him gun the engine and take off. I was starving. There was a box of Kraft Dinner hidden in the drawer under the oven so I took out my earplugs and waited. I didn't want my mom to see me, either. She was always weepy and apologetic after she'd break up with someone. I didn't want to listen to all that again so I waited, listening at the crack of my door until I could imagine she'd passed out.

"After it was quiet for a while, I painstakingly unlocked my door so that the lock mechanism would make the smallest amount of noise, but she must have been listening for me because she called out, 'Petal?' She used to call me Petal when I was little and she was better. 'My sweet petal?' I froze when I heard it. Her voice sounded—strange. Thick. I don't know.

"I felt this little flicker of compassion but it was followed by rage. I wanted to tear that house of horrors off its foundations. I wanted to scream and smash things like they did. I wanted her to feel afraid like I did. But I didn't. I relocked my door and put my earplugs back in. How dare she? How dare she make this our lives? How could she look me in the face and call me Petal, like when I was a little girl. Call me Petal while she was strung out. When she had brought these evil men into my life who I hid from. Parents are supposed to protect their kids, not force the kids to do their homework in the alley behind the garage and climb in their bedroom window so that they avoid detection by the guy with sexual assault charges."

"No—I locked my door. My stomach was growling, but I'd rather starve than let her see me. I wanted to scream all of these things at her until she felt as bad as I did. But I didn't. I was silent but the screams echoed in my head like a siren going off and getting louder and louder. I heard her knocking about in her room and talking to herself. Each sound made me more and more enraged. But it was this cold anger—this coldness settling into my heart.

"I fell asleep eventually but woke to my stomach growling with emptiness. I remember looking at the red numbers on my alarm clock. It was 4:07 a.m. I went to the kitchen and made some tea and toast. The evidence of Mom and Rudy's bender was all over the place. Stuff everywhere. They had burnt a bunch of the spoons. I didn't even know what I was looking at. I don't know what made me look into my mom's room. Normally, I wouldn't have, but when I pushed open her door, I knew she wasn't asleep. I knew she was dead." She stopped walking and wiped at her eyes. "And I knew I hadn't stopped it."

"You were just a kid," I said quietly.

"Doesn't matter," she answered. "I let my mom die. I put in earplugs and closed my door. That's on my card. Every time my stomach growls I remember that. It's always in front of me. I needed forgiveness. But no one owes you forgiveness—least of all, God."

I hugged her because I couldn't stop myself and I didn't know what else to do or say. Iris seemed to accept it for a few moments before she began to pull away.

Iris' eyes looked even bluer as she fought back her emotions. "Do you believe in God?"

"Yeah—I think so."

"You want to know something funny? When I was a kid, I thought God lived in the clouds like the Care Bears. I thought Jesus was on my side and would never let anything bad happen to me. But He did and I hated Him for it and told my dad every time I saw him that I was an atheist just to hurt him. I even bought the jewelry."

"There's atheist jewelry?"

Iris nodded sheepishly. "It's a somewhat insecure movement." She stopped walking and turned to look at me.

"You had a lot to forgive, too, though, and I'm not just saying that because I like you."

Iris didn't say anything in response. She smiled a kind of sad, rueful smile. We walked in silence for a few minutes winding the undulating curves of the river path as it approached Shouldice Park.

"I idolized my dad. It was hard to see him fall and it was hard to face the fallout. Trust me, I felt all the moral indignation possible in such a situation. But being justified—at least, initially—wasn't any comfort. There comes a point when you surrender the moral high ground of righteous anger to bitterness. My dad's affair had collateral damage in my life, for sure; but I was the one who decided how extensive it was going to be."

I started to see where Iris was leading me and it made me feel as though my skin was too tight.

"Did you ever read *War and Peace*?" she asked after a little while. "There is this line in there about a lost battle: 'We lost because we told ourselves we lost.' That was me. I was so focused on how I was losing, how I was being wounded, that I made it harder on myself even than it had to be. I threw away everything that could have helped me. My faith in God. My relationship with my dad and brother. I told myself every day—a thousand times a day—that I was the wronged one. And I thought I was the only good one. I was the only one who had stayed with her, even though I hated it. I was the one who kept putting the pieces back together. Then, suddenly without warning, without changing a single thing, I was the one who didn't save her mom from dying. I was the one who was wrong."

"I wouldn't interpret it that way."

"You would if you had done it," she said bluntly. "And nothing I ever did was going to wash that stain off of me. What I did was wrong—not in itself: putting in earplugs and going to bed isn't a moral or immoral act— but what was inside me, what drove me in that inconsequential act, was nothing but evil wearing a different outfit."

I exhaled heavily. I could see what it was that she was saying about me. I suddenly understood what Sam had been trying to tell me months ago. It didn't matter what anyone else did. None of that was any excuse for what I had done. I had always had the chance to choose something different. Even if it was going to cost me more than was fair or more than I wanted to pay, I had always had a choice.

"Forgiveness is the only absolution," Iris said as we neared the copse of trees that made up the picnic area of Shouldice Park.

I nodded. "I get it. My conscience isn't clear. You win. You also win the shitty life contest. No contest."

"I won because I told myself I won," she said, laughing.

CHAPTER TWENTY

The Greater (Gopher) Good

The path to the picnic area ran parallel to the sloping bank. Gaps in the trees revealed the glistening surface of the Bow River, sparkling under the bright sun. At the far end of the picnic area, I recognized the familiar shapes of my family huddled against the intermittent blasts of icy wind that brought clouds from beyond the horizon to blot out the blue sky and the warmth of the sunshine. Natalie's twin daughters were standing astride an unused picnic table with their arms stretched to the sky before they jumped to the ground with a shout. My sister saw me approaching and gave a wave. I picked up a broken branch and threw it out into the water, watching as it floated in the river swollen with the spring runoff from the mountains.

"Are you okay?" Iris asked.

"Am *I* okay? After what you just told me? Are you okay? How are you this normal?"

"You went quiet. That was just my way of asking what you were thinking about." She looked away and a slight smile touched the corners of her mouth as she watched the girls leaping from the table, their blond hair flying wildly for a moment as they hung suspended in the air, a blur of gold and primary colours.

I stopped walking and she stopped as well and turned toward me. "Iris," I said, the burden of my feelings toward her seeming to grow too weighty to carry in silence any longer. I could see in her eyes that she anticipated what I was about to say. Would she be mortified that I—who hours before had merely been a "client" requiring support—wanted, I don't know, to possess her body and soul? Put it that way and it sounded kind of creepy. I hoped wildly that by the time the words were out of my mouth, I would have come up with something better.

She was looking up at me with expectation. Her cheeks and nose were flushed pink with the cold and it made her eyes seem piercingly blue. It was now or never, a speak-now-or-forever-hold-your-peace kind of moment. In that instant, it seemed to me that everything—from my parents moving out, to bagels and slam poetry, to the house that Dignity built and everything attendant in between—had been about this. Each had been a step in leading me to this moment. This was the precipice to launch from, either to soar or to tumble to my ruin on the rocks below.

I took a deep, slow breath like I used to do when I stood on the starting blocks at the pool before the buzzer sounded. It was win or lose. There was no placing in this contest.

It was then that I heard it.

It wasn't a scream. Some elemental signal reverberated through me like metal ringing against metal. In a moment, the hair on my neck stood on end and I was sprinting away from Iris toward the riverbank. This terrible alert seemed to sound in my whole body, a frequency of warning that I understood instinctually. I was running through the trees to the river. Something was terribly wrong.

"What is it?" Iris's voice was full of alarm.

I saw the green of Bret's jacket through the denuded bushes that lined the riverbank. I knew Michael was in the river without seeing him. The Bow, swollen with spring runoff, had been carving away at the bend in the bank, creating a steep angle of slippery muck. Not much, nothing disaster-film worthy, but enough to take the feet out beneath an eight-year-old boy who had stepped too close to the edge. Whether from the shock or the cold of the river, even as his shoes and jacket grew heavy with the frigid water, Michael never yelled. My heart pounded in my throat as I covered the distance to the bank. Bret's sudden shouts filled my ears. He scrambled along the bank trying to stay parallel to Michael as the current bore him along. The river quickly outpaced him. I saw his contemplation of the water even as I ran.

"Bret! Stay back!" I yelled, pushing him backward as I passed him. "I'm here."

The red of Michael's jacket appeared through a break in the brush a little ways ahead. I ran faster to get ahead of him. There was only one chance that I would be able to catch him. There was only this moment. There were only these interminable seconds. If I misjudged it—well, I didn't think about that.

"Call 911!" I yelled to Iris without looking back.

I jumped down the icy bank, somehow managing to keep my balance, and threw myself into the water parallel to Michael. In movies, people always pull off jackets and shoes before jumping in the water to rescue someone. There was no time. It didn't occur to me until I felt the drag of water filling my shoes. The icy temperature of the water barely registered as I propelled myself across the current after my nephew. His face was turned away from me and the river seemed to taunt me, holding him just out of my reach.

"Michael! I'm here." His head whipped around and I saw for the first time the desperate look of fear on his face that had rendered him mute. His face was barely out of the water and his eyes were wide with shock from the bitter cold of the icy mountain runoff. Each stroke of my arms and kick of my legs fell short of reaching him. His head bobbed under the surface of the river for an eternity before he surfaced again, sputtering.

"Kick off your boots!" I blinked hard to clear the water that splashed in my face. "It's going to be okay. I'm here." I pushed myself harder across the current, my legs kicking against the weight of my shoes so that the current pulled them from my feet. Faster, stronger now, I propelled myself after him.

His voice was weak over the rush of the river. "I can't swim anymore." He was choking on the water or crying. "It's not letting me swim."

I reached out my arms in a desperate lunge against the resistance of the current. "I've got you." My fingers closed on the hood of his jacket and I pulled him close against the drag of the current, looping my arm over his chest and under his armpit so that his face was out of the water.

"It's okay. I've got you," I said it again, surprised at how calm my voice sounded even though everything in me was electrified with adrenalin and cold. "I won't let you go." I adjusted to swimming with only one arm as I held him to me tightly. "You've got to help me out, though, bud. You've got trust me and be brave. I know you are. You just need to trust me and try to relax while I swim us back to shore." The force of the current was insistent and tried to pull him from my grasp.

"You're doing great, Mikey. You're doing awesome." My words were breathless and stilted. Michael's teeth were chattering and he was a limp rag doll in my arms.

"We're almost there," I said, spotting a break in the ice crust that still lined much of the riverbank, where I could see the smooth stones of the river bottom angling gently up. "Talk to me, pal. Let me know how you're doing."

"I'm—I'm cold," Michael answered after what seemed like an eternity. His voice was faint and the words slurred and I felt a renewed burst of fear.

"Almost there. We're in this together. We're almost there. We're—almost there, Mikey—" I was babbling. Trying to convince us both, maybe. I could hear the cold in my voice and struggled against its leadenly effects to my muscles. I hoped for the reassuring sound of sirens approaching but my ears were full with the rush and splash of the river. I didn't know how far away we had been carried from where he had fallen. My progress to the bank was painstakingly slow as the water pushed us farther and farther away from help. I gulped at the cold air that was stabbing at my lungs and sapping my strength. No matter how hard I kicked, it didn't seem to make a difference. The shore remained just out of reach as my arms and legs grew weaker and weaker.

At last socked foot kicked against the smooth stones of the riverbed and my legs scraped along the bottom. I struggled to stand pulling Michael up into my arms. A gust of wind threatened my balance. The cold of the air registered only as pain and the water seemed warm in comparison to the wind and tempted me to sit back down into it. Instead, I stumbled up the icy bank hoping to find shelter from the wind in the trees. Michael seemed almost comatose in my arms.

"We—made it," I said, gasping from both cold and exhaustion. "We gotta—get this—jacket…off," I said, as I tried to get my numb fingers to cooperate with the zipper. "Talk to me…Mikey—you okay?" The words sounded shaky and stilted despite an artificial veneer of confidence. The wind cut into us mercilessly as I tried to shield my nephew from it with my body. Michael's lips were blue, but his face was splotchy with bright red patches.

"You—you need—you need—you need—" I stuttered over the words, as though the cold were shaking them out of me. "Talk—to me—Mikey…"

"Tro—tr—sss—sle…" The strangled, shaking sounds of his barely formed words struck renewed fear into my mind.

"Winston!" Iris's voice, like a beacon of hope, seemed to come from a long way off.

"Her—He—Here!" I managed to rip off my own jacket and held Michael against my chest, rubbing his back with only semi-cooperative hands.

"You're—okay—you're okay, now." I kept saying it over and over. "You're… going to be able… to tell everyone how you—you—you saved me."

"Michael!" Jeremy burst through the trees. "Michael!" His voice was heavy with panic. My brother pulled his son to his chest. "Oh, God! Thank you, God!" His face was torn with fear and stitched together with relief. "Thank you thank you thank you… Oh, God! Come on, son, stay with me, son—"

Within moments the rest of my family came crashing through the trees like waves on the shore.

"The paramedics are on their way!"

"Get him out of those wet clothes."

"Winston!"

"Thank God you were there!!"

Beth was crying and ripping off her jacket to wrap up her son. I clenched my hands at my sides in a vain effort to control the spastic shaking of my body. Everyone was talking. There were too many words, too many voices that blended together into white noise that provided a bass track to the chattering of my teeth. I looked over at Michael, his face buried in Beth's chest. The dark curls of his wet hair still plastered to the side of his head. He was shivering uncontrollably. Time seemed to be congealing in the cold; every moment was daggers and spasms. A wailing of sirens burst upon my consciousness as a fire truck and an ambulance came careening through the park. A paramedic with flaming red hair who looked like he couldn't legally get a drink was suddenly in front of me. He was talking to me. He was asking me questions but I couldn't seem to make out their meaning.

"M…Mi…Michael," I said.

The paramedic called me "sir," but everything else was lost. My brain felt thick and I wanted to lie down. Where was Iris? The cold that had just seemed so unbearable moments before began to dissipate. I was warming up again. That uncontrollable shivering had stopped.

Somehow—though I don't exactly remember it—I was riding in the ambulance the short distance to the Foothills Hospital. Roads that normally felt smooth were suddenly pitted with potholes—or maybe they were gopher holes, I thought idly—as the ambulance bounced over curb and pavement, leaning around the corners with the slightly muted sound of the siren wailing overhead.

"Those damn gophers."

"What?" The young, red-haired paramedic peered into my face with a perplexed expression. "What did you say, sir?"

"Nothing," I answered.

There was nothing else to say.

CHAPTER TWENTY-ONE

Torschlusspanik

Torschlusspanik.

I think I have it. Or, rather, I think I had it. The fear of the closing gate. Fear of being trapped in a choice. Afraid of being trapped outside of one. I had a foundational aversion to being either inside or outside; and I was loitering instead in the entryway as though that was a rational place to stand around. I could see now—or maybe merely admit to myself— that my paralytic response to every choice from career to marriage and the responsibilities of manhood had not merely been the side effects of an affable, laid-back personality. That was a nice idea, a good excuse, but it was only so much smoke to blow out of—well, you know where.

I wanted all my options open all the time. I feared the closing of the gate. I feared pursuing an actual career because it seemed that the excitement, the verve of being alive, was in not knowing what would happen next. Once a decision was made, say, to be a geologist, the mystery of the future would dissipate and I would be a geologist. I would apply that word to myself—nothing really against it, mind you—but the gate on what I *could be, might be,* would clang closed. I dreaded the loss of possibility. It sounds foolish now; it doesn't sound so different from what Robbie was saying about how he couldn't be a dad because it would ruin his life. He imagined the heavy portcullis of potential closing fast and sealing him within high walls and soon he would be some kid's grey-haired dad. He wouldn't be a front-rank model anymore.

Maybe if I had learned German, I would have learned about *torschlusspanik* and its effects on the human psyche. I could have been bold in my decisions. I could have been more like Jeremy and less like me. But even my brother's confident decisions might have had a tinge of *torschlusspanik* about them. Perhaps he strode boldly into decisions and changes because he felt that he was opening more gates for himself rather than closing them.

I didn't stop at myself and Jeremy and Robbie; I began to wonder about others. What about Sam? She was making a big decision, too. Was it because she feared that a gate of opportunity was closing fast and she needed to make a move, that she was getting married? Or did she see marriage as a roadway for adventure that was full of the excitement of the unknown opening up in front of her? I didn't know the answer. But it seemed clear that while the actions on the surface looked the same, it was the perspective that drove them that made all the difference in the world.

I threw myself in after Michael without hesitation. It was one of a handful of moments in my life when I knew without a doubt what I was doing. All the noise, all the static and confusion of my own thoughts coupled with everyone else's opinions and expectations—that noise and mist that cluttered my mental real estate like a hoarder's aggregation disappeared as everything came into a surreal focus that seemed outside of time itself. Who I was, what I was here for—all of it came into focus in one moment of crystal clarity in which all of my self-doubt evaporated into a juggernaut of purpose. This is what the gophers know. They don't think about their actions, weighing risk against reward. They react. They respond to the moment, to the instinct that takes over when the stakes are high. It isn't that the maiden-aunt gophers don't have hopes of their own, but when the clarion call of danger sounds, they react. They stand up so that everyone else can get down to safety. It's what they are made to do.

Something about that dunk in the river, something about the moment when I grasped my nephew and knew that he was going to be okay had set me free from the prison of my own foolhardy perspective.

"Leave."

I traced the letters of the word in my mind with a calligrapher's care. It was time, like when the Littlest Hobo knew that his task was done and now he was free to roam again. "Leave." The word slid back and forth across my conscious and unconscious thoughts like the provincial map abandoned on the dashboard of my car that glides across my vision every time I turn a corner. "Leave." The instruction was so simple it didn't even need a whole sentence. The word carried weight, heavy with purpose like a water balloon that threatened to burst under the pressure of its own significance. I thought that my big move, my *grande* play was in moving out of the Dignity house. That somehow, in the packing up and the mailing in of keys, I had leapt from the precipice and would either fly or fall to my destruction. It had felt that way at the time. Momentous. But only a few days out from that glorious leap and I had landed—safely on my feet and back in my parents' place. It was the absurd pièce de résistance of the whole am-I-or-aren't-I Dignity debacle. It was time to jump off this whirligig; it was time to leap with abandon from this Ferris wheel I'd been comfortably riding in circles for far too long. I was Mary Poppins and the wind had changed.

Untangling myself from Dignity was only the first step. It was the flinging open of the prison door. But freedom isn't standing on the doorstep of a prison; it is losing sight of it far behind in your rear-view mirror.

Leave.

For a week, or a year, or ten years. I could head westward and pick up seasonal work planting trees or fighting forest fires. I could bum around the country and see things I had never seen. I could look for work on a rig or a farm. I could do anything, really. Something about rescuing Michael had lifted my eyes to the horizon.

Leave.

The moment felt pregnant, like if I did not give in to its call, I would miscarry my chance at liberty. I would grow sleepy again and forget.

Leave.

The urgency to obey the command grew in my mind and my chest as I lay on my parents' unfamiliar couch and stared at the knock-down ceiling. Boomer's deep and even breathing beside me counted off the moments as surely as a ticking clock. Time was draining out and the night would soon be over. People who care about you—parents, in particular—want to know you have a plan. They want to hear where you will be staying that night, how far you will be travelling. They want you to call or text them and tell them that you've arrived safely at your destination. I didn't have the answer to any of those questions. I only had the command that only I could hear, the one I had to obey. The road would have to rise up to meet me.

Without turning on a light, I got up and folded up the blanket and sheets. I dressed silently and collected the few things that I had brought into their condo from my car. Boomer never stirred from his sleep. I found the notepad that my mom keeps by the phone and scribbled a quick note to them. I tore it off the pad and curled it into the handle of their coffee carafe, where they would be sure to find it.

For the first time in my life, I felt the irresistible call of the road. I left my parents' building on a night that smelled like cut spruce trees. I breathed deeply and felt the magnetic power of leaving. My car was already packed and ready for wherever the leaving would take me. I put the key in the ignition and smiled as the engine roared to life, as though I was headed out into the wilderness with a faithful beast and a shout of "Heigh-ho, Silver!"

It seemed like the most natural thing in the world as I drove away from the rising sun and toward every possibility. My escape from the prison bars of my own perception was like an unforeseen kiss, or sudden laughter with your head thrown back. Just the most natural thing in the world—those moments that God made us to enjoy. It was seeing the new green-gold in the leaves and the wind moving the long strands of prairie grass like waves in water. It was seeing the Eternal in the temporal and smiling because there He was with me. I'd taken the long way around to satisfaction, but joy welled up from somewhere deep within me that made me want to sing and shout and drive real fast.

I pulled into the Petro-Canada station just past Cowboy Trail, the last turnoff to loop back. I kept my eyes on the western horizon as I pumped gas into my tank. Even in this brief and necessary stop feeling something like how I imagine a stallion feels when a rope is thrown around his neck. *Torschlusspanik* was fear; and I refused to be ruled by it in any way. An infinity of possibilities seemed to stretch to the horizon on every side.

The sweet light of the early morning bathed that heaven land where the mountains rise up from the tableland of the prairies. The grassy fields were flaxen and the sky to the west was a deep grey blue that made me think of Iris's eyes.

Iris.

I would call her from somewhere. Maybe I would ask her if she wanted to swing open the gate and marry the long shot. Something about that made me smile. I liked that I was the long shot. I was the horse no one would bet on to win. No one but Iris. A fleeting sense of wistfulness passed over my eyes and heart as I realized I loved this place—this land, the people in it. It was home, but it would still remain. The mountains would hold down the picnic blanket of the Prairies for rose-gold sunsets and aspen thickets and wilderness. It would remain. I would go away for a while. But it would only be in order to take the long way back home.

The bottle blonde behind the counter did not look up at the sound of the digital bell as I pulled open the gas station door. I scanned the aisles until I found the Longview Beef Jerky and pulled two packs off the shelf. I poured a coffee from the machine. I walked to the till, reflexively scanning the newspaper and magazine covers, remembering headlines I'd imagined should my stint with Dignity be regarded as fraudulent. There was nothing of the kind. The freshly inked pages proclaimed a breakdown in negotiations for a provincial union and the heroics of a local Instagram star. I set my purchases down on the counter and pointed to my valiant steed waiting at pump six.

"Headed out or headed home?" the woman asked as she handed me the receipt.

I looked at the scratch tickets laid out in neat rows descending and ascending under the plastic under my fingers. A brightly coloured array of paper fortunes, each proclaiming the possibility of a new future for people down on their luck. I tapped the scratched case with my fingernails.

"Both," I said.

She didn't ask me what I meant.

45783617R00205

Made in the USA
Middletown, DE
20 May 2019